SOMETHING HAPPENED ON THE WAY TO HEAVEN

SOMETHING HAPPENED ON THE WAY TO HEAVEN

NISH GUNAWARDENA

BALBOA.
PRESS
A DIVISION OF HAY HOUSE

Balboa Press books may be ordered through booksellers or by contacting:

Balboa Press
A Division of Hay House
1663 Liberty Drive
Bloomington, IN 47403
www.balboapress.com
1-(877) 407-4847

Because of the dynamic nature of the Internet, any web addresses or links contained in this book may have changed since publication and may no longer be valid. The views expressed in this work are solely those of the author and do not necessarily reflect the views of the publisher, and the publisher hereby disclaims any responsibility for them.

The author of this book does not dispense medical advice or prescribe the use of any technique as a form of treatment for physical, emotional, or medical problems without the advice of a physician, either directly or indirectly. The intent of the author is only to offer information of a general nature to help you in your quest for emotional and spiritual well-being. In the event you use any of the information in this book for yourself, which is your constitutional right, the author and the publisher assume no responsibility for your actions.

Any people depicted in stock imagery provided by Thinkstock are models, and such images are being used for illustrative purposes only.
Certain stock imagery © Thinkstock.

ISBN: 978-1-4525-3487-9 (e)
ISBN: 978-1-4525-3486-2 (sc)

Printed in the United States of America

Balboa Press rev. date: 5/24/2011

Dedication

My parents and my family
My guides Becca, Meggie, Wibke, and Eilish.
All the systems busters.
You know who you are!

This book is another log
thrown into the fire that
is already burning bright!

A new scientific truth does not triumph by convincing its opponents and making them see the light, but rather because its opponents eventually die, and a new generation grows up that is familiar with it.

Max Planck
Nobel Prize Winning Founder of Quantum Physics

CONTENTS

I can only Be, through you.

CATERPILLAR

"Baltimore airport please," I hurriedly said to the cab driver. I was already late. I recently missed a flight out of DC, so I couldn't help being nervous and jittery.

"Where are you headed?" asked the cab driver.

"Baltimore International! Didn't I say that?"

"I got that! I mean your final destination."

"Final destination? Hopefully heaven. Okay, seriously. I am on the way to Vancouver."

"Ah, the glorious epicenter of BC. The center of the universe."

"What are you, Canadian?"

"Yep, originally from Winnipeg."

"Okay. Cool. I am from south of Minneapolis. Canadian sarcasm, huh? Colder but sweet!"

"What's that all aboot, eh?"

"Self-deprecating too. What are you doing in Baltimore?"

"Unlike you, I am already in heaven. You cannot go to where you already are."

"Oh great! What am I, dead?"

"By death you mean waking up."

"Do I have to pay extra for your theological sermon?"

"Nope, it is a gift from the other side."

"I don't believe in heaven or the 'other side,' as you put it."

"The other side! Canada, my friend, Canada!!"

"Ah! You mingle your symbolic speech with the literal too haphazardly. I get a bit lost in your angle."

"So, does that mean you are 'found' in yours?"

"I don't know! Shut the hell up and drive, will ya? And step on it!"

"Okay, okay! … So, what's the hurry and what's in Vancouver? Some girl?"

"In fact, yes."

"Wife, girlfriend, your friend with benefits?"

"No, she is not my girlfriend, but not just a friend either. It's complicated. The long distance thing is a killer. You are pretty nosy, aren't you? Looking for a taxi cab confession?"

"No. I mean, don't you think life just passes by like a dream and we just make meaningless small talk or text around. Whatever happened to true dialogue? The human communion. John Lennon said, *life is what happens to you while you're busy making other plans?*"

"I see what you mean. To be honest, this is the first time in my life in Maryland of three years now that someone tried to prod this far into me. Most conversations are so superficial and impersonal. You know, 'paper or plastic, cash or credit, you want fries with that.' It's like I am trapped in a shell and just wafting."

"I know. It's like living in *The Matrix* or Plato's *Allegory of the Cave*. I get all kinds of people in here. They say a lot of things. But the fun part is the meaning or its absence. It is never the language they use."

"It's like they are communicating, but the noise of the words is actually obscuring the essence of the message. People often get hung up on words, but never get it. Metaphors misunderstood."

"Exactly! Words are the shadow. Didn't Aesop warn, *beware lest you lose the substance by grasping at the shadow?*"

"Don't confuse the bulb with the light. So what am I saying to you?"

"You are seeking a communion with this girl, something far beyond a mere 'relationship.' You have had plenty of those so far. But you are single and so dissatisfied because in the past you were a *persona*, or a mask in Greek, dating another *persona*. The real souls never really met. *Each has his past shut in him like the leaves of a book known to him by his heart, and his friends can only read the title* – Virginia Woolf."

"Whoa! I communicated that?"

"And more."

"More?"

"You think you have figured it all out many times all over in your life only to have some iconoclastic event topple your cherished applecart destroying your carefully constructed worldview. Now at least you know it is going to happen again, so you are paying attention. It's almost like you are watching it happen just as you expected with lesser attachment to your applecart. Although, you don't know what is truly coming, you have become ready for anything. Now it is the change that is the constant. This new worldview is beginning to fit your life, the one within."

"Next thing you know, you are telling me that you used to teach Existentialism at Johns Hopkins and now drive a cab because the passengers are less obtuse than some of your students. Either that or you are the reincarnation of René Descartes."

"Pretty close. I am not nosy, I am Epi-curious. I did study Philosophy at University of Manitoba and then taught Existentialism at McGill. Unfortunately, my students never learnt as much as I learnt from them. So now I drive a cab. At least I think I am driving a cab, therefore ..."

"... I am driving cab. Nice. Did you minor in clichés, too?"

"That, the Americans taught me. Also, to correct you, Walt Whitman. Not the reincarnation of Descartes."

"You think! Therefore, you are? I figured Walt Whitman would return to *his* America in his many sojourns."

"*You cannot really understand America without Walt Whitman, without Leaves of Grass ... He has expressed that civilization, 'up to date,' as he would say, and no student of the philosophy of history can do without him.*"

"That was his British friend Mary Smith Whitall Costelloe. You sure know your Whitman legacy."

"You know, the secret American Dream is to experience life as a Canadian."

"What is you guys' motto up there, *We are so full of ourselves, eh?*"

"Hey, I am not the one in love with a Canadian soul."

"Wit-man, you are my friend! That you are!! Do you know your America? What's your take?"

"Whitman said, *be curious, not judgmental.* I am curious."

"Well, we have established you are not Epicurus."

"Curious about the meaning of life."

"Did you figure it out? So, what is the meaning of life?"

"Hokey Pokey!"

"Hokey Pokey?"

"That's what it's all aboot!"

"What if, huh? At least it's not 42."

"42! Like in *Hitchhiker's Guide to the Galaxy.*"

"The meaning of life is somehow hidden in the code 42."

"Joseph Campbell, mythologist-in-chief, said that we are not seeking the meaning of life. *We are seeking an experience and rapture of being alive. . . . Follow your bliss!*"

"So, do you miss the academics?"

"Not necessarily the academics, because it is the application that is the living. See the term *philosophy* is usually translated as the Love of Wisdom. This is incorrect. It is Love of Sophia – the feminine aspect of God or Goddess, if you will. She is trapped in all of us."

"I do have my mother's mitochondrial DNA. You could say she is trapped in my cells' mitochondria."

"DNA is like a wound serpent or *Ophis* in Greek."

"It's just a metaphor. DNA is biological creative knowledge written with an alphabet of only four letters. Sophistication from simplicity. Serpent and knowledge or wisdom are always associated. It's just a figure of speech though."

"Like Ophis and Sophia. Her trapped energy is the *Lapis Philosophorum*."

"The Philosopher's Stone? Like in *Harry Potter* and alchemy. Turning base metals into gold. What's that got to do with philosophy?"

"That's what it's all aboot!"

"I don't get it."

"You will. The gold is trapped as base metal. The trapped energy, Sophia, transforms under right conditions. This is *sophistication*. I see this every day. That's why I said I am already in heaven."

"Do you believe in heaven?"

"It is a label, isn't it? Language fails gloriously when trying to convey what just IS. Language cannot contain heaven, for language is but a reflection of heaven."

"So what IS? I guess you are going to telling me that you have already communicated that and that it is communicated transpersonally through the silence between the sounds and the spaces between written letters or some philosophical mumbo jumbo like that."

"You answered your own question. *The spirit of the letter.* That's what esotericism represents. Joseph Campbell once told a story about a western theologian visiting a Japanese Shinto shrine. After observing the activities for a few days the western theologian says to a Shinto spiritual leader, *I don't get your theology; I don't get your ideology.* The spiritual leader answers back and says, *we don't have a theology; we don't have an ideology. We just dance."*

"Like Sufi Whirling Dervishes."

"Whitman said, *a morning-glory at my window satisfies me more than the metaphysics of books.* The Persian Sufi mystic scholar Jelaludin Rumi was writing a metaphysics book. One day a visiting Dervish took this book and through it in a well. His disciples became so enraged by this that they killed this dervish. The shocked Rumi went into isolation and sought solace in mystic poetry. After some years he returned to introduce the whirling ritual to his disciples. He was the founding Whirling Dervish."

"Sorry, I rubbed off on the east coast irreverent cynicism and snarky attitude in the last few years and lost my Minnesota niceness. By the way, I am Raye. R-A-Y-E."

"Like the female version. Sophia is definitely trapped in you. Dr. Raye, I presume. You have that aura."

"Aura! Are you into Kirlian Photography or something?"

"I feel beyond my five senses. It's like in *The Celestine Prophecy."*

"You presume wrong about the Doctor part or I am sure you are going to tell me 'not wrong in one of the parallel realities.' I get it. I just finished my third year at University of Maryland PhD program in Molecular Medicine. My Human Genetics track thesis is interdisciplinary with Neuroscience and Evolutionary Genetics. I study neurogenetic gene expression focusing on 'junk' DNA. I got into genetics back in Minnesota?"

"University of Minnesota? Mayo Clinic?"

"Undergrad at Winona State. It was my work in Biochemical and Molecular Genetics at Mayo Clinic that lead me here. I am what they call a DNA 'deepthroat.' My calling has been from my inner mitochondrial DNA, which we all get from our mothers and their mothers. My dad is Italian. My mother's father is Norwegian and her mother is Australian Aboriginal."

"A recombinant heritage! Why is the junk in 'junk' DNA within air quotes?"

"Because almost everyone in the field of genetics believes that the true function of this DNA sequences are not yet discovered, but definitely existing. We call them *the dark matter of the genome.* Some of them work as 'on/off switches' for the coding DNA."

"What tells the switch genes to turn others on or off?"

"The 'boss genes!' They run the show. But they are only a tiny fraction of the genome. Vast majority is mysterious. I love this mystery. I think it is the potential."

"Have you seen the movie *Phenomenon?*"

"Yes, at the end of the movie the Travolta character, George Malley, says *I am the potential.* It is not farfetched. The science fully allows it. I can explain."

"Please ..."

"Take human abilities for instance. Singing, rolling your tongue, painting, tying the stem of a cherry into a knot with your tongue, running speed, belching the national anthem, cognition, intentional dimples, and so on. Even though we cannot isolate in each case, the field of genetics holds that the variation of these abilities across a population is partially based on the inherited DNA stored within a genome."

"So the DNA genome is only the potential."

"It is. In Quantum Physics, which is now trying to explain a non-material basis for DNA, everything in the cosmos is just a potential. The realization of the potential, in both cases, is driven by the chosen set of behaviors and uncontrollable external factors. I also study diseases, which are either inhibitions of basic human biochemical pathways or over-activation of them."

"That's why we are here."

"What do you mean?"

"Life!"

"Life is a process of realizing that potential?"

"It is an opportunity."

"It really is. Isn't it? In fact let me read you this from a BBC Magazine article from my iPad titled *Is there a genius in all of us*?

New science suggests the source of abilities is much more interesting and improvisational. It turns out that everything we are is a developmental process and this includes what we get from our genes. A century ago, geneticists saw genes as robot actors, always uttering the same lines in exactly the same way, and much of the public is still stuck with this old idea. In recent years, though, scientists have seen a dramatic upgrade in their understanding of heredity. They now know that genes interact with their surroundings, getting turned on and off all the time. In effect, the same genes have different effects depending on who they are talking to.

'There are no genetic factors that can be studied independently of the environment,' says Michael Meaney, a professor at McGill University in Canada. 'And there are no environmental factors that function independently of the genome. A trait emerges only from the interaction of gene and environment.'

This means that everything about us - our personalities, our intelligence, our abilities - are actually determined by the lives we lead. The very notion of 'innate' no longer holds together.

'In each case the individual animal starts its life with the capacity to develop in a number of distinctly different ways,' says Patrick Bateson, a biologist at Cambridge University. 'Like a jukebox, the individual has the potential to play a number of different developmental tunes. The particular developmental tune it does play is selected by the environment in which the individual is growing up.'

David Shenk supports this 'interactionism' in his book *The Genius in All of Us*.

DNA is like the keyboard of a piano. It can remain silent or can play any song if YOU know how to 'interact.'

Apparently you Canadians, especially McGill people, are above US in finding that hidden genius within."

"The Hindu Vedas speak of his hidden potential as a coiled serpent called *Kundalini*. Australian Aborigines speak of and paint this coiled rainbow serpent as the unborn seed of potentiality. For the Celtic Druids this identical concept is also a serpent – The Dragon. In Egypt this energy called *Sekhem* was represented by a serpent was called *Uraeus*. For the Greek it was Ophis, where Sophia comes from. We are all hiding our inner sleeping yet fiery dragon. It is trapped in us."

"This serpent is nothing but a metaphor for a wave of energy. There are reports of people and even kids having incomprehensible strength and power during times of dire straits. Is this a forced 'Kundalini,' 'sekhem,' or 'dragon' wave of energy, figuratively, unleashing?"

"Exactly! The Christian name for Kundalini is God's Grace. These dire episodes are called *Grace Under Fire*."

"Like when blood flow is increased to part of the body that needs white blood cells or nutrients to rebuild."

"The body knows how and when to release this hidden potential, until then the serpent lay asleep like a coiled spring."

"How many of us realize that?"

"That's diversity."

"The variety in the levels of individual realization?"

"Yep."

"Isn't diversity euphemism for chaos?"

"Actually, the original Greek philosophical meaning of Chaos was not diversity, but the exact opposite. Chaos was the pre-existing formless *potential*. Diversity came later, according to, very ironically, the Chaos Theory."

"That's what I meant, taxi driving philosopher. A diverse ever-expanding *Cosmos*, which in Greek means order, arises because any slight disturbance to the initial conditions is exponentially amplified due to the sensitive nature of that pre-existence and its far reaching expansion."

"Butterfly Effect!"

"Exactly! These tiniest shifts in initial conditions as input of numbers can be amplified by seemingly insignificant imprecision or rounding error. The numerical computation of these shifts then will create a diagram, resembling a butterfly, which illustrates widely diverging potential outcomes in the chaotic systems. For example, this is encountered in trying to predict the weather. We are always slightly off because our input values are not perfect. Similarly, all you need is a tiny error like a single point mutation in our genes to cause chaos in our physiology resulting in developmental diseases."

"French philosopher Blaise Pascal asked how different would the history of the world be if the shape of Cleopatra's nose had been different."

"This is how a nose can lead to Chaos."

"In the beginning was the perfectly still caterpillar of nothingness. The wool tickled the inside of the divine nose causing God to sneeze creating untold Chaos."

"Gesundheit! The wooly larva of potential. You certainly walk paths beyond existentialism."

"So the butterfly is symbolic of the realization of the potential."

"It's not that simple. Mathematically the chaos theory says this 'butterfly' once unleashed is not predictive enough in the long-term."

"A truly wild butterfly!"

"Setting off from your Canada to the Michoacán mountains in Mexico. Theoretically the butterfly is deterministic according to initial conditions, but our math is not perfect enough."

"So our embryonic math is the real caterpillar."

"I guess there is some chaos in our math."

"In many cosmologies, including Buddhism, there is the notion that the chaos or the multi-layered universe arose from a singularity of nothingness through the origin of desire to experience that chaotic complex structure. So the gods, that's us, left the initial field of potential nothingness and descended to this illusory creation we call reality to pleasure ourselves."

"Who let the gods out?"

"Gods let themselves out into a lower dimension. Scottish philosopher David Hume and German philosopher Immanuel Kant both assert that time/space is but an illusion – an extremely realistic hologram projected from *The Matrix*. They echoed the mystics including the ancient Egyptians, Kabbalists, Australian Aborigines, Gautama Buddha and René Descartes'

Evil Genius, the basis for *The Matrix*. In the Zohar, the ancient book of Jewish mystical Kabbala tradition, the Tree of life is the dual cosmic structure of the hologram and the matrix. The hologram is the visible tree – the manifested design. The matrix is the invisible subterranean root system – the sustaining blueprint."

"Seth Lloyd, the MIT designer of the quantum computer, stated that *the history of the universe is, in effect, a huge and ongoing quantum computation.* Quantum mechanics does imply holographic nature of reality, projected from mathematical information."

"Aborigines called The Matrix of mathematical information, *guruwari* – the totem design."

"I spent a part of my childhood in Queensland, Australia. According to my Aboriginal grandmother, who lived in Cape York with the Murri, one of the elders described it like this. *In the trance vision one can see a web of intersecting threads on which the scenes of the tangible world as well as dreams and visions are hung.*"

"*A web of intersecting threads*, is, in fact, the hieroglyphic symbol for the Egyptian creator mother goddess Neith, who weaved the cosmos into being with strings. She is often represented with a weaving shuttle headdress, which is used to weave the invisible matrix. Those who access altered states of consciousness see the fabric of the invisible matrix, the source of the tangible world."

"In Quantum Physics this structure, the *web of intersecting threads*, perpetuates the visible and invisible dimensions. The invisible has a higher range of vibration frequency. The invisible can lower their vibration frequency and fall into the visible dimension. That's a big fall though."

"That's the Fall from Grace. It happened when the gods themselves out. But we, the fallen gods, don't listen to the wisdom of the Scotts, the Germans, the Egyptians, the Jews, the Indigenous Australians, the Nepalese or the French. So now we have Fallen from Grace gotten addicted and stuck like a moth to our own holographic web, which we ourselves, as spiders, weaved. We collectively are both the moth and the spider. You could say they or we got kicked out of the Garden of Eden, the higher dimension of non-duality, and became entangled in the web. Now we are trying to free ourselves and return to Eden of unity following the traces we left on our way down *Jacob's Ladder* of *Genesis*."

"So, is this return journey what we label as *Spiritual Evolution*?"

"Basically, it is a return to the original potentiality from which all arose."

"An intentional regression back to whence we came – Eden."

"This the Greek *Apocatastasis* or restoration to the primordial condition. Greek *Apotheosis* or 'becoming god' is a parallel concept. Divine transformation or return to divinity. This is not simply a return, but with the boon of all the wisdom gained from all the experiential lessons. This is the design of the cosmos."

"Have you had a chance to read *The Grand Design* by Stephen Hawking in addition to your philosophical repertoire?"

"Yes, the quest for the Theory of Everything."

"Hawking enjoys pointing out that he has sold more books on physics than Madonna on sex."

"Not surprising with that kind of snarky remarks."

"How do you feel about his comment that *philosophy is dead*?"

"Is it or did science come from behind, I mean from very far behind, and merge with what gave birth to it, in the first place, forming a *quantum entanglement* of the two? After all, the person considered to be the *father of science*, Thales, was a philosopher. Don't forget that."

"Yes. An alignment was inevitable and meant to be. It was a matter of time.

Christopher Potter in his book *You Are Here: A Portable History of the Universe* says that *Quantum Physics has brought us to a place where we can begin to understand what certain mystics have always understood: how a world that appears to be made of separate things arises out of a world of inseparability.*"

"Oneness! It's like King Solomon's judgment depicted in *The Story of the Chalk Circle.*"

"We are cutting life in half into two dead pieces of the body and the soul."

"Science studies the body and religion the soul, both lifeless, trying to understand life. A Quixotic irony!"

"The question is, is science truly aligned with the mystics? And if so, why now?"

"You don't think these days are the most exciting to be alive ever?"

"Sure, with the world ending soon and all. Real exciting!"

"*This* world is ending. This *old* and *illusory* world!"

"You seem happy about it because …"

"A New World is here."

"Yeah right! More like an Illuminati New World Order of corporate slavery."

"Okay, calm down Alex Jones. Wag more, bark less. Be more Eckhart Tolle, who by the way already inhabits the dimension you are headed to: Vancouver."

"What *The Power of Now* and *A New Earth: Awakening to* blah blah blah'?"

"Yes, be here. Be in the Now. That's all the time you have. This moment. This eternal moment."

"Real heavy! I don't know if I have time for this."

"You had the time to read those books."

"I didn't. She did."

"Ms. Vancouver?"

"Yes, she gave me the Cliff's notes on them. I am yet to experience *The Power of Now.*"

"Life is now!! This timeless now. Australian Aborigines, who some say are a higher form of a human species, called it *tjukurrtjana* or Dreamtime, because we dream the world into being, *now.*"

"My mother gave me a book by scholar Robert Lawlor, who was studying among Aborigines. I have the kindle version in my iPad. He writes in *Voices of the First Day: Awakening in the Aboriginal Dreamland,*

None of the hundreds of Aboriginal languages contain a word for time, nor do the Aborigines have a concept of time. As with creation, the Aborigines conceive the passage of time and history not as a movement from past to future but as a passage from a subjective state to an objective expression. The first step in entering into the Aboriginal world is to abandon the conventional abstraction of time and replace it with the movement of consciousness from dream to reality as a model that describes the universal activity of creation."

"They knew dream is the womb where reality is conceived and nurtured."

"The great Swiss psychologist Carl Jung, the founder of modern psychology, said, *space and time seem to have a precarious existence in the minds of so-called primitive people and only harden with the idea of measurement.* Sounds likes Jung agrees with you."

"… and your grandmother's people – the Aborigines."

"This 'higher form of humans,' considered primitive by some, have existed independently in Australia for about 400,000 based on mitochondrial DNA studies. Other humans lived in Asia in parallel, around that time as recently discovered by archeologists of Tel Aviv University in Israel. Evolutionary geneticist Alan Wilson says, *it seems too far out to admit, but while Homo erectus was muddling along in the rest of the world, a few erectus had got to Australia and did something dramatically different – not even with stone tools - but it is there that Homo sapiens emerged and evolved.*"

"They are the earliest humanity, the first people. Dreamtime is the longest continuous spiritual understanding documented anywhere in the world. Primitive literally means the *first*.

According to Anthropologist Jared Diamond, *if the fulfillment and delineation of the human person with a social, natural, and self-transcendent setting is a universally valid measure for the evaluation of culture, primitive societies are our primitive superiors."*

"The irony of all this primitiveness or 'earliness' of the understanding of time is laughing at our ignorance and confusion of reality like a kookaburra in the outback."

"Friedrich Nietzsche explained why the 'primitives' understand reality better. *In our dreams we pass through the whole thought of earlier humanity. I mean, in the same way that man reasons in his dreams, he reasoned when in the waking state many thousands of years — The dream carries us back into earlier states of human culture, and affords us a means of understanding it better."*

"This is a paradox – this idea that dreams harness more clarity than waking reasoning. This implies that dreams are redefining time for us. Though difficult to interpret, the clues are lurking in those blurry night trips, like an undecipherable computer program code – like 42."

"In the book *Buddha in Redface*, a Native American elder from New Mexico tells the psychologist Dr. Eduardo Duran about this Dreamtime. *Human beings required a way to have perspective and reference, and because of that, another energy emerged from the dream, and this is known today as 'time.' It is from the energies of dream and time that the third was given birth to, and that third one is known as the 'dreamtime.' Dreamtime is also known as 'mind.' And the dreamtime mind is reflected by the emptiness of awareness."*

"Time is a construct of convenient perspective?"

"Some call it Zero Time or Null Time. Eleanor Roosevelt called it 'The Present:' *Yesterday is history. Tomorrow is a mystery. Today is a gift. That's why we call it 'The Present'.* Now is eternal!"

"That's a stretch!"

"Isn't it? All the time, all the moments that ever 'existed,' exist, and 'will exist' all simultaneously existing in this eternal Now. That *is* a stretch.

Let me allow Joseph Campbell to define eternity.

Eternity is not some later time. Eternity is not a long time. Eternity has nothing to do with time. Eternity is that dimension of here and now, that time segments. This is it. If you don't get it here and now you will not get it anywhere else."

"Hmmm ... Einstein did say *People like us, who understand physics, know that the distinction between past, present, and future is only a stubbornly, persistent illusion.*"

"Walt Whitman rendered it in poetic form. *Here or henceforward it is all the same to me, I accept Time absolutely.*"

"No distinction; all the same. Time is not rigidly linear?"

"Many ancestors were operating with a very different view of life and time than modern people currently hold. Modern shamans still operate so. In fact, linguist Benjamin Whorf said, in the Hopi view, *time disappears and space is altered*. Time was seen as flexible and changeable and as a locator or organizer of realities, like the internet."

"I didn't know the Internet was invented that far back in time."

"Well, that 'back in time' not back there. There is no back there."

"American physicist John Wheeler of Princeton University said, *time keeps everything from happening at once*. I think what he meant is what you are saying."

"Everything does happen at once, but we isolate ourselves to a specific moment and move on to another. René Adolphe Schwaller De Lubicz, the author of *The Temple of Man*, said, *every day we observe a great mystery: everything that exists has a seed. Time is the passage between seed and fruit*."

"Every moment that ever existed or will exist is like a webpage. You can access it if you know the URL. You can always come back to homepage."

"That 'back in time,' is still here, now."

"The evolution actually means unfolding. Something that is unfolded always exists, either in the folded or unfolded form. It is always there, but not necessarily experienced in this parallel moment. We are moving from one parallel now to another."

"The persistent cyclist, Einstein, also said, *reality is an illusion albeit a persistent one*."

"She told me about Tolle's story of the two monks. I like that because it is a parable."

"Parables do the tricks sometimes. Jesus said in Mark 4:11, *to you it is given to know the mystery of the kingdom, but to them that are without all these things are done in parables.*"

"Subtle. The story … I think I get it, but I am not sure."

"The two monks?"

"Yes, so basically the two monks are walking across this natural landscape into a temple in another city. They see a beautiful young lady all prissy and dressed up near a stream. She is reluctant to cross because she doesn't want to get the dress wet. One of the monks picks her up without saying a word and carries her across. After several hours they reach the city. The monk who didn't carry the lady wants to know why the other one carried a woman, which is forbidden."

"So the first monk says *I put her down a long time ago, you are still carrying her.*"

"So the second monk was not in the now."

"Right! What about you?"

"It's not easy for me. I am a left-brained thinker and a rationale analyst."

"You are a time traveler"

"Well, I don't think it is quite like that."

"Sure it is."

"How so?"

"Time is three dimensional. Every moment is a probability that can be organized into a 3D framework to understand."

"You lost me with your *Brief History of Time.*"

"Okay. Let's say there is a three dimensional room. There is nothing there except all of the moments of what we call past, present and future. Except for every moment of the 'past' there are also parallel moments of 'pasts' that you were not aware. Think of them as past parallel reality potential or probabilities that you didn't realize. You recall experiencing only one of them. The present is also the same. Think of this 'present' as one of many probabilities, but you are only consciously experiencing this and not others."

"Because I chose this?"

"Exactly. There are millions of web pages now on the net, but you choose one in your iPad for now. The others exist whether you are aware of them or not. But you are here, now."

"So there are other parallel now realities where Elvis is alive and Paul is dead. The future is the same. That part is plausible, but I struggle with the parallel pasts, because you are saying there were parallel pasts where Hitler or Jesus did not exist."

"That is true. But those parallel parts were only potentials. So your this life is a journey from one end of the room to the other on one of the infinite number of probable paths. The path you are on continued from one of parallel paths where both of them did exist. However, remember the room is a visual aid or a metaphor and not reality."

"Okay, you are saying time travel is just more like space travel and not only can you go to the past that you once experienced but also others that you consciously didn't."

"Yes. How different would the history of the world be if could go back in time and edit one word in the original copy of the book of Genesis? What would be the Butterfly Effect?"

"Like in the movie *The Butterfly Effect* when Evan Treborn travels to the times written in journal."

"Then he lives in alternative future realities. What if *created* became *became*? What if you swapped those words in the first line in *Genesis*?"

"This is science fiction and theory, even though the implication is profound. No one does it in real life."

"Everyone does it."

"What?"

"Dreams, imagination, and visions."

"But those are not real."

"As opposed to this?"

"Yes, this is real. I am here. I am in the Now. At least sometimes."

"This is your waking dream."

"You mean daydream? Doesn't make any sense."

"Daydream is one within the waking dream. That's the non-visual version. The visual dream is the Feature Presentation."

"The visual dream? You mean what I am seeing right now with my eyes?"

"Sure, let's say light is penetrating your eye lens and hitting your retina, this is what you perceive to be out there with your brain."

"It is just like vivid visions that you see with your eyes fully closed."

"Exactly, how does your brain know the difference between your 'vivid vision' and your 'eye vision' of what is perceived to be in front of you?"

"Yes, but the vivid vision is rare and imagined. These reveries are obviously fake."

"Exactly, what if the vivid visions are not rare and happening all the time?"

"They do ... to schizophrenics."

"So if the schizophrenics, whose visual cognitive processes are not under full endocrinological control, are 'confused' about the two interjected forms of vision, at least according to the normal, then this means the 'normal' are being sold a convincing picture, with no oscillating confusion."

"So you are saying that we are not necessarily more aware of the reality than a schizophrenic. We are watching one set channel. Their TV uncontrollably switches between two or more channels."

"Exactly, this is why when we dream, we are convinced it is real and that we are awake. The dream reality channel is off when we are 'up.' But all channels are equally real when we are solely attuned to that particular channel."

"Except when we are not, like lucid dreaming. Then we know it is a dream."

"Right, but see what happens when you try to retrieve the memory of a lucid dream or one of your past waking events. What happens to the memory image?"

"It is not vivid. Looks fake. An obvious reverie and not a real event."

"Right. So which one was real, if they both seem equally fake now?"

"Good point. Hence, the condition we call 'false memory.' We cannot tell the difference between a real memory and false memory, unless you are Eidetic."

"Yes, eidetic memory, commonly called *photographic memory,* makes us ask the question: Why it is so rare?"

"Because it is an evolutionary mechanism. If all of our recalls of dreams, past events, and imagination were vivid we would be in real trouble. We would be bombarded with multiple 3D vivid imagery and we would not know where we are, what is happening, and why there is a humongous T-Rex in my living room?"

"Yes, so it is controlled. Your whole life is under control."

"By who? *The Truman Show.*"

"You are so close my friend, so close. This Truman, this Descartes' *Evil Genius,* is YOU."

"I wish, if that was true, I would already be in Vancouver."

"Well, you are."

"I didn't realize your cab has a name called Vancouver. I meant the city in British Columbia, by Burrard Inlet."

"Okay, back to dreaming. In the waking state everything seems real and vivid because the pineal gland in the middle of your brain is secreting DMT at a controlled specific concentration."

"Dimethyltryptamine."

"Yes, Dr. Rick Strassman of University of New Mexico called it *The Spirit Molecule* in his so titled book and its new groundbreaking and stupendous documentary version. But the science is still a little 'blurry', pun intended, on the exact function of DMT."

"And the Pineal gland."

"According to René Descartes, it is *the point of mediation between the material body and the immaterial soul.* Dr. Raja Dove describes it in terms of Quantum Physics. *Pineal gland converts waves into particles, producing particle pattern – pictures, visions, configurations – in accord with one's holographic belief system.*"

"It's a signal converter attached to an antenna."

"Perhaps, it is the tether of the soul of consciousness to the body."

"We are not exactly sure why it is produces DMT in the waking state, but we know its secretions rise dramatically in the states of vivid imagery like hallucinations including psychedelic, near-death experiences, mystic experiences, reveries, and altered states of consciousness brought about by meditation and perhaps dreaming."

"To those who have attained altered states of consciousness through increased secretion of DMT it is none other than the chemical mechanism for *Jacob's Ladder* in the biblical book of *Genesis.*"

"Was Jacob's sleeping or in an altered state? Either way when he woke, there was no ladder."

"So when you try to recall those you see blurry fake representations. Have you ever tried to recall your memory of your current reality within a lucid dream?"

"No, I haven't even thought about it."

"I have. The dream stays vivid and the recollection of this reality seems fake. So much so that once I returned to waking I couldn't tell if both are fake or both are real. Somehow both seemed the same."

"DMT is speculated to 'vivify' the waking visual process as well. It is present in the waking state, but much smaller compared to, say a near-death experience when the pineal gland is gushing DMT and your whole life is flashing in front of you. I heard it's very 3D and very real."

"You go through the serpent rope, silver chord, stargate, or the picture puzzle pattern door."

"Picture puzzle pattern door? Like the Dick Van Dyke chalk drawing portal in Mary Poppins?"

"You think, you wink, you do a double blink, close your eyes, and jump into an altered state of consciousness."

"Not just altered states. DMT vivifies what we perceive as the waking reality."

"So DMT makes visual cognitive process vivid or realistic. I think it also enables the human brain to interact with the cosmos that lies outside the frequency we perceive. It's like 3D glasses when you watch an IMAX 3D movie. Have you ever taken the glasses off and looked at the other viewers?"

"Yes, it seems a bit ridiculous how serious they are looking at a meaningless blurry blob of red and blue."

"Then you place your glasses back and fully immerse in the reality they collectively buy into."

"It seems to be that way. Now there is question of LSD. I have never done any drugs in my life. However, I once had an extremely vivid hallucination caused by hypothermia while climbing Mt Shasta in Northern California. I saw some sort of beings. They were really nice. The males looked like the older version of Obi-Wan Kenobi hologram with a white robe and a golden sash."

"Like the beings in *The Book of Revelation*?"

"To put a picture on them, yes. I swear one of them looked like Lawrence of Arabia with a goatee. I heard the name of a place called Serapis Bay. I don't know where it is. There were females too. Of course, you are going to say this is my fantasy and I wouldn't blame you. One female was this gorgeous long haired blonde with a Star Trek like tight uniform in dark greenish/grayish color standing in front of a craft. She had a belt and some gadgets on them. The texture of the uniform was not smooth but like elephant skin. Weird! She was really sweet to me. I felt this amazing bliss with them. She gave me the impression that she was a warrior on a mission to save mankind from itself. I call her *Joan of Arcturus*. Funny thing is I was on my way to 'heaven' or death."

"I thought you didn't believe in heaven."

"I pragmatically don't. *Shut up and calculate*, said physicist Richard Feynman. I am a scientist, a molecular geneticist, and an atheist. I read Richard Dawkins."

"No wonder. I read *Aesop's Fables*. The difference between Aesop and the scientists is that Aesop does not need to update his fables every year."

"Hollywood does it for him."

"Dawkins is the Oxford evolutionary biologist and staunch atheist, right? I guess you don't read the Bible."

"My stuff is *The God Delusion* and *The Blind Watchmaker: Why the Evidence of Evolution Reveals a Universe without Design*. The other guy I read is Carl Sagan. *Cosmos* and *Demon-haunted World*. But, I have read the whole Bible, which is some truth and history muddled with a lot of superstition. Even Sigmund Freud said, *the truths contained in religious doctrines are after all so distorted and systematically disguised*."

"Henry David Thoreau said, *men are probably nearer the central truth in their superstitions than in their science*. Perhaps, superstition is truth systematically disguised."

"I'm not so sure. I don't consider myself a Christian either. My hero Francis Crick, Nobel Prize winner for the co-discovery of the DNA double helix structure, is famous for saying, *Christianity may be okay between consenting adults in private but should not be taught to young children*."

"Crick also said, *an honest man, armed with all the knowledge available to us now, could only state that in some sense, the origin of life appears at the moment to be almost a miracle, so many are the conditions which would have had to have been satisfied to get it going.* It seems what separates a theologian and an atheistic molecular geneticist is the small word *almost*. Do you happen to find *any* of the Bible agreeable?"

"I would welcome a new better species of humans on earth. So I found Matthew 5:5 kind of refreshing. From the Sermon of the Mount: *Blessed are the meek, for they shall inherit the earth.*"

"Psalms 37:29 echoes it. Even Eckhart Tolle finds that *a new species is arising on the planet. It is arising now and you are it.*"

"This seems like a fantasy though, like a hallucination when presented in this way. We need science."

"You were talking about LSD."

"Yes, even Crick confided before his death that his discovery of the double helical structure of DNA came to him in a vision as two woven serpents during an altered state of consciousness brought about through his secret use of LSD.

LCD and other hallucinogenic drugs like ayahuasca, peyote, San Pedro cactus in the Americas, ibogane in West Africa, *Wisdom Potion* of the Druids, and soma in India stimulate the pineal gland to release DMT at higher concentrations. Hence, the vividness of the visions. Vedas say the poets drank large quantities of soma before composing the verses based on their visions."

"So what about the waking dream?"

"Why do you call it the dream? The waking state!"

"Okay, what happens if DMT or other endocrinological controls of the waking states are malfunctioning?"

"That's when our world visually begins to dissolve and we see something akin to a blurred recollection of a dream."

"Reality seems like a dream. Dream state is a kind of an alternative reality. Now the different alternative realities have become indistinguishable. That's a clue to the nature of reality."

"I thought it was 42."

"Maybe it is."

"Let me read you page 42 of *The Grand Design* by Stephen Hawking. I have Kindle in my iPad.

A different kind of alternative reality occurs in the science fiction film The Matrix, *in which human race is unknowingly living in a simulated virtual reality created by intelligent computers to keep them pacified and content ... Maybe this is not so far-fetched, because many people prefer to spend their time in the simulated reality of websites such as Second Life. How do we know we are not just characters in a computer generated soap opera? If we lived in a synthetic imaginary world, events would not necessarily have any logic or consistency or obey any laws. The aliens in control might find it more interesting or amusing to see our reactions, for example, if the full moon split in half, or everyone in the world on a diet developed an uncontrollable craving for banana cream pie. But if the aliens did enforce consistent laws, there is no way we could tell there was another reality behind the simulated one. It would be easy to call the world the aliens live in the 'real' one and the synthetic world a 'false' one. But if-like us-the beings in the simulated world could not gaze into their universe from the outside, there would be no reason for them to doubt their own pictures of reality. This is a modern version of the idea that we are all figments of someone else's dream."*

"In Hinduism, the universe is being dreamt into being by Vishnu."

"Australian Aborigines say, *we are dreaming within a greater dream.*"

"The Indian guru Paramahansa Yogananda said, *you are walking on the earth as in a dream. Our world is a dream within a dream.*"

"*What Dreams May come.*"

"Lewis Carroll:
Ever drifting down the stream
Lingering in the golden gleam
Life, what is it but a dream?"

"*You may say I'm a dreamer.*"

"But I'm not the only one."

"Is anyone awake?"

"The Awakened are. Buddha means awakened."

"Prince Siddhartha Gautama!"

"After he became Buddha, he realized that there is no way he could communicate and teach others what he had realized about reality. He was convinced that people would find his words simply crazy and nonsensical."

"If you are one step ahead of humanity you are a genius, if you are two steps ahead you are considered crazy. The latter are often put to death."

"Jesus was killed awake by those still sleeping. His last words were, *they know not what they do.*"

"Apparently, *they* still don't. *Be in the world; not of it.*"

"That's how the awakened live, a life in the context of surrealism. They know *The World* is an illusion. They know they are just *in it* and *not of it.* Sufi Muslim master Hazrat Inayat Khan knew exactly how Gautama Buddha felt. This is from his book *Awakening: A Sufi Experience.*

Imagine that you are awake and walking about amongst people who sleep; how can you communicate with them? You realize that they can have no idea about your awareness because they are still sleeping. You used to be like that yourself. But now you are awake."

PETROSEXUAL

"Are you awake, Raye?"

"Sorry, I dosed off for a second."

"That's how boring I must be."

"No, I am a bit tired."

"Any dreams?"

"In fact, yes. How long was I asleep?"

"About five minutes."

"No way!"

"Way!"

"The dream seemed like it was almost two hours."

"I am sure it was. Time dilation! Relativity!!"

"There was no way all that happened in five minutes, even considering time is relative."

"I will let Einstein's aphorisms explain: *When you are courting a nice girl an hour seems like a second. When you sit on a red-hot cinder a second seems like an hour. That's relativity.*"

"Relativity indeed!"

"What was the dream?"

"I wish it was *a nice girl.* I was in a tropical island in this breathtaking, yet elegant outdoor area of a hotel. I was drinking tea and chatting with this old British man named Arthur."

"Was he a knight in shining armor?"

"No. Actually he was dressed like a local in one of those long man-skirts."

"Must be an island thing."

"Or he was gay."

"Maybe he was an island metrosexual."

"He did all the talking. This was not a lucid dream. I really don't remember everything he said, but what he said seemed like he was describing some aspects of my thesis projects."

"Specifically what?"

"See my interest was sparked back in Minnesota and Wisconsin by Dr. John Hawks. He is a Biological Anthropologist at UW Madison. In his research into the genetic basis of evolution, which is my area, he found out that contrary to what some people or scientists think, the human species is not only evolving, the evolution process is speeding up."

"Counterintuitive if you watch the news, but hopeful."

"Evolution is often misunderstood. It is simply a process of unfolding. The potential remains folded like a dormant seed. The unfolding reveals that. Vedics and Aborigines knew this unfolding. In Sanskrit it is called *lila*. For Aborigines this is the uncoiling of Dreamtime, *tjukurrtjana*, into this reality, *yuti* – the tangible hologram. Our potential is the coiled rainbow serpent. She is spitting out the potential into actuality in a hurry now."

"Why the hurry?"

"The cause of the speeding is currently debated."

"But it is real?"

"Empirically so! It was published by the National Academy of Sciences. We are apparently in the *evolutionary fast lane and are becoming increasingly different*. The research shows that in the past 5,000 years, which is a geological flash, genetic change has occurred at a rate roughly 100 times higher than any other period."

"Now this is physical evolution and not cultural, right?"

"Yes, we know the technological and cultural evolution is at a crescendo. The physical evolution is understood to be so slow that it is measured in geological terms. But make no mistake about it. Things have significantly changed genetically since the Egyptian times. I know this sounds preposterous to many but we can be considered a new sub species, at least."

"Genetically, and not just technologically and culturally!"

"According to Professor Henry Harpending of University of Utah, Salt Lake City, a co-author with Hawks, the genes are evolving fast everywhere, but not every geographical group is heading into the same directions. He stated that we are getting less alike. It is like a bifurcation."

"So much for the melting pot."

"Actually the melting aspect is there, but so is the bifurcation. Melting is even more because of globalization. This bifurcation, called cladogenesis in evolutionary biology, is not racial, but generational and at the level of intelligence."

"The new and smart gets smarter. Sounds controversial."

"All new discoveries are, at first. However, corroborating studies in psychology strongly mirror this. The famous *Flynn Effect* is nicely elucidated by Dr. James Flynn, of the University of Otago in New Zealand, in his book *What is Intelligence?* He discovered that the average IQ of every new generation is higher than the last. This was done with abstract and geometric concepts that are trans-generational to eliminate bias. Since the mean IQ must be 100, the scale has to be revised every time to adjust for the 'evolution.' He partly ascribes the Flynn Effect to increased cultural sophistication. In other words, we've all gotten smarter as our culture, especially the techno-culture, has sharpened us."

"That can't be so bad if we are all turning smarter. It is a welcome change."

"Of course this is the average IQ shift. Remember there is a bifurcation or a polarization."

"Humanity is now increasingly bipolar. You could have fooled me."

"Yes, so not everyone is getting smarter, but the smarter are skewing the spectrum data. When you take the 'top half,' the deviation is paradigm shifting."

"Wow!"

"This half has new genes. It appeared between 100 and 200 generations. It gets dramatic in the top 20 to 30 percent. Seven percent of human genes are undergoing a revolution."

"How do they know they are new genes?"

"Good question. They studied genetic variations called single nucleotide polymorphisms. These are single-point mutations in the DNA sequence on chromosomes. If the random mutation is advantageous then it is 'selected' and rapidly introduced into the population, along with DNA on either side of the mutation. If the same chromosome in multiple individuals had a segment with an identical pattern of mutations this would indicate that the segment of the chromosome had not been broken up or recombined recently and therefore definitely new. Old genes in the chromosomes are broken up and reassembled."

"What is the cause? Is it because the physical evolution is catching up to the technological and cultural evolution?"

"Philosophically that makes perfect sense. Biology is materialistic. It does not work that way. One hypothesis proposes that it is nutrition, environment, and increased population size. Biology has to learn from physics. It has hit a huge roadblock in trying to understand the cosmos solely in materialistic terms."

"The cosmology was hopelessly incomplete?"

"In the new book *The Edge of Physics* Anil Ananthaswamy, a writer for *New Scientist* and *National Geographic*, point out that nearly 90 percent of the mass of the universe is made of invisible dark matter, which is only understood to be present due to its apparent gravitational effect. Speaking inclusive of dark or invisible energy he says, *roughly 96 percent of the universe cannot be explained with the theories at hand. All our efforts to understand the material world have illuminated only a tiny fraction of the cosmos.*"

"*Most of the Universe is Missing*. We are experiencing 4 percent or less."

"The book *The 4 Percent Universe: Dark Matter, Dark Energy, and the Race to Discover the Rest of Reality* by Richard Panek elaborates all of this well.

Cosmos here means the multiverse, where *our universe is just one of the possible 10500 universes, if not more.* Quantum Physics had to grow up to illuminate beyond the material cosmos. It is not materialistic anymore."

"It is the older, wiser, more spiritually enlightened brother of the two. Interestingly, the ancient practice of alchemy saw the visible material and the spiritual world as a unified system. St. Augustine knew that the concept of time only began with the advent of perceived material."

"Personally I am a bit offended by geneticists being called the 'less enlightened.' The father of Genetics is an Austrian Augustinian monk named Gregor Mendel and the father chemistry Robert Boyle was a student of the Egyptian religious text, *Emerald Tablet*, attributed to god Thoth. Take that, mediating particle shooters."

"So then where did the materialism come from? Was the mother of genetics a shopaholic? Ms. Black Friday?"

"I see what you mean, but you must understand that the monk Mendel didn't know anything about what we call DNA. He knew its manifestations, so to speak. He knew phenotypes, but not the genotypes."

"Yes, genetics is still 'Third Eye Blind.' Random mutations are not random. Nothing is random. A Zen proverb says, *No snowflake ever falls in the wrong place.*"

"*Every freckle on my face is where it's supposed to be.*"

"Video?"

"India Arie. Remember we talked about the entanglement or alignment of philosophy and science. Well, guess what, it is happening to genetics and quantum physics as well. So your idea of a driving force that pushes physical evolution to catch up to technological and cultural evolution is not unobserved at other levels, especially in microscopic level, including microbes. This is the principle of self-preservation. Balance or death!"

"Hasn't it happened in the past?"

"Countless of times. In fact the study indicated that so some time we have been at an evolutionary lull between two storms. Dr. Hawks studies Neanderthal genetics. One storm happened about 40,000 years ago."

"Art?"

"Actually yes. But you are jumping ahead. At that time there were two main species. Possibly more if you include another possible species in China and *Homo floresiensis*."

"The hobbit?"

"Yes, for simplicity let's focus on *Homo sapiens* and Neanderthals so I can illustrate the bifurcation. All of a sudden there was an outbreak of tonal languages, practices like burying the dead with food and artifacts for the afterlife, and what seem like religio-spiritual-shamanistic and herb & spiritual healing tendencies among most known human populations round the planet. These were the 'medicine men,' if you will."

"The tonal language is where the frequency of the vibration is fine tuned to achieve a specific spiritual effect."

"This is basically shamanistic chanting. These practices were significant because these populations were isolated, shown by the studies by Dr. Spencer Wells of Oxford University. The paintings by shamans are incredibly beautiful and complex. They seem to represent their mythologies, cosmologies, and possibly altered states of consciousness."

"Joseph Campbell said, *myths are clues to the spiritual potentialities of the human life*. George Lucas wrote *Star Wars* based on his work on myths worldwide.

Star Wars is a hero's quest of initiation. Luke Skywalker is another face. He wrote the ultimate self-help book."

"Something that could be tilted *Myth for Dummies*."

"In *The Hero with a Thousand Faces* he writes, *myth is the secret opening through which the inexhaustible energies of the cosmos pour into the human cultural manifestation*."

"The communication of this, in this art form, was unprecedented and abrupt. The cave man began to decorate their caves."

"These were just the *Homos*?"

"Okay. I prefer 'petrosexual.' 'petro' meaning rock, because the petroglyphs or paintings and carvings were on rock caves."

"I know. I know. I meant, didn't the Neanderthals do that?"

"We know they buried their dead. And ultimately were themselves dead … altogether."

"It's a decorate-or-die world. The brawny tough guys are defeated and eliminated by the interior decorators."

"Well, the interior decorators had an advantage."

"Queer eye?"

"Okay. That's enough Bravo jokes. To quote Darwin *it is not the strongest of the species or the most intelligent that survive but the most responsive to change*."

"Change is initiation. What was the change?"

"It is a paradox. We see that in the surviving species expression of new genes. Eventually over three hundred unique *Homo sapiens* genes were identified. These are not present in any ancestors."

"Did they come from the *missing link?*"

"The link was not missing. It's the *geneticists* that inserted it that's missing, figuratively speaking."

"The *inserted link.*"

"One of these genes is called microcephalin. It appeared around this time, about 40,000 years ago. Microcephaly means small brain. This is the paradox. Smaller but denser. This result was higher cognitive abilities and its expression in tonal language, art, healing, burial of the dead with artifacts for afterlife, and awareness of multi-dimensional spirituality."

"The pre-historic Indigo children!"

"Leonardo Da Vinci said, *where the spirit does not work with hand, there is no art.* All of a sudden the spiritually themed art was everywhere. Lascaux, Chauvet, and Aurignacian near Haute Garonne in France. Arnhem land, Ku–ring-gai, Mutawinthji in Australia, Hohlenstein-Stadei in Germany, some in Italy and several, including blombos cave, in South Africa. The number of sites in France and Spain alone number almost 350. It was truly a sudden explosion of creative impulse and power. These art were so sophisticated at portraying perceptive depth that Pablo Picasso, after visiting the caves, pointed out that *we apparently invented nothing; it was all done before.*"

"Is it just art or were they trying to convey their view of reality?"

"Joseph Campbell called them *temples* and *landscapes of the soul.*

This is what Aboriginal scholar Robert Lawlor wrote in *Voices of the First Day: Awakening in the Aboriginal Dreamland.*

Aboriginal painting in Carnarvon National Park, western Queensland, are considered some of the finest and most colorful in Australia still in their natural state. The spattering of pigment outlining a hand or implement, creates an inversion between the negative background space, which appears as a positive activated surface, and the object, which then becomes an empty silhouette. This sort of inversion is basic to the Aboriginal view of reality. As in the cosmologies of modern physics, Aborigines conceive that space and its contents have no physical existence independent of the activity of the perceiving mind. Therefore space must be primarily considered and described as an aspect of consciousness."

"So any theories on the stimulus of this great shift in consciousness?"

"There is. It is very good in my mind actually. There is a pre-Inca archeological site called Chavin de Huantar in Peru's Conchucos Valley."

"40,000 years old?"

"No. About 3000, but it gave a tantalizing clue. There are these deep dark underground passages that lead to these 'sacred' spots. The idea of sacredness is due to amazing carvings and paintings. There was a huge problem for the archeologist though."

"Snakes?"

"No. There was no soot anywhere."

"Obviously the Interior Decorators were ultra clean."

"I see you still got the sssssnakessssss. No soot or any sign of use of fire. There is no way that these carvings were done there in that darkness. No way!"

"So how did they do it?"

"They found many snuff pipes made of dear bones and sculptures of faces with what looks like mucus coming out the noses. Also, the modern day local shamans known as kuranderas use a hallucinogenic ayahuasca drink to enter into psychoactive states. It was discovered that a human entering the deepest darkest areas of the caves can still see the walls of inner chambers. This seems impossible because what they saw was not a vivid vision of an alternate reality, but what the place they are standing in would appear with a significant light source."

"Some light is there?"

"No, definitely no external source. In normal consciousness it is pitch black. You cannot see your hand in front of you."

"Wow! So ...?"

"A completely unrelated work of research shed some light on it. Pun intended."

"Nice!"

"NASA and labs were researching to see any particles from space can penetrate the earth crust, specially the top milestone thousand feet. They thought perhaps nothing would make it that far, but they were happily wrong. In several thousand foot deep underground station, when they pointed their detectors upward they observed a light signal from space in the shape of a cross."

"Jesus?"

"In fact it was a constellation known as the Northern Cross or Cygnus, meaning swan, some 6,000 light years away. They were detecting cosmic rays, specifically X-rays and gamma rays. These rays were named cygnates, meaning the *children of the swan*."

"The swan is a sacred symbol in many ancient cultures around the world."

"Right! The source of these rays was a binary star system. One of the stars is active and the other one had exploded and collapsed. In 1975, Dr. Stephen Hawking bet Dr. Kip Thorne, an astrophysicist at Cal Tech, that this Cygnus X-1 would not turn out to be a black hole."

"The bet was a subscription to *Penthouse*."

"Yes, Hawking lost, to Throne's wife great annoyance. The thing is Cygnus X-1 is the source a relativistic jet. It's like a two way cone shaped cosmic ray emission machine. There are many of those, but this one was special. One of the sides of the jet was aimed right at earth. It is now the most studied astronomical object of its class. Even ancient Egyptians knew that earth was a receiver of such rays. They have a hieroglyph called *Ta Mari* to mark that."

"Where are you going with this shooting swan?"

"Well, studies showed that these cygantes produce flashes of light when they hit the retina and this is highly enhanced under the influence of hallucinogenic substances."

"So the stoned petrosexuals got impregnated by the swan sperm, like Leda, Queen of Sparta, by Zues disguised as a swan, in *The Iliad*, giving birth to Helen of Troy.

"Something like that. Data shows that 40,000 years ago cosmic rays reaching earth was more than double the base rate."

"So cosmic rays invented art. I knew it!"

"Well it's not the rays themselves but the artists that responded to that stimulus. I am sure it was not the whole population either. It's like Dr. Hawks's study. The genetic evolution hits the most sensitive and those responding positively, who become more and more common and ultimately become the majority."

"I am sure the 'artists' were thought of as weird at first by the jealous dull ones."

"And even mistreated or even persecuted. You know how we initially treat the iconoclastic revolutionaries among us."

"Joan of Arc. Jesus. Akhenaten. Galileo Galilei."

"Mahatma Gandhi. Martin Luther King. John Lennon. Princess Diana"

"Indigo children."

"These artists were way beyond that. Joseph Campbell said that these cave were the wombs of the earth, sites used in rites of passage in the initiation of the new young children into wisdom keepers or shamans. He said a shaman is *someone who has turned totally inward. The whole unconscious has opened up and he has fallen into it.*

"When the shaman enters the cave. He enters his subconscious. Womb of Mother Earth, Pachamama. Belly of the whale. The labyrinth. A rite of passage. A rebirth."

"Yes, in fact I am involved with a project testing the DNA of these gifted and precocious 'New Children' right now. This is to develop the findings by a 2005 University of Chicago study that children born since the mid-1980s have two newly identified genes. One of them is new version of microcephalin and the other is ASMP, Abnormal Spindle-like Microcephaly-associated Protein. They are related to brain neurogenesis and densification. Once again don't let the name fool you. The result is denser brains. ASMP codes for the so called IQ domain. One is present in 70 percent and both in 30 percent of these kids. Their IQs are reaching 160, while anyone with an IQ of 130 is considered a genius. For evolutionary geneticists this correlation is extremely significant, because we had thought genetic evolution had slowed down."

"So, this is like a new dramatic step in human evolution?"

"Let me give you a background of evolutionary history. There are these major events. Evolution is not truly gradual, uniform, and slow. This phyletic gradualism is an illusion. Evolution is better understood as quantum. Change comes in leaps with no liminal state. We call it punctuated equilibrium."

"Punch what?"

"Stephen Jay Gould built upon the work of Ernst Mayr to develop this. Species are more often than not evolutionarily stagnant. This corresponds to periods of stability in their immediate habitat as well as the global and cosmic conditions. These conditions are obviously not without end, but interesting because a sort of a species dysfunction or tension builds up towards the end of some of these events. The tension is however, not always great enough to be a critical mass exceeding a threshold."

"But something gives, sometime."

"Precisely, some stimulus. They can be subtle or catastrophic."

"Cosmic rays or an asteroid."

"Intra or extra planetary. Some are not well understood. But consider PC operating systems, they go through a punctuated upgrade. New codes get introduced to the software and often hardware must be reconfigured to accommodate this."

"The software leads and the hardware follows. But these upgrades are not random mutation. They are carried out by purpose driven intelligent beings, who then live their lives through them."

"True. An external stimulus is always postulated."

"Didn't Carl Sagan say something about Cosmic rays having a role in human evolution?"

"He wrote that in his book *Cosmic Connection: An Extraterrestrial Perspective.*"

"The children of the swan. I have seen symbols of ancient cultures. The one that strikes is the Entangled Swans forming a Double Helix or spiral from Sri Lanka. It is called *Hansa Puttu*. Sagan said we are all made of star dust."

"Well, ultimately we all came from one single source."

"Goddess! The womb of Sophia!!"

"Well, I was thinking something like the Big Bang."

"… which resulted in the creative cosmic orgasmic childbirth."

"But lately The Big Bang theory has gone quiet in the light or noise of quantum non-locality formulated through the wave function collapse. The double-slit experiment with sub atomic particle, in 1909 by British physicist Geoffrey Taylor, and later 60-carbon molecule called the Bucky ball, short for buckministerfullerene, proved that particles, atoms, and molecules do not exist as such. They are just potential existing as a cosmically pervasive wave."

"The Big Potential. The Aboriginal Dreamtime is the wave function."

"Dreamtime is the non-local big potential that collapses into the particle world we see in our version of reality. They knew the wave function collapse and expressed it metaphorically through the rainbow serpent myth."

"So if molecules, I mean biological, are non-local wave functions, then are all biological species subject to the same law of quantum physics?"

"Naturally. George Simpson of Columbia University called this rapid emergence of new species due to drastic changes in conditions literally *Quantum Evolution*."

"Instantaneous change."

"Geologically speaking under 50,000 is instantaneous."

"You said we are changing into a new species in under 5,000 years. A flash!"

"Well, I didn't say that. Dr. Hawks' research indicates that. It *is* a flash."

"This is a forced response to the technological and cultural evolution?"

"This stage of evolution began with the development of written language, spread of agriculture and development of cities, roughly correlating to the mean estimated age of the emergence of the ASMP gene of 5,800 years ago. Since then we have observed a highly rapid spread of the gene. According to a hypothesis called a 'selective sweep', the rapid spread of a gene through the population indicates that the mutation is somehow advantageous to the individual."

"It's a keeper."

"Advantage is the capacity to advancement. We can see that those advancements are now unprecedented and exponential. We are deep into The Age of Information, which is supposed to have begun on 14 February 1946, the day of the unveiling of the first electronic general-purpose computer. In 2005, information was doubling every 36 months. By 2008, it was every 11 months. In August 2010, Google CEO Eric Schmidt said: *Every two days now we create as much information as we did from the dawn of civilization up until 2003.* By the end of 2010, information was doubling every 11 hours. Now even faster."

"Whoa! TMI."

"Too Much Information!"

"Is this crescendo sustainable?"

"The imbalance cannot be sustainable."

"It must happen. How is it going to happen?"

"The next punctuating equilibrium!"

"The next realignment!!"

"Paul Hawken, one of my favorite eco-entrepreneurs and founder of WiserEarth, finds that the earth has an immune system like an organism. An immune system always fights back. We are none other than its own white blood cells. His book *Blessed Unrest: How the Largest Movement in the World Came into Being and Why No One Saw it Coming* spells this out. Here's how he words it.

... the growth of a worldwide movement that is determined to heal the wounds of the earth with the force of compassion, dedication, and collective intelligence and wisdom. ... They share no orthodoxy or unifying ideology; they follow no charismatic leader; they remain supple enough to coalesce easily into larger networks to achieve their goals. While they are mostly unrecognized by politicians and the media, they are bringing about what may one day be judged the single most profound transformation of human society."

"French philosopher, paleontologist, Jesuit priest Pierre Teilhard de Chardin since 1920 wrote his philosophy in his works such as *The Divine Milieu* and *The Phenomenon of Man*. He was ahead of his peers in stating that mankind is evolving, mentally and socially, toward a final spiritual unity that he called the *Omega Point*. The most well-known quote from his is:

For the observers of the Future, the greatest event will be the sudden appearance of a collective human consciousness."

INCEPTION

"I completely forgot about the dream I had."

"Oh yes, having tea and scones with King Arthur in front of the hotel in the tropical island."

"His accent was very English. It sounded exactly like that TV show from the 80s called *Mysterious Universe*."

"One with the rotating crystal skull theme."

"In the dream he said all these random and weird stuff. *I've been designed to tell the truth, I cannot lie. Touch me now and feel my force, I will give you life.*"

"Hmmm."

"Something about *a cosmic design. An alien messenger. The bringer of a new day. Harbinger of a new race. Evolving soon. See the world through the all-seeing eyes. Another dimension. Perception expand. Evolution of man?*"

"2001: A Space Odyssey"

"Arthur."

"C. Clarke."

"Oh yes. The Stanley Kubrick movie."

"The monolith."

"Yes, that was the symbol for the quantum leap in evolution at the beginning of the movie."

"The ape men touch the monolith. One of them throws the bone tool in the air."

"The next thing is a transformation of the tool from a bone to an extremely sophisticated space center."

"Talk about a quantum leap."

"No doubt!"

"The monolith reappears at the end of the movie. Doing the same thing again."

"Yes. Yes. It is also in his sequel book *2010: Odyssey Two.*"

"And its movie *2010: The Year We Make Contact.*"

"The spacemen apparently, symbolizing the mankind, has now explored space, and landed on the moon. He is wealthy and living in an opulent yet sterile room."

"More like dying in an opulent and sterile room."

"Yes, but apparently mankind survives. In *2010: The Year We Make Contact*, the cosmonauts are asked to go back to Earth because *something wonderful is about to happen*. In *2001: A Space Odyssey*, Then you see a human embryo in a transparent egg floating towards the earth. The monolith is some kind of an intervention/conception. This theme was first introduced by him in his 1953 pioneering book *Childhood's End*."

"An intervention/conception. An Inception."

"An Inception is an event that is a beginning."

"I have that song, you want to listen?"

"What song?"

"Starchild.

Touch me now and feel my force
I will give you life
History will change its course
Man will survive
Chorus: Something's strange, I'm so confused, I don't know why
(secrets have not been told)
I've been designed to tell the truth, I cannot lie
(when will the truth unfold?)
I heard the news, a mystery, a strange device
(what does the future hold?)
I'm so afraid, I just can't see through all these lies
(behold this alien messenger)
is this a cosmic design?
(the bringer of a new day)
one by four by nine
Reach out to me and seal your fate
A new phase is near
Come to me and cross the gate
No pain, no fear
Chorus:

A strange signal, beamed out in space
From the face of the moon
Harbinger of a new race
We'll be evolving soon
I see the future, a new star will rise
I see the world through the all-seeing eyes
Of the Starchild
I have entered another dimension
My perception expands
Transcending beyond comprehension
Evolution of man?
I see the future, a new star will rise
I see the world through the all-seeing eyes
Of the Starchild
Time has come, a brand new sun
Shining down on you
The reign of peace has now begun
Dreams have come true
I see the future, a new star will rise
I see the world through the all-seeing eyes
Of the Starchild"

"That is what Arthur was saying. He also said *you will wake up in time*."

"Indigos."

"What about the them?"

"They are the starchild. *Childhood' End* introduced them first."

"You are saying they are the inception."

"They are the conception. The modern *children of the swan*. The conception has happened."

"This is science fiction."

"Actually the book of revelation talks about the same *floating embryo*; the swan sperm. *The Great Sign in Heaven.*"

"This is religious mythology."

"Joseph Campbell understood most of the episodes in religious text only have relevance with respect to the role they play in transformation of oneself. They are the facilitators of the rites of passage that initiate you."

"This is indigenous mythology."

"See what this means.

Revelation 12:1 & 2. *A great sign appeared in heaven: a woman clothed with the sun, with the moon under her feet and a crown of twelve stars on her head. She was pregnant and cried out in pain as she was about to give birth.*

Mayan prophecy says the same."

"So we are just unborn embryos?"

"According to the interpretation of the Mayan Calendar by their chronicle Popol Vuh, the Planet Earth was impregnated somewhere in the 1980s. Think of Earth as an egg or ovum penetrated by a cosmic 'swan' sperm, of course symbolized by the monolith in *2001: A Space Odyssey*, with the conception of a new inhabitant."

"Starchild?"

"They are the indigos and/or as Mayans call them 'men of wisdom' and 'ancestors.' These children are wise beyond their years."

"Wisdom *out of the mouths of babes and sucklings?*"

"Exactly. That's in Mathew 21:16. According to the time measure of the Mayans called 'kin' the time about 260 'days,' according to their time units, represents the planetary gestation period. As any obstetrician would do, the Popol Vuh gives a rough 'due date' of the new baby. It falls around the winter solstice of 2012. De Chardin's *Omega Point*. However, we all know that those 'due dates' are not exact. But we know we are in the third trimester of this pregnancy. Any expecting mother would tell you that the third trimester is time of great discomfort and restlessness. The earth is now in labor. She is about to have to an explosively orgasmic childbirth."

"Is that why there is extreme pain and pleasure there today in the same breath?"

"Also, remember the babies are not very pretty at birth. But give it a nice bath and you have brand new life."

"Does the Popol Vuh address constant crying and changing diapers, too?"

"Nice! I guess it's your turn to be snarky."

"I know genetics is solid on rapid evolution. And the 'indigo' DNA is certainly skewed to one end of the intuitive ability spectrum. In psychology terms this is superconsciousness. How would Arthur C. Clarke know all this beforehand?"

"Which one of his coded and cryptic science fiction prediction has failed to realize?"

"Among his accurate predictions were humans landing on the moon in the 60s. He described the geostationary communication satellite years before like he was looking at it. He even foretold something akin to the Internet and its sites like Wikipedia called the *Global Library*. In the book, *2010 Odyssey Two*, written in the late 70s he casually mentions major tsunami in 2005 that the dolphins in the book predict, by not making their annual visit. The tsunami happened on December, 26 2004. He was off by six days."

"Maybe he was looking at it."

"You are talking about the parallel 'future' probabilities and how we time travel in dreams and visions."

"Also, intuiting."

"Like Einstein did."

"Everyone knows everything, but not everyone knows it."

"Like genetics now strongly suggests that *there is a genius in all of us.*"

"They are looking for the reading glasses that are on their heads."

"Intuition is this realization and the unfolding."

"That's clairgnosis!"

"Clairgnosis? You mean superconsciousness."

"And channeling."

"Channeling? Like a medium or an oracle."

"I have heard the basis of *Star Trek* came from such intuited material."

"From where?"

"From elsewhere."

"That's clear as mud."

"Muddy water, let stand, becomes clear. – Lao Tzu. Think of them as *foreign exchange students."*

"Here to learn and teach a *foreign* idea?"

"Like *peace* and *balance.* Think about the Great Imbalance you were acknowledging. Look at the world today. Is it living up to the potential?"

"No. It is in self-destructive dysfunction."

"The Hopi calls that imbalance *koyaanisqatsi."*

"That's what that movie *koyaanisqatsi,* produced by Francis Ford Coppola, was about."

"Yes, but why? A civilization anywhere near its potential would function with a reasonable balance of technological, physical, and spiritual evolution. Our technological evolution is advanced for one segment of the population. Physical evolution is stagnant and is not in line with the technological evolution. Spiritual evolution has been dismal."

"We have placed the cart before the horse."

"The society reflects the individual imbalance. An initiated individual has power, wisdom, and compassion, the personal Trinity, in correct balance. These are politics, science, and spirituality in a societal parallel of balanced Trinity. It is analogous to technological, physical, and spiritual evolutionary stages of existence. An imbalanced person may have too much power and some wisdom with little no compassion."

"Sounds like Wall Street and the Military."

"This is an archetype exemplified by Prometheus and later the *American Prometheus."*

"You are talking about UC Berkeley theoretical physicist Robert Oppenheimer, the father of the atomic bomb. I have read his Pulitzer Prize winning biography *American Prometheus: The Triumph and Tragedy of J. Robert Oppenheimer*. It's about the Manhattan Project and its sad consequences for him and basically all of us."

"Remember how he quotes the Indian epic poem Bhagavad Gita after watching the first atomic bomb test explosion at Trinity, New Mexico."

"Now I am become Death, the destroyer of worlds."

"He was the *American Prometheus*. Prometheus stole fire from the Zeus and gave it to mere mortals. This is basically going ahead and stealing wisdom and power and giving it to those that lack understanding of vulnerability of those at your mercy. Understanding that vulnerability, for example what it is like to be a child playing in Hiroshima on that fateful day, is compassion. The lack of it results in severe long lasting pain for self and others."

"Prometheus opens the Pandora's Box and suffers heavily for it. A very angry Zeus then punishes him by having him bound to a rock while an eagle ate his liver every day only to have it grow back to be eaten again the following day continuously. It's like a Halloween horror version of *Groundhog Day*."

"Now, it is not just Oppenheimer that is the Prometheus, it is the entire mankind. We cannot blame Pandora, Prometheus, Oppenheimer or even Zeus, it is us, who opened the box releasing the potential for trouble. We have acquired the bombs but not the empathy of vulnerability. If we do not acquire that understanding, that understanding will acquire us."

"Does not sound pretty at all."

"Humans know the content of Pandora's Box is out. That's why we see fear everywhere. The Axis of Evil is but a projection of our collective fear exploited for political gain. Many are on this dreadful the *path of fear*."

"The path of fear?"

"It's simple. The two paths to take in life: The path of fear and the path of love. The paths in your consciousness manifest in the physical world around you.

Let me tell you an old Cherokee story.

A Cherokee elder is teaching his grandson about life. *A fight is going on inside of me*, he said to the boy. *It is a terrible fight and it is between two wolves. One evil. He is anger, envy, sorrow, greed, arrogance, self-pity, lies, false pride, superiority and ego. The other one is good, he is joy, peace, love, hope, kindness, empathy, generosity, truth, and compassion. The same fight is going on inside of you, and inside every other person too.*

The grandson thought for a while about it and then asked his grandfather, *which wolf will win?*

The Cherokee elder simply replied, *the one you feed.*"

"A personal Armageddon of fear and love within all of us?"

"Armageddon and Apocalypse are not the same thing."

"Apocalypse is Greek for Revelation."

"The Apocalypse brings about the Armageddon. But there is no evil as such. I see it as the path of fear, which is characterized by looking for opportunities to find weaknesses to bring others down, manipulate, insult, and cause dysfunction. This path suppresses the truth, seeks to realize full potential only for self and a secret group, but still never happy, and therefore bitter, angry or fearful, extremely materialistic, compartmentalizing, lost in duality or separation mentality or 'spiritual death,' and believes media are portraying the world accurately. 'Third Eye Blind.' – Basically, Illuminati-like."

"And the path of love …"

"Looks for opportunities to lift others up, seeks the strengths to fortify them even more, have a healthy concern for the well-being of others, seeks to realize full potential for everyone, are happy and have no unhealthy fear, asks every possible questions and turns every stone, strives for a harmonious existence for all living beings, spreads the truth, seeks avenues of enlightenment and try them, knows media are creating a worldview conducive to those who own the media, see frivolous events as they really are, seeks simplicity, see the material illusion as it is and uses it to realize potential, treats bad events as opportunities to grow and turning points in life, see the whole Cosmos as One, know oneself as an individual is chimerical and truly everyone is One with All That Is, welcomes the truth, seeks the harmonization of physical, technological and spiritual evolution. Basically, Luminari."

"I suppose you are Luminari."

"Luminari is just a label. We need balance. The polarization is the path to extinction. Virginia Woolf said, *it is fatal to be a man or woman pure and simple: one must be a woman manly, or a man womanly.* Fatal because the Path of Fear resorts to attack."

"All attack is a call for help."

"*A Course in Miracles.* Brilliant! More of the sacred feminine is the help required. Luminari is the lunar feminine energy, the Yin. Look at the male dominated world. Wars. Bombs."

"More and bigger bombs."

"I read Jane Roberts. She wrote a book called *The Chestnut Beads.* I know it's her feminist fantasy, but the message poignant. It's about a bomb and a college sorority.

This college sorority's initiation rite is actually a ritual of subliminal suggestion. The women are given instructions on how to survive the coming holocaust and take over the world so that men could never again have the chance to destroy it. The initiates are consciously not aware of the inner message embodied in the ritual. They carry it within them, like an invisible mental fetus. Then they go above life through the rites of marriage and childbirth and house cleaning — until the Day comes. A Bomb is dropped and this triggers the release of the message to the consciousness of the female survivors. They rebuild a peaceful civilization."

"I am all for end of violence. But it is impossible with the fear that is everywhere."

"The technological, cultural, physical, and spiritual evolutions are completely out of line. There is much buildup of potential energy of tension. There is too much Yang and not enough Yin. Lao Tzu said, *know the masculine, keep the feminine.*"

"This has only gotten worse. Look at the ecological imbalance. It's all in the book *The Last Hours of the Ancient Sunlight* by Thom Hartmann. In environmentalist and New Age circles subscribe to the Greek concept of the Earth as a feminine conscious entity Gaia, promoted by Chemist James Lovelock."

"Gaia concept is older than Greece. There is an ancient legend of an underground race where the inner earth men are called Ana and the women are called Gaia. The naturally Mother Earth would be called Gaia. She is an exemplar of the Earth Mother Archetype. There were exemplars included Cybele in Phrygia or modern day Turkey, the Anatolian Kubaba, the Minoan Rhea, and the Hittite Hebat. All of them were honored in bloodletting rituals called *sanguinaria*. Even some of the Virgin-Mother-of-God symbols in Rome were originally attributed to Earth Mother."

"The idea of the earth as a living organism with a circulatory system of energy *blood* was central to the Australian Aboriginal tribes. This is from *Voices of the First Day.*

... connecting these tribes was a circulatory system called songlines. Directed by a complex, unwritten calendar of ceremonies and rituals, tribal people would move along

these songlines and interact with people of other regions. ... This universal culture was like the blood that unites all the functions and parts of a living organism.

Following a songline is what is known as a *walkabout*. Outside the Aboriginal world this internet of kinetic energy is malfunctioning. Blockage is causing buildup of potential energy to a dangerously unsubstantial level."

"What does the Universe or Mother Earth, if you will, do when the imbalance reaches critical mass?"

"Some mechanism of equilibrium."

"Charge polarization causes lighting. Plate tension is released by earthquakes. Sexual tension leads to 'volcanic' orgasmic eruptions. Snow buildup in mountains causes avalanches."

"In chemistry, the addition of one chemical to a reacting solution eventually reaches equilibrium."

"Universe is self-aware and self-corrective in its intelligence. A planet is no exception. It, being a mini-universe follows a common universal course."

"So Yin is to be restored to balance."

"Rightfully! All things are in a rhythmic cycle. Few understand the rhythms of life more than women."

"The ultimate feminist Woolf said, *arrange whatever pieces come your way.* Go with the natural flow."

"Women are in sync with life itself and therefore are better candidates to find the more harmonious pathway of human progress. We need the return of Isis."

"Does this cab have a *Palin 2012* bumper sticker? You seem to be under the spell of Isis."

"My Head of State is a Queen. Even Incan cosmology speak of *Pachacuti*, the 'upheaval of earth.' Pacha means Earth. This is a reference to the restoration of the feminine leadership. This is written in the Jewish Kabbalic Zohar. Israeli Kabbala scholar and Chasidic Rabbi Ohad Ezrah writes this.

Sixteenth-century Lurianic codes prophesied the feminist movement of the 20th and 21st century and the awakening of the feminine nature. ... women have been very small and under the control of the masculine. Now is the time when the feminine will be divided from the masculine to develop until she becomes equal, totally equal, to the male, the masculine. Only when she is totally equal to the masculine will the male and female turn face to face.

The return of the Queen."

"Right. We Americans always forgot about the British constitutional monarchy part. God Save the Queen, eh!"

"Queen and later Egyptian deity Iset or Auset, or as we know her, Isis, means 'of the throne.' She was also called Juno. Her archetype was also known as Ishtar in Iraq-based civilizations and the Etruscans, Astarte in Canaan, Athena in ancient Greece, possibly Sumerian Inanna, Hindu Nari, Cypriote Cypris, Minoan Ariadne, and later Madonna and Child. She was the embodiment of that missing Yin energy of wisdom and creativity. That Holy Grail of creative blood.

This is in the writings of Roman Apuleius:

I am nature, the universal Mother, mistress of all the elements, primordial child of time, sovereign of all things spiritual, ... the single manifestation of all gods and goddesses that are ... Though I am worshipped in many aspects, known by countless names ... the Egyptians who excel in ancient learning and worship call me by my true name Queen Isis."

"Maybe we all have an Oedipus complex wanting to be with our universal Mother and Queen Isis, who is perhaps too busy with more celestial matters. How about the return of Eleanor Roosevelt? That was true Yin leadership potential. How did she say it?"

"Women are like teabags; you never know how strong they are until they're put in hot water."

"I think the water is beginning to boil. I see bubbles."

"The consequences of the heat of imbalance imply the unthinkable. Sometimes an intervening trigger can set off the tension release and realignment of unbalanced elements. In Canada, little canons are used cause mini avalanches to protect highways."

"Without the trigger the realignment process could be so destructive that it could wipe out life on planet Earth."

"This is one of the 'future' probable parallel realities. To quote Jesus, *those with eyes to see can see it.*"

"Planetary Equilibrium is natural and inevitable."

"The path to equilibrium that it was on, with a possible extinction of humans, was 'not meant to be.' Life preserves life. God equals life. Life equals God. Aristotle said, *knowing yourself is the beginning of all wisdom.* Look within you. See Life. See God."

"Life preserves life. Arthur C. Clarke said, *any path to knowledge is a path to God—or Reality, whichever word one prefers to use.*"

"Now do you see the ultimate source of all wisdom?"

"Wikipedia? Oprah??"

"It is within you."

"It is definitely within *you.* How come you are such a know-it-all?"

"I was raised by the Woolfs and dolphins."

"Leonard and Virginia? Makes perfect sense of your down to earth delivery of unearthly intelligence. You listen like Spring and talk like Juno."

"All knowledge is eternal and internal. It is always available to mental sympathy."

"Mental sympathy?"

"Knowing how to tune your mental Wi-Fi antenna to the frequency of the cosmic Wireless Network that houses the piece of information you need at any given time."

"Is there anything you do not know?"

"I know everything except the Knower."

"Maybe everything and Knower are one and the same."

"You know. Hindu philosophical texts *Upanishads* say *duality is whereby the Knower knows Himself.*"

"You remind me of Wilson."

"From *Castaway?*"

"No. *Home Improvement* with Tim 'The Toolman' Taylor."

"Heidi Ho neighbor!"

"And interestingly I am yet to see your face for your long hair and those drops of Jupiter. Did you fall from a shooting star?"

"It doesn't matter how long my hair is or what color my skin is or whether I'm a woman or a man. – John Lennon."

"You convey timely incisive magic with your seductive mystery. How do you remember stuff so well?"

"I meditate. We are containers into which the infinite cosmic intelligence can flow, but the thinking mind is a lid. To meditate means to remove the lid and let the stream flow in. Science backs this. A study on Buddhist monks showed brain growth and restructure through their *Anapanasati* breath meditation. It's in Matthieu Ricard's *Why Meditate*. Another MRI study on London cab drivers showed an enlargement of the section of the brain that functions in memory."

"The London study is by neurologist Professor Eleanor Maguire. It showed enlarged posterior hippocampus."

"Yes, the study showed that the longer the driving career, the larger the posterior hippocampus."

"You must be as old as Yoda. Your youthful look is a disguise. Apparently I need to meditate more and maybe find a cab job in Vancouver for the summer."

"The knowledge you need is within you. Friedrich Nietzsche said, *the body is a great intelligence, a multiplicity with one sense, a war and a peace, a herd and a herdsman … There is more reason in your body than your best wisdom*."

"In the book *Talented Teenagers* authors Mihaly Csikszentmihalyi, Kevin Rathunde and Samuel Whalen imply that intelligence represents a set of competencies in development. They write, *high academic achievers are not necessarily born 'smarter' than others, but work harder and develop more self-discipline*. There is a genius in all of us."

"It is like a trapped cellular memory potentially unleashed with intent."

"Like your mother's mitochondrial DNA – your Sophia!

Dr. Carol Dweck of Stanford University demonstrated that students who understand that intelligence is malleable rather than fixed are much more intellectually ambitious and successful."

"This great intelligence was not stimulated enough to be released because not everyone understands their intelligence potential. Sophia is trapped, indeed. The Inception was unavoidable.

That's why they are here!"

THE TWIST

"Do you ever find time to mediate with your doctoral studies?"

"Well, about ten minutes a day, and not really everyday either. I do a little yoga. It helps me concentrate during research and lab work."

"That's not bad. I do that for about thirty minutes, every day without fail. Fifteen in the morning and fifteen in the evening, that's after my long walk. That's how I get entangled."

"Entangled with what?"

"The mind of God."

"Ah! That explains your infinite wisdom. Say hi to Him next time you mediate."

"See our 'mind' can be perceived as three parts: Subconscious, conscious, and superconscious. The Trinity. Subconscious is fully aware of the 'past,' although they are hidden in the Now. Superconscious is fully aware of the 'future' probabilities, although they too are hidden in the Now. Conscious can be aware of the present now, but it wonders. Meditation brings all of these aspects to Now and you are aware of it ALL, as you progress. Trinity unites in *The Celestial Marriage*."

"All?"

"She is All There Is!"

"She?"

"Oops! Woolfian slip."

"Figures!"

"The Prime Creator is a feminine vibration, man. Nice lady too."

"Okay, whatever. Philosophers! You think, therefore, She Is. I am scientist and a geneticist. Where is the proof?"

"Fortunately, I speak your language – DNA. Where does your mitochondrial DNA come from?"

"My mother."

"Where do hers come from?"

"Her mother."

"And hers?"

"Okay, I get it. So no matter how far back you go, the ultimate source of our blueprint will be feminine. I should know better than that to debate with a philosopher. A Lover of Sophia!"

"We are all primarily of the same gender. Feminine!"

"So what are the masculine, a sub-gender?"

"Well, we are all mothers as creators. We give birth everyday, even the guys at Apple *creating* the next iPhone. They conceive, gestate, and next thing you know Steve Jobs is on a stage having severe labor pains."

"You are saying even male scientist and technologist are injected with that creative ideal."

"Yes, recognizing your inner Sophia is a form of freedom. It is really a free and an integrative approach. You integrate your inner Father, Son, and the Holy Spirit. That Holy Spirit or Holy Shekinah in Hebrew is your inner Divine Mother – the Creator aspect. It is really Father-Son-Mother!"

"I know that mankind has had various approaches to the truth. I understand that the compartmentalization is the problem and basis of all dysfunction. We study different layers of the same puzzle as different sciences. Molecules are one such layer. The study of it we label Chemistry. The study of the layer within it we label physics. The outer layers are studied by geology and biology. Further outer layers are studied by ecology and astronomy. It is dangerous and foolish to be oblivious to the seamless holistic nature of the system we study. That's why geneticists like me are working with quantum physicists to reconfigure our working model of the truth to a more collaborative or integrative one. The field of Integrated Medicine is such an example."

"The consciousness driven evolution?"

"More like *Creative Evolution*. That's a book by Dr. Amit Goswami, the quantum physicist who wrote the text book on the subject. The subtitle of *Creative Evolution* is *A Physicist's Resolution Between Darwinism and Intelligent Design*. It is an interesting time we live in when quantum physicists write books on evolution and as some geneticists are shifting from their materialistic paradigm. While some are still crystallized in the dense illusion, others have begun to understand what Anaïs Nin meant when she said: *We don't see things as they are, we see them as we are.*"

"Where do you stand?"

"Evolutionary geneticists used to look back at the Cambrian Explosion to the origins of their field because before that event, that inception, there was no life to study."

"So where do you look to now?"

"*Now*, I guess. That's *All There Is*, isn't it?"

"You have done well, grasshopper."

"We have been forced to look further back to the beginning of it all."

"Woodstock!"

"Funny! You have to go far beyond that to the Cambrian Explosion for a different creative or constructive explosion."

"As opposed to a destructive explosion, like a bomb. So, the Cambrian Explosion was *Make Love Not War* moment? The biological Big Bang?"

"More like the Big Potential.

The elite in the physics have known for about hundred years about the non-local existence of the universe and wave function collapse when awareness comes into play. The Cambridge Astrophysicist Sir Martin Rees said this back in 1942: *In the beginning there were only probabilities. The universe could only come into existence if someone observed it. It does not matter that the observers turned up several billion years later. The universe exists because we are aware of it.*"

"In the movie *What Dreams May Come* Chris says, *I have a sort of a voice in my head, a part of me that thinks and feels that is aware that I exist at all.*"

"Then Albert says, *so if you are aware you exist, then you do.*"

"This is Descartes' premise reworded. In the book *Buddha in Redface*, a Native American elder tells Dr. Eduardo Duran about this awareness.

There has always been a dream. Everything is still the dream. All that we call creation and Creator is the dream. The dream continues to dream us and to dream itself. Before anyone or anything was, there was a dream, and this dream continued to dream itself until the chaos within the dream became aware of itself."

"*The Nothingness* begins to gain appearance of something and suddenly it is aware of it."

"Kogi people of Colombia, who live in a mountain called *The Heart of the World* and consider themselves the *Elder Brothers of Mankind* says this: *In the beginning there was blackness, only the sea. In the beginning there was no sun, no moon, and no people. In the beginning there were no animals, no flowers, only the sea. The sea was the Mother. The Mother was not people; she was not anything, nothing at all. She was what she was. Spirit. She was memory and possibility."*

"After Einstein came up with E = MC2, Princeton theoretical physicist and cosmologist George Gamow realized that since energy and matter are equivalent a star could be created out of nothing as the energy of its misty mass is exactly balanced by the energy of its gravitational field. Why stop there? This can be applied to the whole cosmos, whole total energy is zero."

"Sea-ro was the Mother. *She was memory and possibility."*

"Stephen Hawking clarifies Gamow assertion of creating a star as the creation of the whole cosmos in *The Grand Design.*

If the total energy of the universe must always remain zero, and it costs energy to create a body, how can a whole universe be created from nothing? That is why there must be a law like gravity. Because gravity is attractive, gravitational energy is negative: One has to do work to separate a gravitationally bound system, such as the earth and moon. This negative energy can balance the positive energy needed to create matter, but it's not quite that simple. … Bodies such as stars or black holes cannot just appear out of nothing. But a whole universe can."

"Afar down I see the huge first Nothing. I knew I was even there, I waited unseen and always, and slept through the lethargic mist, And took my time."

"Walt Whitman."

"Yep."

"Over time the possibility gives rise to existence of what we are aware. But you have to understand this caterpillar metamorphosis is an ever replicating premise. It's not like there was one instance of potential caterpillar and leading to the existence of the butterfly. This is just one layer of the process. The replication of the process is without a perceivable end."

"An eternal process."

"It's all layers in fractals."

"Like Mandelbrot Set or trees."

"Benoit Mandelbrot of Yale University developed the Mandelbrot Set as one of the most well know example of a fractal, which is something that repeats or replicates as layers of ever varying scale. Each fractal is one of infinite permutations. It's pure and simple mathematics. Stephen Hawking said the whole cosmos can be explained with mathematics. Newton implied the same thing. Galileo said, *mathematics is the language with which God has written the universe.* Nobel Prize winning physicist Paul Dirac, *God used beautiful mathematics in creating the world."*

"So did Pythagoras, whose school, which was like a brotherhood of strict vegetarian monks, was called *mathematikoi,* meaning those who study everything. They knew the basis and essence of all reality, music, astronomy, geometry, as purely mathematical. Geometry literally means measurement of earth. A game of repeating numbers, not as attributes, but as the mystical essence of origin. The Chinese *I Ching* and the Jewish *Kabbala* both emphasize the mathematical basis of all existence. The book *Sacred Geometry: Deciphering the Code* by Steven Skinner is a decent piece of modern work on this subject."

"The ultimate geometric phenomena, the Mandelbrot Set, is a repeating fractal. f(z) = z2 + C. You plug in the numbers, let the answer repeatedly feedback as input. This loop is capable of infinite iterations. Voila! Spontaneous generation!! Francois Jacob, Nobel Prize winner in Medicine, once said, *every cell's dream is to become two cells.*"

"So geneticists and theoretical physicists are on the same page. The same as the esoteric mystics and philosophers as pointed out by Fritjof Capra in his wonderful book *The Tao of Physics: An Exploration of the Parallels between Modern Physics and Eastern Mysticism.*"

"This is about trying to fit old answers to new questions to see if they are on the same page."

"John Lennon said, *there's nothing you can know that isn't known.* The old answers that have been mostly ignored by the West except of those far ahead like Einstein, who said, *the ancient knew something which we seem to have forgotten.* Not just Indian, Sufi, and Chinese mystics but the understanding of reality by the Australian Aboriginal Dreamtime.

"Aboriginal scholar Robert Lawlor writes, *disguised in the language of astrophysics and geology is the essence of the Dreamtime creation. ... The active fields in the Dreamtime creation myth are fields of consciousness. The kinetic and psychic energies of the fields are symbolized by the ancestor' ability to alternate between animal apparitions and pure spiritual powers.*"

"The ancients knew it and we are just remembering it."

"For example, the idea of wave function collapse into particles of matter in Quantum Physics is depicted in the Dreamtime story of honey ants appearing from earth and disappearing into their wave shaped holes of concentric circles."

"They are on the same page. Honey ant is a metaphor for particles of matter."

"Except, this 'same page' is every page."

"Joseph Campbell said, *the flavor of the ocean is contained in a droplet and the whole mystery of life within the egg of an ant.*"

"Same but different. Fractals are not banal. All layers of the cosmos are consisting of units that are very similar but unique. Like snowflakes, which are symbols representing infinite permutations. Each layer that is created through replication of the previous is very similar but different. This because every value of *phi* or divine proportion or golden ratio/mean generated as you go higher on the Fibonacci sequence is very similar but different. For example, let me use my iPad to show you the sequence

1.618033813, 1.618034056, 1.618033963, 1.618033999, 1.618033985. If you round them you will get 1.618034, but that masks the uniqueness of every layer."

"Same but different. Like all Katie Perry songs or the next iPhone."

"This continues infinitely. Phi is named for the Greek letter *phi*, the first letter of the name of the celebrated sculptor *Phi*dias. Phi value can never be determined, only approximated. Such numbers are called incommensurate numbers. You see this geometrically demonstrated in the Mandelbrot Set and everything in the cosmos whether it's DNA or positrons or snowflakes. In fact, take the ratio of the length of your arm to your forearm, upper arm to forearm, whole finger to the outer two thirds, middle third to the outer third. Each one approximates to 1.618034, but they are never the same. This is true if you take ratio of the width of DNA to one complete turn of DNA strand. In fact, no two things in the cosmos have the same *phi*."

"Yes, Heraclitus said, *you cannot step twice in the same river.*"

"He also said, *man is the measure of all things.* All the DNA needed to recreate a human is found within one of millions of cells. In that cell, there is more potential than you could use in your entire lifetime. The part is a whole in miniature. In fact the Quantum Physicist, David Bohm added, *in some sense man is a microcosm of the universe; therefore what man is, is a clue to the universe.*"

"Mosikei Ueshiba, Founder of the Martial Arts Aikido said, *all the principles of heaven and earth are living inside you.*"

"Bruce Lee echoed it by saying, *all types of knowledge, ultimately, means self-knowledge.*"

"Sufi Islamic master Hazrat Inayat Khan said, *the fulfillment of this whole creation is to be found in man. And his object is only fulfilled when man has awakened that part of himself which represents the master, that is God himself.*"

"So, you can replicate the larger scale structures of the cosmos by iterating the miniature."

"With a twist!"

"Hmmm?"

"The spiral."

"Oh yes, nice. The double helix structure. The twist!"

"The twist is replicating."

"The twist is replicating. The spiral is everywhere in the universe. It's in living organisms such as the biocomplexity spiral and beyond. It's in DNA, the evolutive shells of all mollusks including the 'living fossil' the nautilus, ferns, horn of a ram, horn of an narwhal, broccoli, branching of trees, flowers like honey suckle and morning glory, growth of leaves on a branch, pine cone, pineal gland, colony of salps, vortices, tornadoes, hurricanes, galaxies, and universes. Also, our moon is spiraling out at an undetectable deviation. Of course, it is in the Mandelbrot Set."

"A gentle flowing stream. Every possible ancient petroglyph site around the world has a spiral, from New Grange in Ireland to Chaco Canyon in New Mexico. There is no ancient site that does not have a spiral marking somewhere. When I meditate, I light an incense stick in a still room and watch the spirals endlessly self-generate. It's like watching the first day of creation. In fact many descendent of ancient cultures insist that incense smoke is multi-dimensional. These are exact words of a Maya elder. *Incense is very powerful. It is the food of the gods. It's a way to communicate directly with the dimensional world of gods.*"

"The spiral shape in everything is based on the ratio phi or golden ratio. It is the default. It's difficult to explain in words. In a nautilus, for example, the ratio of the whole length to the length from one end to where the structure touches its side is phi. Then you will see the smaller segment is an exact replica of the larger in lower scale. This repeats infinitely. This is called the Fibonacci spiral. There is a picture of it on page 120 of *The Grand Design* by Stephen Hawking."

"The phi, this 1.618034 number rounded, is basically derived from the Fibonacci sequence, right?"

"I see you have read your *The Da Vinci Code*. Yes, the Fibonacci sequence are these numbers of the order 0, 1, 1, 2, 3, 5, 8, 13, 21, 34, 55, 89, 144, 233, 377, 610, 987, and so on. Each number is the sum of the previous two numbers."

"I see. 144 is 55 plus 89. It's like the two numbers join to reproduce the next generation, over and over."

"Sex!"

"Sex?"

"That's how it was discovered."

"Who was doing it?"

"Rabbits!"

"Rabbit sex led to the discovery of the Fibonacci sequence?"

"The Italian mathematician Leonardo de Pisa, who studied in Arabia, had to deal with a burgeoning rabbit population. The uncontrolled copulation led to a number of rabbits in each generation following a sequence he had learnt in Arabia. This is the Fibonacci sequence."

"This is how the cosmos reproduces itself."

"In 1753 Scottish botanist and mathematician Robert Simson observed that the growth patterns of plant were governed by the Fibonacci sequence. This was done partly to maximize the exposure of leaves to sunlight. In a sunflower the number of interlocking spirals was always a number in the sequence. Same was seen in a pine cone. Count the number of petals in a lily, buttercup, delphinium, marigold, black-eyed Susan, pyrethrum, aster novi-belgii, and Miachaelmas daisy."

"You get 3, 5, 8, 13, 21, 34, 55, and 89?"

"It was observed from Arabia to the land of the Celtic Druids."

"Have you read the writings of Drunvalo Melchizedek?"

"I didn't know you read the writings of Druids."

"A modern day one from Sedona, Arizona. Not Glastonbury. The book is *Serpent of Light*. It talks about the Flower of Life, which is based on the phi ratio, the sacred geometry on earth, and the implications of the distortion on the course of human civilization. The great shifts follow the fine tuning of the geometric nodes."

"The phi is continuously fine-tuned by taking a number from the Fibonacci sequence and diving that by the previous number. Then you get the sequence 1, 2, 1.5, 1.666666, 1.6, 1.625, 1.615384, 1.619047, 1.617647, 1.618181, 1.617977, 1.618055, 1.618025, 1.618037, 1.618033, 1.618034, and goes on. But now the number is constantly approximates to 1.618034, but as I showed earlier with each step it is very similar but different. So when the cosmos replicates itself it uses a finer tuned number with every layer of replication. This is a scientific fact. This beauty is everywhere."

"Whirling Dervishes. The Sufi Muslims. They whirl and whirl to the mystical music, as their physical meditation takes them into harmonic resonance with this amazing cosmos."

"And we inside our bodies we have little Whirling Dervishes we call electrons whirling through the space of an atom completing billions of trips around the nucleus each millionth of a second! Now if there are more than 10 billion atoms in a speck so small that you have to view it under a microscope, how many atoms do you think are in you?

"A bigillion? That is why little children like to spin. Because they are closer to the true nature than adults, who have had more time to forget and buy the illusion and lose the freedom by becoming trapped in the spider web matrix woven, in Egyptian cosmology with strings by goddess Neith. The adult are *of the world*; the children are just *in it*."

"It's in the strings of the superstring theory, the smallest unit of the cosmos that have been understood so far, postulated by Theoretical Physicist Dr. Leonard Susskind of Stanford University. First, the strings were theorized to be patterns of vibrations 10-35 meters across. In size, a string is to an electron what a ping pong ball is to our solar system. However, it is not the size, but it is the mathematical signature energy frequency of the vibration that determines the type of matter it will comprise."

"How do you measure such a small size?"

"A good question. This size was only one possible size the vibration can achieve. A consistent size turned out to be undeterminable definitely, due to the lack of permanency of the strings and the width it can attain. Let me read the explanation of strings by Stephen Hawking in *The Grand Design*.

Strings are *patterns of vibration that have length but no height or width – like indefinitely thin pieces of string. String theories also lead to infinities, but it is believed that in the right version they will all cancel out. They have another unusual feature: They are consistent only if space-time has ten dimensions, instead of the usual four. Ten dimensions might sound exciting, but they would cause real problems if you forgot where you parked your car."*

"I know the feeling. It happens all the time."

"The universe is made of these strings of energy at various vibrations. All geometric arrangements are made possible due to the diversity in spinning frequencies. This makes the universe explainable through mathematics."

"So the math just the renders in numbers of the geometric arrangement of the universe through an endless feedback loop of creation and re-creation."

"The whole universe is a Mandelbrot Set! If you look at various levels of the Mandelbrot Set you can see everything you see in the universe. I can see leaves, trees, beetles, stones, rivers, seahorses, meditating monks, Beatles, Stones, Einstein's hair, and Beyonce 's bottom."

"Did you lose your virginity to the Mandelbrot Set?"

"I was lonely and it was bootylicious!"

"I believe that. It should not surprise you that even what we perceive as time or history is based in fractals. Gregg Baden explains that in his book *Fractal Time*."

"Makes sense. As space repeats, so does time, similar events, but different. Déjà vu, but *different*. Already seen … sort of."

"Yes, time is a geometric spiral. As in time the sacred geometry is everywhere. The phi, the divine proportion, is the basis of every design, including atomic structures within larger forms. They are arranged according to the geometry of the flower of life. This symbol is found in every religious or spiritual structure around the world. And we revolutionized our computer technology using our knowledge of fractals. That suggests a single creative mind. One!"

"A single creative mind! The collective unconscious *that we all share* of legendary Carl Jung. In the documentary *The Colors of Infinity*, Arthur C. Clarke, after wonderfully explaining fractals, states that *the computer revolution would … give new impetus to the Jung's theory of the collective unconscious, the idea that there is a well of consciousness compounded of primordial universal images that we all share, the substructure or background of awareness. The mind clearly finds resonance in the Mandelbrot Set … this mathematics offers new insights into the way the way the universe works.*"

"Spiral is primordial to the collective unconscious that we all share."

"Even solar systems are spirals. No one notices, but Earth and all other planets orbiting the sun are in fact spiraling towards to sun. It's so minute to our perception that it creates the illusion of a consistent elliptical orbit."

"So someday we'll be reunited with the sun."

"Our solar system itself is heading into the galactic core, the *Galactic Central Sun*, the source, up our spiral arm."

"Native American mythology finds that there will be a reunification of us and all the rest with the Source, which in Chinese is called the *Tao*. The Vedics called it Brahman and the Buddhists Dharmakaya. An Italian Proverb says, once the game is over, the king and the pawn go back into the same box. Qur'an 21:105 says, *remember the day when we shall roll up the heavens like the rolling up of scrolls.*"

"Sounds like the Italians, Arab & other Muslims, and Greek philosophers like Aristotle and Epicurus are in agreement with the wisdom of the Red man."

"Naturally! Very similar but unique. Even our mythologies and cosmologies are Fibonacci fractals. It is the Greek *Apocatastasis*. It is also in Stoicism,

Judaism, Christianity, and Gnosticism. *The One who became many is becoming One again.* It means all will return to the original or primordial conditions whence it came from. A reunification with the Source. A return to Eden."

"So theoretically we are allowed to 'return to Eden' or do anything else we want even in this neatly organized universe. How do we do that? Where's the map that contains the path of return to Eden."

"Clarke concludes by saying *the Mandelbrot set is indeed one of the most astonishing discoveries of the entire history of mathematics. Who could have dreamed that such an incredibly simple equation could have generated images of literally infinite complexity? We have all read stories about maps that revealed the location of some hidden treasure. Well, in this case the map is the treasure.*"

"Infinite complexity from incredible simplicity! Who could have dreamt that?"

"The way the universe works is summarized in that documentary by Dr. Michael Barnsley, whose name was given to the famous fractal, the Barnsley Fern, saying, *this is how God created a system which gave us free will, it's the most brilliant maneuver in the universe to create something in which everything is free. How could you do that?*"

"In the book *You Are Here: A Portable History of the Universe*, Christopher Potter writes, *it is often said that free will is impossible in a deterministic world, but it's as if the world has set itself up in such a way that the illusion of free will is guaranteed. It's the complexity of the evolved world that makes that illusion compelling, as if nature is determined to save us from existential despair.*"

A FAIRY TALE

"In the beginning there was nothing. The total energy of the cosmos is zero. What existed was potential or probabilities."

"Genesis 1:0. The caterpillar returns."

"The perceived reality is an illusion, a mask or an effect of what is actually there or not there. When you try to see an electron through a microscope you do not see it. It is not there. Nothing is there. To quote co-founder of Quantum Physics and Nobel Prize winner Werner Heisenberg, *atoms or elementary particles themselves are not real; they form a world of potentialities or possibilities rather than one of things or facts.*"

"So is there is no electron?"

"We know it is there because of its effects perceived as a little colorful bump in our sophisticated microscopes. It's a shadow. Shadow defines the light."

"So is there an electron."

"Well, you quoted Aesop who said, *beware lest you lose the substance by grasping at the shadow.* No one has ever seen or claimed to have seen one. There is no perceivable substance."

"So, Emperor has no clothes!"

"Someone has to voice it."

"Okay so, more people have supposedly seen the Loch Ness Monster, Yeti, Yowie, Elves or Wood Nymphs?"

"So, this potential is identified as consciousness. Consciousness is a potential state that is capable of thoughts, ideas, and decisions. It has the potential to imagine or to conceive an idea or a concept. It is basically formless information of what can become as form."

"In the beginning was God, with Him was the Word, the Word was truly God. The Hindu Veda Krishna Yajurveda."

"In the beginning was the word, and the Word was with God and the word was God! John 1:1."

"The word is not just a sound or a written symbol but a force full of expressive and creative power."

"The word, in Greek *Logos,* was like an unorganized binary code organizing itself into a meaningful pattern. Meaningless letters become a meaningful word. This is the Greek concept of *ex nihilo*: *Cosmos* from *Chaos* or Order from Nothingness. The numbers themselves mean nothing. However, they have potential to create virtual manifestation that can be perceived to be real."

"So real that people cry at movies. *Everything you can imagine is real.* — Pablo Picasso."

"I wonder if Picasso knew that the Aborigines had no word in their language for our words fiction, fantasy, and imagination. My grandmother indicated that they don't distinguish between realism and surrealism either."

"Reality leaves a lot to the imagination. - John Lennon. Everything real is imagined."

"We *Imagine* that what consciousness conceives, according to the String Theory – the predecessor of the M-Theory, to be a string. Not any string, but a spiral wound up, often depicted as an egg shaped entity."

"So which first came first? The String Theory or the egg?"

"The egg of strings is generated by pure theoretical mathematics. You feed the equations and the computer program spits out these forms and shapes. The form corresponds to what is observed in nature. Therefore, since the math is held to be solid this form is very plausible and even likely. In fact there are no other candidates."

"The egg wins. Sound like the math agrees with the Sanskrit Vedas, which speak of *hiranya garba* or the golden egg of creation, the seed of the cosmos."

"These strings are not still. They vibrate. In fact the vibration came first."

"In the beginning was the sound, the Word enunciated. Hindus call this vibratory frequency Ohm! Druids called it the vibration of Melchizedek."

"It's the mysterious disturbance of the initial conditions. Physicist Armand Delsemme said the universe arose out of a *spontaneous rupture of the pre-existing grand symmetry of nothingness.*"

"Maybe the initial conditions were cold and God was under the weather and sneezed."

"Did he bless Himself too?"

"He had to. No one else was there. Cold and lonely. And oh my God. An eternal and Holy Boredom. No wonder we are here."

"Now the strings can vibrate at different frequencies, just like electromagnetic radiation. The frequency matters. They determine what they are perceived to be. Nicola Tesla, the genius inventor of electricity, said, *if you want to find the secrets of the Universe, think in terms of energy, frequency, and vibration.*"

"Universe is a guitar. Then Jimmy Hendrix pulled a string."

"Think of vibrating strings as information."

"Thoughts! Word!! Sound vibrations!!! *Logos*!!!!"

"Okay. When the thoughts of words cause a vibration and create what we call photons – units of light."

"In the beginning was the Word. The word was *let there be light*!"

"This *Word* is an idea or a concept, something conceived."

"Sophia is impregnated by Logos. Not a bad *idea*! Concept!! Let there be candle light!!!"

"And light was. This light as photons, although perceived to be particles, are truly temporary manifestations or collapse of a wave function potential. They are definitely not particles. They do not have a speed. The speed of light is a misnomer if they are thought of as particles. The 'photon' does not travel per se. However, the wave can have a speed. A water molecule in a pond with a wave does not travel with the wave. So basically, light or a photon does not travel. Light is simple a displacement in the matrix or space/time continuum."

"A wiggle! A dance!!"

"Think of the space/time continuum as a perfectly still pond. Some call it the Field. Indigenous people like the Kogi of Colombia call that initial condition the Ocean. We know from cymetics that any sound disturbs that perfect symmetry. In a pond the effect is a wave of a specific frequency."

"A disturbance like sneezing!"

"Nothing moves from one end to the other. There is a temporarily displacement in position, but almost immediately there is a replacement. Now imagine that every little displacement of the fabric, the surface of the pond, causes light to appear. The light, for simplicity, is formulated as a 'particle' called a photon. All it really represents is a localized dense spinning collection of energy sustaining the displacement in the fabric. If it is not perpetuated with energy the wave returns to perfect symmetry of nothingness."

"Back to the initial boredom."

"This disturbance and re-creation literally happens everywhere all the time. Have you seen the documentary about Stephen Hawking called *Theory of Everything*.'"

"No. *Theory of Everything*? Like everything everything?"

"Everything everything! So not all the light that appears, immediately disappear without doing anything else."

"So what do they do?"

"Do you know what happens when a particle and anti-particle collide? Say like an electron and a positron."

"They annihilate themselves, after making out for a while."

"Very good and the annihilation is not final. It conceives and generates a photon, for simplicity. A photon can be considered a subatomic embryo."

"Sounds like they more than made out, like Logos and Sophia!"

"Apply this in reverse. Now the photon can return to matter and anti-matter in equal amounts. This also happens everywhere all the time. It or rather its effect is observed in labs. So matter and anti-matter are created and eliminated all the time, out of nothing. This spontaneous creation is like the cosmos is flexing its muscles before a real task is given. A real task is what we call imagination. When we conceive an idea we cause a vibration or a wave, which is a disturbance, in the potential field of this still space/time continuum which creates light."

"Let there be light! Sophia is in gestation. Light Conception!!"

"Australian Aboriginal mythology says the universe was sung or vibrated into existence, a vibration still heard from a didgeridoo – the world's oldest known musical instrument."

"I always found the Tibetan guttural tonal chants to resemble the didgeridoo vibration too uncannily."

"Vibrations create displacement in the fabric. This is well demonstrated by cymatics, where the visible effect of various sound vibration frequencies is observed on a membrane, like a canvas."

"Cymatics! That's where they drop a random bunch of sand grains onto a sheet, or membrane as you call it, and these amazingly intricate patterns form and change according to the variations in the vibration frequency. Even a note on violin produces a specific geometric pattern corresponding to the sound."

"Information can manifest as numbers, sounds, and patterns. This is how the world was sung into being. This is a two way process. Robert Lawlor explains this in his book *Voices of the First Day*.

In the Aboriginal worldview, every meaningful activity, event, or life process that occurs at a particular place leaves a vibrational residue in the earth, as plants leave an image of themselves as seeds. The shape of the land – its mountains, rocks, riverbeds, and waterholes — and it unseen vibrations echo the events that brought that places into creation. Everything in the natural world is a symbolic footprint of the metaphysical beings whose actions created our world. As with a seed, the potency of an earthly location is wedded to the memory of its origin. This is 'Dreamtime.' This dreaming constitutes the sacredness of the earth. Only in extraordinary states of consciousness can one be aware of or attuned to, the inner dreaming of the earth."

"The inner dreaming is the blueprint, the matrix, that is expressed as a sound vibration. *Let there be light.*"

"The displacement in the fabric from the vibration is light. Light creates matter."

"Stars don't create light; light creates stars."

"Precisely! Sophia gives birth, if you will. The photon embryo is made manifest as physical matter. This is a continuous creative process."

"In the early Gnostic Christian mystical consciousness all creation was the result of an interplay between the feminine and masculine aspect of the cosmic force. The feminine matter was Sophia; The masculine spirit was Logos. They mate. They conceive. They gestate. They give birth."

"They rinse! They repeat!!"

"The Native Americans call it *Them* Mother Earth and Father Sky. Earth represents the realm of matter born out of Sophia. Sky represents the spirit realm containing the cosmic DNA blueprint information, Logos, which codes for what is born. We are here from the union of Heavenly Father and the Wise Mother. Then we do as they do to propagate."

"Rinse and repeat!"

"An endless spirit-matter dance of mating and life giving."

"Ultimately though this 'spirit' and 'matter' are light at different levels of energy density. They are both energy string vibrating at different frequencies. They, or rather, we are all light conceiving light."

"Mexican Medical Dr. Don Miguel Ruiz, writes in his book *The Four Agreements: A Toltec Wisdom Book*, that the Toltec master *came to the conclusion that human perception is merely light perceiving light. ... matter is a mirror – everything is a mirror that reflects light and creates images of that light – and the world of illusion, the Dream, is just like smoke which doesn't allow us to see what we really are. The real us is pure love, pure light.*

This is the knowledge passed down from their ancestors."

"Thought vibrations create matter and anti-matter around us through light."

"Thoughts create reality. When I meditate I focus on the didgeridoo vibration. I learned that in Sedona. We know it creates light matter, but what about dark matter?"

"We don't see them and we can't detect them by any means. But mathematically they must exist. Equations that derive cosmic gravity say so."

"So they do exist! We have seen their mathematical foot print."

"Australian Aborigines knew of their existence. Physicists David Ash and Peter Hewitt explained this in *Science of the Gods*.

Aborigines understood energy frequencies faster than the speed of light comprise of a world of super-energy and a super-physical energy.

Super-energy is dark energy. Super-physical energy is dark matter. They say when these super-energies decelerate, substance and form materialize. This is the origin of the material world. Dreamtime is the realm of Super-energy or, dark energy and super-physical energy or dark matter. Ancient Egyptians called it Duwat. For the reality we are familiar with they are but potentialities. We perceive Dreamtime only when it decelerate and is compatible with the vibration frequency of this dimension."

"Dreams have now come true. Before this material manifestation there is intermediate form of light, right?"

"Yes, they are like holographic matter."

"What is really light, then?"

"To us it is the visible portion of what is created by the strings/thoughts, the vibrations that disturbed the initial stillness or nothingness of potentiality."

"So paradoxically, there is invisible light."

"The light we see is electromagnetic radiation that is visible to us. So you could say that there are other 'light' forms that we don't see. In fact you can think of UV, X-rays, Gamma rays, cosmic rays like cygnates, infrared, microwaves, and radio waves as 'invisible light'."

"So what do these invisible photons create?"

"They also create matter and anti-matter. We cannot see or detect them. We called them dark matter and dark anti-matter."

"So if we cannot see them, then where are they?"

"They are all around. Roughly 96 percent of the estimated cosmos is made of them and dark energy. We know their existence theoretically and indirectly."

"Indirectly?"

"Yes, when dark matter and dark anti-matter collide they produce energy. Nobel laureate Austrian physicist Wolfgang Pauli identified missing energy in beta decay as 'neutral particles.' Neutral as in no charge and not Swiss."

"How do you identify missing energy? Hiding within the cheese? Swiss cheese!"

"The law of conservation of energy seems to be violated in beta decay. The discrepancy, the holes in the cheese if you will, was the undetectable energy. Italian theoretical physicist Enrico Fermi called these neutral energies, neutrinos, or *little neutral one* in Italian."

"Okay so even neutrinos are not directly detected but are missing pieces that must be there. They are an effect of dark matter, and therefore, indirectly they indicate the existence of dark matter. Sounds like an Austrian-Italian conspiracy against the Swiss, I mean, neutral ones."

"Then the Americans dropped a bomb."

"Shocking!"

"The shock was the extremely high rate of emission of neutrino, about 1013 per square centimeter per second, when nuclear weapons were tested at Los Alamos Lab facilities in New Mexico. This made way for the Hiroshima and Nagasaki tragedy. Neutrinos were much greater than normal background concentrations present due to cosmic rays and the dark matter the cosmic rays create."

"So even cosmic rays and their resulting dark matter are detected by the neutrinos they emit. But they are hard to detect due to low concentration."

"Exactly. Even though neutrinos can pass through matter or even right through the entire earth undetected due to lack of charge, when present in high concentration one eventually collides with nuclei of atoms, contributing in some way to the nuclear energy. The Swiss do have a role in facilitating these collisions at LHC."

"Large Hole Cheese?"

"Large Hadron Collider. Hadron is a collective term for all subatomic particles, which the physicists like to call the *particle zoo*."

"Large Hadron Collider? What an awful name. They should call it Particle Zoo Demolition Derby Race Track."

"Maybe it was taken. The collision emits another subatomic particle called a muon. A muon travels faster than the speed of light producing the light version of a sonic boom called the Cherenkov cone, which is visible as light. Frederick Reines and Clyde Cowan Jr. won the Nobel Prize for the detection of neutrinos."

"It was a 'matter' of time. Even this discovery is an indirect effect of dark matter and dark energy. We still cannot see this dark or invisible stuff."

"The heart of the matter is invisible. This is where membranes come in. When strings/thoughts vibrate or spin at various frequencies the like attracts like."

"St. Francis of Assisi said, *what you yearn for also yearns for you.* Today, we call this the Law of Attraction. *The Secret* that everyone knows. So a thought is a vibration of energy. Energy and mass are two phases of vibration. So a thought has mass?"

"Yes, theoretically. However minute, mass has gravity and gravity attracts."

"Thoughts have gravity and attracts. The Law of Attraction. The thought counts. Be careful what you wish for. The cosmos is always conspiring with you."

"Conspire literally means to breathe together. This means strings/thoughts of equal and very similar frequencies clump together to, in a relative macrocosm, form layers or membranes. This gives rise to multiple membranes vibrating at different frequency ranges corresponding to the frequencies in the electromagnetic spectrum. So because we cannot see the light in say gamma rays, we cannot see the matter that this 'gamma' light creates. They form a membrane of a higher frequency than what we are capable of seeing. This higher frequency range membrane can be thought of as strings of a higher frequency clumping together to form a gamma level membrane, giving rise to gamma light and then to gamma level matter and anti–matter."

"We cannot see any of this?"

"Yes, but mathematically they exist. This is the Membrane Theory or M–Theory for short. Some call it The Matrix Theory."

"Chief Seattle called the Matrix the web. He said, *whatever man does to the web he does to himself.*"

"The M–Theory mathematically requires the existence of 11 minimum dimensions."

"According to Buddhism there are 11 *lokas* or worlds, realms or planes. Four lower realms and seven heavens as Plato's nested structure and the Qur'an. We apparently live in several of the lower realms transcending the first or bottom heaven. So like I said I am already in Heaven, not the Seventh though. Even the next Bodhisattva Maitreya is only in the 5th Heaven, corresponding to the 9th dimension or membrane."

"Quantum Physics would, inevitably, corroborate to the esoteric cosmology."

"Buddhism is only one line of convergence. There are 11 dimensional levels or sephirot in the Kabbalistic Tree of Life recorded in the Zohar."

"Like the famous Tree of Life cut of crystals used in communication technology."

"Tree of Life is a symbol for the entire existence: Creator and Creation as One. Its Divine and Mundane aspects cohesively unite to form All There Is."

"This is fractals. A tree is a fractal. The Cosmos is a super fractal."

"The exemplar is the archetype. If you have seen one, you have seen the other."

"The unit is a replicate of the whole. They are both arranged according to the same geometric laws and ratios."

"Tree of Life has two parts. The visible tree above the ground and the invisible root systems mirroring the fractal iterations of the bifurcation above. The invisible root is the matrix within the Source Creator, the Divine. The Tao. The Brahman. The Dharmakaya. *Tjukurrtjana.*"

"The cosmic genotype."

"The projected visible Tree is the Creation, the Mundane. The hologram. *Yuti.*"

"The cosmic phenotype."

"But that's simplistic labeling. The visible and the invisible are One tree, divine all the way through. *They is Us.*"

"So Buddhists *lokas* are visible and invisible aspect of the same structure."

"Joseph Campbell defined the basic theme of all myths as an announcement of *a plane of being behind the visible plane, which is somehow supportive of the visible one to which we have to relate. That is the basic theme of all mythology.*"

"He said the all burial rituals began in acknowledgement of this truth. He defines a ritual as an enactment of a myth or metaphor. To ascertain how advance the Australian Aborigines are one must understand their metaphor. They were aware of the visible and invisible ranges of the electromagnetic spectrum, which they called the rainbow serpent."

"The expression of the existence of multiple realms in myth and metaphor was even older than the Vedas and Buddhism. This invisible realm was Duwat for Ancient Egyptians."

"They were aware of the multiple realms and the fact that the senses only perceive one of them at a time."

"Exactly as in Buddhism, we perceive the lower realm called Malkuth in Kabbala and Malakut in Sufism. It is the visible Kingdom, which is nevertheless no less divine than the Invisible. It is simply the perceivable expression or reflection of the Source of Divinity."

"*Thy Kingdom come, thy will be done on Earth as it is in Heaven.*"

"As above, so below. These same unified visible and invisible dimensional structures are echoed in pretty much all indigenous cosmologies including Australian Aborigines, Pleroma of Christian Gnosticism, Asvattha or Tree of Life in Hindu Bhagavad Gita, Ancient Egyptian Duwat, and to some extent in Chinese Taoism."

"Robert Lawlor elucidates us the Aboriginal multi-dimensional cosmology in my grandmother's book *Voices of the First Day.*

For Aborigines, humans and the earth have physical and spiritual dimensions that are all symbolically reflected in one another. This relationship is like that of a pregnant woman to the child within her; the woman changes both physically and psychologically as the child develops, and the fetus derives all of its capacities to grow from the mother. As the earth's atmosphere and soil change in relation to the life on its surface, this life in turn reflects the changes that occur in its earthly milieu. ...

All creatures — from stars to humans to insects — share in the consciousness of the primary creative force, and each, in its own way, mirrors a form of that consciousness. In this sense the Dreamtime stories perpetuate a unified world view. This unity compelled the Aborigines to respect and adore the earth as it were a book imprinted with the mystery of the original creation. The goal of life was to preserve the earth, as much as possible, in its initial purity. The subjugation and exploitation of the natural world was to do the same to oneself."

"This is an echo of Chief Seattle in this neck of the woods, down under – the land that time dreamt."

"The Dreamtime stories extended a universal and psychic consciousness not only to every living creature but also to the earth and the primary elements, forces, and principles. Each component of creation acts out of dreams, desires, attractions, and repulsions, just as we humans do. Therefore, the entrance into the larger world of space, time and universal energies and fields was the same as the entrance into the inner world of consciousness and dreaming. The exploration of the vast universe and knowledge of the meaning of creation was experienced through an internal and external knowledge of self.

Every land formation and creature, by its very shape and behaviors, implied a hidden meaning; the form of a thing was itself an imprint of the metaphysical or ancestral consciousness that created it, as well as the universal energies that brought about its material manifestation. These aspects of Dreamtime imply a world in which the spiritual and physical are held in symbolic integration. One cannot consider the visible and invisible worlds separately. The Aboriginal language that emerged from this world view are rich in a metaphoric flow integrated physical, psychological, and spiritual levels of experience."

"So the whole cosmos is an integrated multi-membrane 'structure' or 'organism,' even portrayed in the metaphors of Buddhist, Kabbalistic, Gnostic, Hindu Vedic, Egyptian, and Aboriginal cosmology. We know we are one of those membrane levels because that is what's visible to us."

"That's why the force of gravity is so weak because it is applied to all membranes and thus diluted."

"We are left with residue gravity."

"We call these membrane levels densities or dimensions. The word density was use in the 1950s through 1980s. It is very descriptive as opposed to dimensions, which means something else, hence the confusion."

"The Law of Confusion!"

"Levels of density imply variation throughout."

"Or Chaos!"

"Yes, things at different levels can have different densities. Ice, liquid water, and water vapor have different density levels due to the different vibration frequencies, in the form of varying kinetic energies. So membranes are of different densities.

Our membrane/density/dimension has a certain high density due to its relatively lower frequency vibration. So we perceive a 'solid' world around us and our bodies seem solid. The majority of mankind has bought this holographic illusion. Although, this number maybe decreasing, hopefully."

"Hence, we have a frivolous materialistic worldview that dominates. People are obsessed with illusory material creations."

"They are unaware that even this very dense membrane/dimension is ultimately of thoughts that arose from a consciousness potential. Everything exists because conscious beings like us desire them and are aware of them. Everything can easily return to that potential from which it arose."

"You live the life you think you live. I think, therefore I am."

"This would be a good application of a cliché."

"Or Wikiality. A word invented by Steven Colbert to denote a Collective Consciousness. Which means essentially *we think, therefore we are*. We are unconsciously telepathically connected in an agreement on our

perceived reality. So *we agree, therefore, we see* an apparent comparable reality, which is in essence an overlap of each one's own parallel reality."

"A dream you dream alone is only a dream. A dream you dream together is reality. – John Lennon."

"Cognition researcher Donald Hoffman puts it in more poetic terms. *I believe that consciousness and its contents are all that exists. Space-time, matter and fields never were the fundamental denizens of the universe but have always been among the humbler contents of consciousness dependent on it for their very being.*"

"I am going to use the word dimension for membrane because that is the common usage. So we live in a multi-dimensional cosmos. Most of it is actually seemingly inaccessible to us.

In fact French mathematician Henri Poincaré said, *it is impossible that there is a reality totally independent of the mind that conceives it, sees it, or sense it. Even if it did exist, such a world be utterly inaccessible to us.*"

"What is in these other *inaccessible* dimensions that apparently do exist? Do people live there?"

"Mathematics does not prohibit it. If they do, their bodies would be less dense and of higher frequency vibrations such as light or dark matter. That means there could be being of various levels of body density. We can think of them as light beings."

"With light bodies like the Egyptian Ka body. So then, why are all human mythologies, ancient and modern, across the planet full of stories of various light beings? Why do these stories claim that they appear and disappear at will? Does that mean there are multi-dimensional beings? Can they lower their vibration frequencies to be compatible in our dimension?"

"Technically, yes. Also, can humans raise their vibration frequency to be become less dense and have more of a light body or Ka body and enter a higher dimension? Theoretically all of this is possible."

"Have you read the book *Supernatural: Meeting the Ancient Teachers of Mankind* by Graham Hancock?"

"No, what's that all about?"

"He takes ibogaine, the West African pygmy psychoactive substance and South American ayahuasca, then he *travels to other dimensions.*"

"You mean hallucinate? Those substances increase the level of secretion of DMT above normal."

"Yes, but the supposed hallucinations across a sample population is so consistent that consciousness research scientists have begun to consider the possibility that such vividly real hallucinations may be real perceptions of and experiences in other 'dimensions' and parallel realities of space and time. Some of them made of dark matter."

"So DMT could be thought of as Dark Matter Television."

"Or as a computer program."

"The brain is the computer. High DMT is a program needed to run certain applications."

"The dark matter in other dimensions are these 'files' that cannot be operated in without the program. Need to be high on DMT."

"So, install and run the DMT program to watch the 3D movie application."

"Inca shamans see four levels of parallel realities. Physical, which is the chemical body reality. Second is Symbolic, which is the mind of words and thoughts. Third is Mythic, which is soul travel through images. The last as the most elusive to us is Essential, which is spirit energy."

"What did Hancock see? Fairies?"

"Yes, sometimes fairies in circles."

"So, this book is just *a fairy tale*."

"Einstein said, *if you want your children to be intelligent, read them fairy tales. If you want them to be more intelligent, read them more fairy tales.*"

"Metaphors! John Lennon asked, *I believe in fairies, the myths, dragons. It all exists, even if it's in your mind. Who's to say that dreams and nightmares aren't as real as the here and now?*"

"Hancock saw Light beings. Man-beasts called therianthropes. Talking snakes and other intelligently communicating animals. Aliens and their crafts. Teaching female spirit beings. That's why he calls it *Supernatural*."

"Reminds me of those prehistoric cave paintings in France, Spain, Italy and South Africa. Those were painted by shamans under those conditions with help of the cygnates. The earlier inception."

"That's his theory too. He claims that these 'supernatural' beings depicted in the painted caves are possibly the ancient teachers of mankind. These human students were the children of the swan if you will. He touches on human evolution, not just as a 'meaningless' random process that Darwin identified, but as something more purposive and intelligently driven by the inception you imply."

"Wow! The current paradigm comes full circle and collapses into within."

"Spiraling into a new dimension. This is the old paradigm. Imagine that you have a radio that is playing only one radio station, KOPD. K Old Paradigm Dimension. Obviously this radio signal is broadcasted at a specific frequency, but delectable across a narrow range. You are not aware that there are other radio stations. But there are many, most of them better than the only one you are forced to hear. You have been told all your life that this is only radio station that exists and people who believe anything else are considered nuts and ostracized. You are sick and tired of this radio station because it only plays songs by the band 'Third Eye Blind' from the album 'You are stuck in 3D, too bad, so sad. It sucks to be you. Na na naaa …'

You are so sick of it that you carry this radio with you on a bicycle to throw it into a river. Because you are holding the radio with one hand you lose control and have a bad fall. The radio and your head hit the pavement really hard. The middle of your forehead cracks open and an indigo light hits your brain. The radio is now playing songs you have never heard. You absolutely love the new music. Even the DJ is the sexiest voice you have ever heard.

You realize the object on the front of the radio that looks a Mayan calendar has changed its orientation. You try to restore the original position. It works. It's like a dial with which you can use to change the frequency. You hear Third Eye Blind again. So you change it a different station. You hear the song 'Starchild' from 2001 A Space Odyssey. '… *Is this a cosmic design? … Harbinger of a new race. We'll be evolving soon. I see the future, a new star will rise. I see the world through the all-seeing eyes Of the Starchild. I have entered another dimension. My perception expands. Transcending beyond comprehension. Evolution of man?*'

All of a sudden you realize that your 'radio' is in fact a television. You couldn't see before 'cause you were 'third eye blind.' The whole time you were stuck on VH1's 'Where Are They Now?' You play with and discover a myriad of channels. Each one is playing a movie. One of them is called DMT – Dark Matter Television. You can watch *2001, 2010, Avatar, Sixth Sense, Déjà Vu, Phenomenon, Powder, Ghost, The Truman Show, Kundun, Indiana Jones, Whale Rider, Contact, The Matrix, Stargate, Lord of the Rings, Back To The Future, Men In Black, Life of Brian, What Dreams May Come, Abyss, Always, Batteries Not Included, E.T., City of Angels, Cocoon, Defending Your Life, Star Wars, Heart and Souls, Heaven Can Wait, Star Trek – The*

Voyage Home, Willow, Groundhog Day, Multiplicity, Close Encounters of the Third Kind, and many more. There is an eerily similar theme going on. A Dream. A Holographic Illusion, A Return of the Ancestors and Wise Men. An Intervention. A Revelation. A True Understanding. A Paradigm Shift. Realizing Potential. A Harvest. A New Race. A New Earth. New Golden Age."

"This is like Plato's *The Allegory of the Cave*, the basis if the movie *The Matrix*."

"The Allegory of the Cave in his *The Republic* is *The Matrix*. In a fictional conversation between Plato's teacher Socrates and Gaucon, Socrates describes a group of people who have lived chained to the wall of a cave all of their lives, facing a blank wall. The people watch shadows projected on the wall by things passing in front of a fire behind them, and begin to ascribe forms to these shadows."

"The shadows are their limited idea of reality."

"A philosopher is one who is freed from the cave."

"Unplugged from *The Matrix* like Morpheus."

"He comes to understand that the shadows on the wall are not the true reality at all and the true reality constitutes other dimensions beyond the two dimensions of the shadows. Then he becomes a creator."

"Like a spider."

"The spider weaves the web, it is the moth that get caught in it. The spider is never caught in his own web. Be the spider and not the moth."

"Plato's based this on his *Theory of Forms*, right?"

"Its premise is that the material world of change, his *Forms*, known to us through sensation is not the most fundamental kind of reality, but only the knowledge of the Forms constitutes real knowledge. The current materialistic and dimensionally challenged worldview is not only limiting the realization of our higher potential but also a debilitating threat on our advancement and very survival."

"The M-Theory or the Matrix theory is gateway to whole new realms, dimensions, and possibilities. In *Theory of Everything* Stephen Hawking says: *I think the years ahead will be a Golden Age of discovery. I think we are acting in reckless indifference to our future on Planet Earth. At the moment we have nowhere to go. But in the long run the human race shouldn't have all its eggs in one basket, or one planet. I just hope that we can avoid rotting the basket until then.*"

ENTANGLED

"Tell me about your girl. Ms. Vancouver?"

"Well, she is not 'my girl'"

"Apparently, she is. You are planning to spend the summer with her."

"That's true, but she is not quite ready."

"Where did you meet her?"

"It was that hiking trip to Mt. Shasta."

"The trip you saw *Joan of Arcturus*? Apparently, Ms. Vancouver has that similar vibe you yearn for."

"Maybe I am not ready or that's how she feels."

"She is still testing you."

"Yeah, it's hard to explain. We don't talk much."

"Tension?"

"There's definitely that. See, she works with dolphins at the Vancouver Aquarium as a part of her grad school program in Marine Biology at Simon Fraser University in Burnaby."

"Isn't that where they filmed the sci-fi series *Stargate SG-1*?"

"Yes. She also spends a lot time diving with dolphins and whales in Queen Charlotte Sound, Hawaii, and Kaikoura bay in New Zealand, for her thesis in cetacean communication and neuroscience. She is amazed by their brain sizes topping humans. The brains sizes are key in their communication. The whale songs are long and complex. Carl Sagan once said, *the whale songs are like reciting The Iliad in 90 minutes then repeating it phoneme-perfect all over again.* So she has over time moved away from human speech as a way of communicating into pure aquatic snazz."

"Does she speak dolphinese?"

"Apparently they speak us. Carl Sagan also said, that *some dolphins are reported to have learned English – up to fifty words used in correct context – no human being has been reported to have learned dolphinese.*"

"So what do dolphins have to say?"

"They communicate using synchronized movements, sonar, and acoustic vibrations. She thinks that dolphins, who seem to operate out of a different paradigm, feel we take life too seriously and end up making it too difficult, complicated, and painful for self and others. I was told of an incredible number of occasions of dolphins displaying unearthly intelligence and a remarkably sophisticated and unique brand of sense of humor. It's almost like she is getting this unexpected tongue-in-cheek lesson in life. I have seen her change dramatically."

"Douglas Adams, who wrote *The Hitchhiker's Guide to the Galaxy*, would agree with her observation. In the book, he wrote, *man had always assumed that he was more intelligent than dolphins because he had achieved so much – the wheel, New York, wars and so on – whilst all the dolphins had ever done was muck about in the water having a good time. But conversely, the dolphins had always believed that they were far more intelligent than man – for precisely the same reasons.*"

"The American poet Barrie Gellis wrote, *the universe is a casual place, not a suit and tie affair.*"

"Gellis will probably tell you that higher you reach in the celestial hierarchy the more ordinary things get like with the dolphins. We have it all backwards. It's not that we are ordinary and they are *extra*ordinary. They are ordinary. It is us, who are burdened by the *extra*."

"She loves John Lilly's *The Day of the Dolphin*. When we are together she doesn't treat me a lot different from a Pacific Ocean cetacean."

"Something's gotta give. You guys need an inception."

"There will be no conception for sure. We don't go there."

"I got that from the *tension*, but something is brewing."

"She wants me to be different than the last ones. I feel the same. We are both nervous you know."

"So I guess you are not going to use a line."

"I am holding it back."

"What is it?"

"*If you weren't real I would make you up.*"

"Nice! Where did you steal that from?"

"*The O.C.* soundtrack."

"You are a west coast soul lost in an east coast hole. That's sad. So what are you going to do?"

"Wait."

"You don't know what lies ahead. You think it will be nice, so the expectations are high."

"It's like we are at this stage. There is definitely a swaying between ordinary lull and ecstasy. The ecstasy is in the silence."

"It's called a *nonversation*. Is it deafening?"

"In fact, it often is. This may sound weird, but I can truly loudly detect constant vibrations. I think that every human can do this to varying degrees."

"But most can't hear it for their noisy thought chatter. What the Buddhist monks call the *Monkey Mind* and the Red man calls *Coyote Mind*."

"Right, we often go on these long hikes in the island, you know, across the Strait of Georgia."

"Main island?"

"And Meares. Her grandma lives in Tofino. She is part Tlingit. … It is so quiet there. I silence my mind and I can hear the trees. The vibe of each sound is different, but together they make music. Pythagoras called this *the symphony of the spheres*."

"Britney?"

"Trees! Each one has a story, like a parable with a subtle underlying teaching given. I never walk away the same person."

"Plato's first academy was a grove of trees belonging to a man named Academos. So was the school of Pythagoras. Moses, Jesus, Siddhartha Gautama, and the Druids all spent time among trees searching for wisdom. Gautama Buddha attained Nirvana under a Bodhi tree. In fact, Druids mean *wise ones of the oak*. Buddha was called *Muni*, meaning the *silent one*. Maybe they all knew how trees and silence could teach."

"Druid lore imply that *divine powers of the cosmos dwell in its eternal silence.* Sometimes I will spend an hour listening to a flower. The life in it somehow finds resonance with every one my cells pulsating with a vivacious stream of life. I often lose track of time losing myself and dissolving into the mist of the island."

"Maybe she is putting you under some mesmeric Tlingit magic spell. I think she is your Isis!"

"I only complain when I am not under it."

"Is she flirtatious?"

"She doesn't need to be. She just gazes at me with her deep sensuous dark brown Tlingit eyes as if I was just a line in a poem she casually wrote. She gave me this book to read."

"What is it called?"

"*In the Presence of High Beings: What the Dolphins Wants to You to Know.*"

"Did you read it?"

"Some of it. It was a bit boring and I didn't quite get it."

"I think that is what she wants you to know on your own. Her silence is purposive."

"There was an exception to the silent treatment."

"The only exception?"

"It was totally unanticipated. One warm evening, last summer, we walked in silence to a meadow of mystical charm. As the sun began to set we both laid down on a lush grassy stretch. That night there were no clouds. This is rare for that neck of the woods. The stars seemed even more magical for this is first time this happened. She began speak. We ended the conversation watching the sun rise over the canopy of the woodland."

"What did you talk about?"

"Who we think we are."

"And?"

"She felt that we were watching ourselves be."

"And you were."

"She wants me to always have this mind state. It's fleeting. I am definitely there when I am with her."

"These states of mind never happen in Maryland?"

"Very rarely. In Baltimore, I have been more of an academic machine or a cybernetic organism – a cyborg. Humanity awaits the human. *The Unbearable Lightness of Being*."

"Milan Kundera. And what's different in Vancouver, Canada - the Higher Dimension."

"It's like my vibes realign with her every time we are together. In that timeless stillness we don't speak for we fear what T. S. Eliot did. *Do I dare disturb the universe?*"

"Your speech is in collective singular. You guys are entangled. Here you are alone. Something is missing. There ... well, *wherever two or more gather in my name, there am I with them.*"

"Isis?"

"Wherever human passions converge, the divine queen springs her magic."

"In fact, our friends call us Neraye."

"Neraye?

"Her name is Nera."

"Raye and Nera no longer exist. Neraye, the resonating collective consciousness, does. The two different vibrating frequencies meet halfway and then there is one shared frequency and voila, you are one."

"I don't like the labels, but she calls it Pod Mind."

"Like Group Mind in *Childhood's End* or Collective Mind of Paul Hawken and De Chardin."

"It's like that Phil Collins song. *Two hearts* ..."

"*... just one mind.*"

"Sometimes I feel even the heart beats synchronize. The dolphins certainly seem to operate as One – a collective consciousness in perfect communion."

"There is this First Nations lore that says a group of dolphins became so permanently entangled as one that when they died and they were reborn as one whale. That's what some whales are – collective dolphin complexes.

Greek historian Plutarch knew it ... *to the dolphin alone, beyond all others, nature has granted what the best philosophers seek; friendship with no advantage."*

"When we are together it is a sublime trance! Nothing matters!! *We* and *I* become synonyms!!! Language approaches full redundancy."

"What is it like?"

"It's almost more manageable when you analyze it from an academic or a philosophical point of view. Being in it is so hard."

"How so?"

"It is not really being in it. It's the lack of it the rest of the time."

"You want all or nothing."

"I want all. Nothing is not an option. Unless Nothing and All are one and the same."

"Do you know how she feels now?"

"Right now the entanglement is more subdued. It feels like a separation not from each other but from the collective state of resonance. When it happens the separation seems as elusive as the communion feels right now."

"She is your soul mate, huh?"

"I don't know. I have never found the importance of seeking a validation like that."

"What's the first thing you are going to say to her when you see her?"

"What does a soap bubble say to another soap bubble when they collide?"

"You smell like clean linen."

"It's like a dissolution of surface tension and a formation of a shared complex. It's like remote access of a computer where there is only one monitor and one cursor, but two mice and keyboards. We often wait for the other to initiate a thought."

"Telepathy."

"I think of as an extreme case of intuitive ability. The capacity to understand the noumenal."

"Something that can be only felt, but not always proven."

"Science does back it. There was a study done at Brown University. They took patients paralyzed from a stroke and placed a small chip wirelessly connected to a computer in their brain. It only took three hours to train these people to read and send e-mail, do crossword puzzles, play video games and surf the Web."

"That's just astonishing."

"Intuition usually works with no man-made computer involved. This intuition of the noumenal is an enhanced state of something everyone already has."

"Ah! A very generously inclusive worldview. Intuition is the ear of the soul."

"It's like the two wings of the butterfly. Once as a caterpillar there was only one. Aren't they still? Entangled!!"

"Can't fly with one wing. You will not get anywhere."

"Exactly. I feel incapacitated without that synergistic energy exchange. I seek it constantly. I know it's transient, but I feel that's what we, I mean all humanity, strive for."

"How come you don't believe in God?"

"You mean why am I not suffering from *The God Delusion*?"

"Yes, why?"

"Because if I cannot commune with Him in the true sense, as a real life consciousness that is ever present and readily accessible. Not as beliefs full with doubt or blind faith. This to me is as good as non-existent. Religion does not appeal to me. *La ilaha*, as Sufis say, meaning there is no Divinity."

"Religion is based on belief. Spirituality is based on understanding. Religion is the embodiment of duality, us versus them mentality – separating you from your God and coming in between. Spirit means God. Spirituality means Godliness. Union with God without the mediation of another. DIY. The Sufi saying *La ilaha* uttered by those who practice dhikr actually means *there is no other Divinity.*"

"Just the fact that there are so many religions is proof that all of them wrong. Some of them breed fanaticism. People should stop going to church. DIY. No Assembly Required."

"I wouldn't say that. Church and God are metaphors. It's not that people should not go into church, it's that they should not come out of it. John Lennon said, *you're just left with yourself all the time, whatever you do anyway. You've got to get down to your own God in your own temple. It's all down to you, mate.*"

"He also said, *I believe in God, but not as one thing, not as an old man in the sky. I believe that what people call God is something in all of us. I believe that what Jesus and Mohammed and Buddha and all the rest said was right. It's just that the translations have gone wrong.*"

"I would say incomplete and in complete disarray. I think God played a really clever teaching joke on humanity. She created a puzzle out of the truth with that divine sense of humor, broke it into pieces and gave each group of belief a piece. The truth will only be revealed only if humanity unites into a collective consciousness."

"I think science has the biggest piece of this joke."

"Like the butt of an elephant.

Gautama Buddha once told a parable of a group of blind people. They were all asked to describe an elephant. Each grabbed a part of the animal and described an elephant as a tail, trunk, leg, belly, ear, and, of course, butt."

"The butt of the joke is …"

"They were all correct. Butt …

Ibn al Arabi, a Sufi Muslim master from Spain captures this truth masterfully.

Beware of confining yourself to a particular belief and denying all else, for much good would elude you – indeed, the knowledge of reality would elude you. Be in yourself a master for all forms of belief, for God is too vast and tremendous to be restricted to one belief rather than another."

"I understand that the truth is segmented but does exist in the collective human consciousness. However, this personification of the truth as God does not resonate with me."

"You are alive. Life spirit is within you. You are in communion with life. Joseph Campbell said, *God is a metaphor for a mystery that absolutely transcends all human categories of thought, even thoughts of being and non-being.* That's how the understanding is invoked."

"God is a metaphor for life, which, however, is temporary. You only live once!"

"Do we?"

"Do you believe in reincarnation?"

"Your favorite author Milan Kundera, who wrote *The Unbearable Lightness of Being* said, *if we have only one life to live, we might as well not have lived at all.*"

"Oh wait, this is a Déjà vu. I have had this same moment before. Yep, it was yesterday at the Deli with the raw vegan, tripping, tree-hugging, dirt worshipping, New Age, Reiki master, hippie nut case – the reincarnation of Ra, the Pharaoh of the ancient Kingdom of Ra-Mu."

"Ancient books and science in the form of regressive hypnosis in psychology address this multiple incarnation concept thoroughly. By the way, I am a raw vegan suffering from constant recurring multiple rawgasms. *Le Petit Mort* – The little death. And rejuvenation!"

"Actually, I was watching *Quantum Activist*, a documentary about Dr. Amit Goswami. I understood everything except one thing in it. Have you seen it?"

"No. What was the thing?"

"He is a serious physicist, in fact, wrote the text book on Quantum Physics. But he once got some sort of a message in his head. It said, '*Tibetan Book of the Dead* is true and you have to prove it.' He ignored it but was repeated as what he calls 'an admonition.' It kind of gave me chills."

"Yes, Padmasambava wrote the *Bardo Thodol* or Tibetan Book of the Dead to help souls deal with the immediate afterlife or *Bardo*. It describes the immediate liminal spirit state of existence as a potential lucid dream. Lucid after you have realized it is. This is where you recognize the monsters you are faced with as truly your inner fears or 'demons' reflecting outwards."

"Mark Twain said, fear or a *problem is an issue of mind over matter. If you don't mind, it doesn't matter.*"

"Joseph Campbell spoke of our fears eloquently. He said, *our demons are our own limitations, which shut us off from the realization of the ubiquity of the spirit … each of these demons is conquered in a vision quest.* Bardo Thodol describes such a vision quest."

"This, I mean conquering fear, is a tough ask from modern humans, without outside help."

"Campbell's *ubiquity of the spirit* refers to the transcending collective consciousness. This is where the fear needs to be expelled from. This, of course, needs outside help and it is a challenge to expel the fear from within."

"Where and when is the outside help coming from?"

"I guess you don't believe in the rapture or the Second Coming either."

"I don't even believe in half of the first coming."

"You think Jesus was real, but what is written about him is not completely reliable. The *truthiness* is diluted."

"Exactly. Colbert fan huh? I know he knew what is really going on, but the teaching is muddled."

"I didn't realize you believed in Colbert that much."

"Jesus. When I read the Bible or any other esoteric theological document, some things ring true. Some are obviously recurring motifs if you read Joseph Campbell."

"Basically, the name Jesus is a Latinized and Greek version of his name Yeshua."

"Right. Both Mathews and Isaiah says he was named Immanuel. You see all the names like Moses, Isis, Osiris, Horus, Augustus, Marcus, Matthias, Lucas, Johannes, end with *es*, *us*, or *is* to be consistently correct in Greek and Latin grammar. So Horu became Horus. Moishe became Moses. Yeshua became Jesus."

"Do you believe he was the Son of God?"

"It certainly wasn't Brian."

"Monty Python's *Life of Brian.*"

"*He is not the messiah. He is a very naughty boy.*"

"You think he was the Messiah?"

"Brian?"

"No, Jesus."

"Messiah and Christ both mean the *Anointed One* in Hebrew and Greek respectively."

"It simply means king. This goes back to Egypt. The crocodile was considered a powerful and mysterious creature with mythic status, an emblem of sovereignty, royalty and protection symbolized by their god Sobek. A coronation of a new Pharaoh was ritualized by the anointing of the head with crocodile oil. This was to impart that power, protection, and awe. One of the Egyptian names for crocodile is *Msha*, son of Set. The one anointed with crocodile oil was the Mshiah, which in Hebrew is Masiah and later Messiah. This is the Greek Khristos and for us Christ, which is an office, not a person."

"I do not see the person of Jesus or Yeshua as an ordinary man. According to all the Gnostic gospels in Nag Hamadi Scrolls, discovered in Egypt, he was a child with powerful abilities. He stretches carpentry wood, give life to clay birds, temporarily causes his friends to appear as goats, and it is written that he even causes a child to lose consciousness just by simply uttering words."

"Yes, that alleged story is in *The Infancy Gospel of Thomas*. Maybe he didn't know what he was doing."

"Then when he was tortured and about to be killed he says, *Father, forgive them, for they do not know what they are doing.*"

"Luke 23:34. This is a lesson in the dangers of judging."

"Some of the writings about him don't make any sense."

"Like the miracles?"

"No. I mean Einstein said, *there are only two ways to live your life. One is as though nothing is a miracle. The other is as though everything is a miracle.*"

"Philosopher Prentice Mulford said, *possibilities and miracles mean the same thing.*"

"Even Dalai Lama once said, *a miracle is something unexpected.* Jesus himself scoffed those amazed by his deeds that said, you *will do the works I have been doing, and they will do even greater things.*"

"Greater things. That's us. *Anything is possible.* Remember Neo's last line in the movie *The Matrix*?"

"Yes. Arthur C. Clarke said, *any sufficiently advanced technology would be indistinguishable from magic.*"

"Future technology is inevitably tied to the mastery of the nature of consciousness."

"In the 2011 BBC Two documentary *What is Reality?* MIT Cosmologist Dr. Max Tegmark says, *we will only be limited by our own imagination,* talking about how mathematics explains the multiverse."

"If we think we can't then we can't. Fortunately the opposite is also true. Unfortunately, some think we can't because of imagined limits."

"Dr. Leonard Susskind, the father of the String Theory in *What is Reality?* says, *old people always think there are limits to what we can understand. It's the young people, who push past those limits.*"

"Old people believe in God. Young people believe they are God. Old people drew a line between them and God. Young people are erasing it."

"What don't make sense is this old people's God ordering the death of people, judgment, eternal hell, and neglect of helpless humans suffering. I am with Virginia Woolf who said, *I read the book of Job last night, I don't think God comes out well in it.* Even more absurd is the concept of inheriting sin."

"Those are made up, by the *Evil Genius*, to suppress people. The only sin that is real is being SIN – Stuck In Negativity. That is the proverbial hell."

"I understand the metaphor of hell. Most intelligent people do. It's the people that believe there is a literal hell for those judged by God as sinners that makes the concept of personal God repulsive to me. What kind of a horrific God would condemn his own children to eternal torture and suffering? If we are made in his image, then that does not make any sense, because most of us will never do that to our children. In fact, many of us make life-long sacrifices for our children."

"Hell is a metaphor for spiritual darkness, which is being Stuck In Negativity – SIN. People have the free will to believe in whatever the hell they want. Pun intended! This belief however, manifests as consequences in their immediate life. That's sad to watch. Free Will is an existential conundrum."

"Also, the temptation attempt of Jesus by the so called Satan is very dubious. I think Jesus retreated for mediation and focus on and preparation for his mission."

"So what happened to him when he died in your view?"

"My view? What do you need my view? Read the Bible. Hebrews 6:20."

"Our forerunner, Jesus, has entered on our behalf. He has become a high priest forever, in the Order of Melchizedek."

"Whatever the Order of Melchizedek is. Melchizedek is mentioned all over the Bible. Psalm 110:4, Hebrews 5:10, 7:11 & 17. He once blesses Abraham in Genesis."

"Druids of Ancient England considered him to dwell in the center of the Earth. Indigenous people of the Americas often speak of this Melchizedek. In Genesis 14:18 he is mentioned as the King of Salem or Peace and as a *Priest of the God Most High.*"

"Well, I don't believe in God as such."

"You don't believe in Satan either?"

"I do believe in Santa."

"They get mixed up all the time. I think it's the red uniform."

"Satan is a fake bogeyman monster character invented by religions to instill fear and hatred in order to control people."

"It's like when parents make up monsters to control children through fear."

"It's conditioning. One day God asks a recovering Catholic, *so if Satan did not exist would that make your life a living hell?*"

"Sounds like your God is a lot of pun! That's one of the best puns I have ever heard."

"I do have enormous sympathy for the Catholics though. Joseph Campbell was formerly a Catholic. He recovered well enough say that most religious people *do not know what a metaphor is.*"

"Satan is a metaphor. The simple fact of not knowing what metaphor is bondage to a survival mentality in a life of fear and hell, which is separation from the ubiquitous Spirit."

"Guess who knows what a metaphor is. Vatican versus Uluru. Catholics versus Aborigines This is Lawlor from *Voices of the First Day: Awakening in the Aboriginal Dreamland.*

A story that illustrates this point is told by an early-contact Catholic missionary. The priest had decided that in one grand gesture he would change the 'uncivilized, primitive' behavior of the Aborigines who had been forced to live on his mission. One day he took a group to a nearby stream, where he commenced to baptize them, telling them that the splash of water would remove the invisible stain of sin that was upon them, and from that point on, they would be and act like completely different 'civilized people.' The following Friday he observed one of the baptized Aborigines enjoying a meal of kangaroo steak from an animal he had just captured. The priest said to him, 'you know that since you have become a Christian it is wrong to eat meat on Friday.' The man smiled and said, 'this is not meat, it is fish.' The priest was angry and told him he was compounding the sin by lying about it. The Aborigine looked at him very sternly and replied, 'last week you sprinkled water on me and told me I had changed into a completely different person, so I did the same thing with this kangaroo. I sprinkled water on it and changed it into fish.' He then laughed as if he had pleased the missionary by going along with his joke."

"Sin and baptism are metaphors. It is fitting who made the point to whom. The recovering religious need major healing after being held captive in that medieval mind dungeon."

"String Theory itself is metaphor. It is our modern myth for something that transcends even our modern thoughts. So let me put a modern spin on spinning strings. Sin is metaphor for a lower vibrational frequency caused by a sense of unworthiness and guilt, which when personified is a metaphor called Satan. This sin or sense of unworthiness can be minimized by a multi-dimensional transformation of the energy vibration to a higher frequency. The metaphor for this is a ritual, an enactment of the myth."

"An example of such a ritual would be baptism or communion at mass."

"Think about it. The church is the protective middleman. No Satan. No sin. No guilt. No fear. No Church. Out of business! Defunct!!"

"They are like insurance companies. Its survival and control is in the fear."

"Little babies, Kalahari bushmen, and dolphins do not believe in these monsters."

"To be like an infant in God's bosom. To be a child of the moment. That is the answer given in the book *Awakening: A Sufi Experience,* when asked, 'what does it mean to be a Sufi Muslim.'*

Jesus said, *truly I tell you, unless you change and become like little children, you will never enter the kingdom of heaven.* Mathew 18:3"

"*Let the little children come to me, and do not hinder them, for the kingdom of heaven belongs to such as these.*

That's the Bible of the land."

"Does Nera read the Bible of the water?"

"It would say unless you change and become like dolphins, you will never enter the kingdom of heaven. Her 'Bible' is a book called *The Sea Around Us* by marine biologist Rachel Carson, who is more known for her genius work, *Silent Spring.*"

"It's those who have been subjected to the religious and political brainwashing, the Adult-like, living in deep-rooted fear and hatred of this imaginary devil. That's a sad waste of life. It's difficult to help them because they are so adamantly defensive and closed minded."

"The bumper sticker on Nera's Subaru has some advice for them. *Be Ocean Minded.*

They are misled and lost. One of them wrote a letter to *The New Yorker* magazine protesting the publication of a series on *Silent Spring.*

Miss Rachel Carson's reference to the selfishness of the insecticide manufactures probably reflects her Communist sympathies, like a lot of our writers these days. We can live without birds and animals, but, as the current market slump shows, we cannot live without business. As for insects, isn't it just like a woman to be scared to death of few little bugs! As long as we have the H-bomb everything will be O.K. P.S. She's probably a peace-nut too."

"Fear through and through! Not *childlike*. Lost on earth!! What about those lost in 'space'? What's your view on demons?"

"I suppose they are like misled and angry souls. No one is a permanent demon. They are just lost and barking."

"They just need help to find their way and help is always sent to those who ask. I once saw a bumper sticker that said. *Wag More, Bark Less!*"

"That makes sense to me. At least, that's the way it should be and is for some. An anthropologist said, *no one has ever met a lost aborigine.* He meant physically, but the meaning is spiritually applicable."

"Demons are angels, who haven't realized their angelic nature yet. They are that way because they are stuck in unworthiness of God's love."

"I sometimes feel more for them than the judgmental self-righteous *holier than thou* folk."

"Jesus said *the tax collectors and the prostitutes are entering the kingdom of God ahead of you.* So those who judge get behind them in the path towards God."

"To me that makes sense. The squeaky wheel gets the oil first."

"My highest worlds are responsible for the lowest, being bound unto one another through Me for the resurrection of ALL."

"The last shall be the first."

"Love conquers ALL! So what do think happens when you die?"

"I think, it's curtains!"

"Didn't you learn from studying evolution all these years that when one door closes another one opens?"

"That how it should be. That's how it is on Earth."

"As above. So below."

"Well, I don't want Heaven to be too true of a mirror. I do like my life on Earth to a great extent. But there is definitely something missing, especially in the leadership and collective consciousness."

"Thy Kingdom come, thy will be done on Earth as it is in Heaven."

"I don't demand perfection to be happy. The evening news getting better day by day and a truer portrayal of a more reasonably balanced world in every aspect would be nice."

"But the media is not a reliable indicator of the true nature of humanity. There is a lot of good out there. Perhaps, news should be divided into equal half of war and peace. So the two halves of the population can choose to watch the version of their worldview, their own parallel reality. Personally, I don't have cable. John Lennon said, *if everyone demanded peace instead of another television set, then there'd be peace.*"

"Yes, I don't think denial and suppression is healthy either. We need a momentum shift."

"You don't think God wants that?"

"If there was a God in Heaven He or She would want that."

"There is no God in Heaven."

"What else is new?"

"Heaven is in God."

"That's like saying the Kingdom of God is within you. Not sure what it means."

"Have you read *Communion* by Whitley Shrieber?"

"Isn't it some alien being encounter book? What's that got to do with Heaven?"

"After one episode his little son tells him *Reality is God's Dream.*"

"So Heaven equals all Reality. It is a figment of God's imagination. At least, according to the extraterrestrial theologians."

"In Hinduism the universe is Vishnu's dream. Doesn't the M-Theory redefine the scientific paradigm of reality?"

"The M-Theory is sometimes called the Matrix Theory."

"This requires cosmic intelligence, *the red pill.*"

"Actually Max Planck, the father of Quantum Physics said, *all matter originates and exists only by virtue of a force which brings the particle of an atom to vibration and holds this most minute solar system of the atom together. We must assume behind this force the existence of a conscious and intelligent mind. This mind is the matrix of all matter.*"

"May the Force be with you."

"And with you."

"Doesn't every culture accept the presence of this Force?"

"Native American Wakan Tanka, Incan Wiraqocha, Chinese Chi, Japanese Ki, Indian Prana, Tibetan Lhung, Egyptian Sekhem, Hebrew Ruach, Greek Pneuma, Christian Holy Spirit, Druidic Nwyfre, Kalahari bushman N-*click*-um, orgone energy, dragon force, and I am sure there are countless other names."

"Do you ever practice the art of *Feng Shui*?"

"Not strictly, but I get it. You try to control the flow of energy where you live to enhance your life like in *Tai Chi*. It is analogous to finding the best spot to receive frequency signal, like Wi-Fi or Radio."

"The best spot to connect to the *Serpent of Light* of the Tibetans and South Americans, dragon of the Druids, and Rainbow Serpent of Aborigines, who knew that some spots of land had a thinner veil covering the original spirit blueprint, from which the land is never separate. This spot channeling the energy from the ultimate Source, the *Tao*, is called *hsueh* in Chinese, meaning the dragon point. *Feng Shui* was originally used by Chinese masters to enhance their sex lives."

"Did it work?"

"Is China under-populated?"

"Yes, and the Indian *Kama Sutra* addresses this energy too."

"And does the Indian population reflect that?"

"I don't know if the quantity of copulation is a good indicator of the tantric quality."

"I agree. The link to sex is apt, because it is a creative force."

"If not, we would not be here."

"The divine sneeze is an euphemism for something more hanky panky."

"Lawlor finds an echo of the Chinese use of the art of Feng Shui in the sexuality among Australian Aborigines in *Voices of the First Day*.

Aborigines consider the natural environment to result from sexual potencies of spiritual beings and that these potencies continue to vivify of creatures and process of nature. They also know that the quality, variety, and intensity of human eroticism can deeply affect the surrounding life processes. The notion that sexual energies of human beings and nature affect each other remains in our thinking today. We acknowledge that moonlight, the thundering of waves on the shore, the color and scent of certain flowers, or the shape and feel of stones possess sexually stimulating qualities. ... Aborigines place on their sexuality are directed towards the reciprocal exchange between human sexuality and the erotic forces of nature."

"Holy Spirit or Force, Holy Shekinah in Hebrew, is a creative and sexual energy that sustains life in its vitality."

"See, for me the Force and God are not the same. God is a judge. Force is neutral."

"You speak the truth my friend. You speak the truth."

"I don't need faith to accept the existence of a life force. This so-called God is made up, as far as I am concerned."

"Life is God. God is Life. Are you familiar with Sufism?"

"Yes, I used to date a Turkish girl in Minneapolis. Celem! I used to call her my Byzantine Magic."

"The Sufi precept is *Not only there is God, God is All There Is*."

"Everything? Matter, Anti-matter, Dark matter, dark energy, potential, consciousness, my dog, your dog, Jesus, Elvis, Tobey Keith, Dixie Chicks, and your hat are altogether God?"

"Wheresoever you turn, there is the face of God. Qu'ran sura 2:115.

Ye Are Gods. Psalms 82:6. That's there is to it."

"*Ye Are Gods* is also a book, right?"

"A wonderful piece of writing by Annalee Skarin."

"So what God does is what everything does?"

"I can only Be, through you."

"That's the nicest thing you have ever said to me."

"Sufi master Vilayat Inayat Khan finds that *God discovers Himself by revealing Himself to you in the form through which He projects His attributes as your unique physical countenance. God's actuality is a virtuality that becomes a reality as ourselves. … Sufis see God as being awakened not just in us, but as us.*"

"Many faces, One Organism! Quantum physics now knows that we cannot find where one cloud of energy ends and another begins."

"That means we cannot find where you end and God begins. There is only one of us."

"One of us? Like the song?"

"Song?"

"*What if God was one of us?*"

"One Being. In *Timaeus*, Plato implies that the universe is musical and has one soul. One Song! Uni-Verse!!

... a single solitary universe, whose very excellence enables it to keep its own company without requiring anything else. For its knowledge of and friendship with itself is enough.

One self-sufficient self-aware harmonious organism. There is only one fundamental cosmic consciousness expressing and experiencing itself through innumerable forms, including you and me. This also the principle premise in Druidry. This cosmic consciousness remains essentially entangled in its diverse expressed form as it was in its unexpressed form of potentiality. This is quantum entanglement, which is unrealized in the current chaotic form."

"And the chaos separated and stratified the harmony. Martin Luther King said, *each of us is something of a schizophrenic personality, tragically divided against ourselves.*"

"This is when the duality divides into indiv*iduality*. Individual, from the Latin root *individuus*, means divided into fragment."

"The Latin word *indivia*, means to envy or more precisely *to look wantonly upon that which is outside one.*"

"Once the fragmentation is in effect come the forgetting! Oh them not remembering who they really are. It's tragic my friend to watch the way people live their lives. They have forgotten that we are all in this together as One. They are not living; they are dying."

"So true! But how does the Life Force gives tantalizing clues to the Oneness?"

"They are everywhere. That's what life is. To find the clues."

"Life is somebody's game? A *Truman Show*?"

"Sufi Muslim master Ibn Arabi said, *at an advanced stage God reveals Himself without using these clues.* Jesus did say *Father and I are one.*

Until this is fully realized there is nothing else to do except play this game. This poker game of life. Hindu Vedics called this interplay of cosmos force through us *Lila*. Life is an opportunity to figure it all out and by getting better at it. The potential is there. The name of the game is fulfilling the potential in the play of unfolding – *Lila*."

"The Universe is all made up. Shakespeare did say that life is but a stage and we are all actors in it. We are players in a greater drama."

"A series of dreams. Dreams within dreams. Your waking dream is main stage. The book *The Four Agreements: A Toltec Wisdom Book* explains this Dreamtime beautifully."

"The same Dreamtime as the Aborigines?"

"The same. Towards the end of his life visionary biologist Gregory Bateson intuited the existence of the Dreamtime.

The individual mind is imminent but not only in the body. It is imminent also in pathways and messages outside the body, and there is a larger mind of which the individual mind is only a subsystem. This larger mind is comparable to God and is perhaps what some people mean by God, but it is still imminent in the total interconnected social systems and planetary ecology."

"We are subsystems of a greater interconnected biological and ecological system."

"In John 15:1 Jesus says *I am the vine and you are branches*."

"This goes beyond biological oneness."

"The individual mind is a character played by the larger mind, the Cosmic Consciousness or God. That's the Cosmic Joke."

"I guess I ought to laugh out loud. Nice one Cosmic God!"

"We are here on Earth to participate in and contribute to a collective remembering experience: to realize that we are one with the cosmos and the earth."

"Not everyone has forgotten. An Aboriginal woman once said, *with your vision you see me sitting on a rock, but I am sitting on the body of my ancestor. The earth, his body, and my body are identical.* This is in the book *Awakening in the Aboriginal Dreamtime.*"

"So that is the Awakening that Eckhart Tolle was taking about in his book *A New Earth.*"

"Awakening to the reality of Dreamtime, being one with all there is, here and now."

"Right, so after you figure it out that *Ye Are God*, an individualized expression of God, you still have to play the game."

"How come majority of people seem to be powerless and stuck in a herd mentality?"

"One reason is that our individualized consciousness is diluted enough to forget that Ye Are God. In the book *The Doors of Perception* Aldous Huxley explains the mechanism of this dilution.

To make biological survival possible, Mind at Large has to be funneled through the reducing valve of the brain and nervous system. What comes out at the other end is a measly trickle of the kind of consciousness which will help us to stay alive on the surface of this particular planet."

"So this creates vulnerability, which is exploited in some way."

"Programmed Guilt! Our freedom is tied to our two forms of creativity: spiritual creativity and biological creativity, which is sexuality. The Austrian-American psychiatrist Wilhelm Reich gave a dire warning.

Sexual suppression supports the power of the church, which has sunk very deep roots into the exploited masses by means of sexual anxiety and guilt. It engenders the timidity towards authority. This results in adult subservience to state authority and to capitalistic exploitation. It paralyzes the intellectual critical powers of the oppressed masses because it consumes the great part of biological energy.

Finally, it paralyzes the resolute development of creative forces and renders impossible the achievement of all aspirations for human freedom. In this way the prevailing economic system, in which a few individuals can easily rule entire masses, becomes rooted in the psychic structures of the oppressed themselves."

"This sounds like Orchestrated Oblivion!"

"It is the father of fear if you ask Emerson. Those who seek to identify the Anti-Christ or Descartes' *Evil Genius* at this time should look inside the collective mind of those who live in fear because of programmed ignorance and cosmic naïveté. That's where he lives – in that version reality of *The Matrix*, based on Descartes' premise."

"The author of the ultimate book on programmed dumbing down, *Brave New World*, Aldous Huxley said, *most ignorance is vincible ignorance: We don't know because we don't want to know.* Unfortunately that's the majority of today, who swallowed *the blue pill.*"

"They are easily distracted from spiritual matters because of orchestrated distractions by large corporations."

"People aren't wearing enough hats."

"Have you ever noticed that large billboard before?"

"The meaning of life!"

"That building was not there yesterday."

"Why does the top on your dashboard *never stops spinning?*"

"What took you so long?"

"You know Americans watch *Saturday Night Live* and not its British predecessor *Monty Python* to get this joke, right?"

"Sorry I was distracted by the *falling buildings.*"

"At least this distraction was orchestrated by us ... or is it? YouTube has a clip of 'People aren't wearing enough hats' skit. It makes this point of orchestrated distraction."

"In the book *1984* by George Orwell echoed the Huxley warning. Orwell said, *during times of universal deceit, telling the truth becomes a revolutionary act.* Mark Twain added, *whenever you find yourself on the side of the majority, it is time to pause and reflect.*"

"Virginia Woolf would agree on being locked in the majority. *I thought how unpleasant it is to be locked out; and I thought how it is worse, perhaps, to be locked in.* People don't pause even for a moment to reflect this."

"In the movie *Waking Life* there is this guy that says every moment that arrives is an invitation from God, but we keep saying to 'No' every moment. And one day, eventually, we *pause* and accept that invitation. Jesus said, be in the world, not of it."

"Henry David Thoreau was an example of someone who was unplugged from *The Matrix*. He said, *if a man does not keep pace with his companions perhaps it is because he hears a different drummer. Let him step to the music he hears, however measured or far away.*"

"Thoreau, Twain, Campbell and the gang walked their talk; they stepped to the music they heard. I am still looking for that drum."

"I am still not convinced of the power this imparts. It doesn't seem real based on the dysfunctional conditions, sorrow, and fear in the world."

"Everybody wants to rule the world."

"Tears for Fears."

"In the book *Conversations with Seth* by Susan Watkins, Seth eloquently ties the conditions on earth and our responsibility for its manifestation.

The gods did not conceive the universe in sorrow; this earth did not come from a tear. You have formed your own tear."

"How can a single person turn the tear from sorrow to joy?"

"People don't realize their own power and status because of limiting belief. Listen to what Seth adds.

It is not that your being exists in a lesser reality. It is that you have not learned to recognize the extent of the reality in which you do exist."

"We occupy and transcend more than we perceive."

"You are a leaf in the tree of life."

"Like in *Avatar* or Kabbala?"

"Let's go with James Cameron here. You are still part of the tree. The tree can only be through you. The trunk cannot have the experience you have and make that same sustaining contribution."

"So I am like an incarnation of a greater intelligence."

"You are an Avatar of the Cosmic Consciousness. One of many. Are you with me?"

"When have I not been with you according to your philosophy. We are the *Tree*. Entangled as One."

"Indeed, my other self, indeed. This is fun. There is nothing in life like watching Our other selves wake. More the merrier!"

"Maybe you can start a new movement."

"I have. It's a very small group. There is only one of us."

SAMADHI

"Apparently we need more and more because I hate to be the voice of doom and gloom and the bearer of *The Inconvenient Truth*. There have been five mass extinctions Earth's history. We are in the sixth. Human population may be growing in wisdom, but also in size. Some may be evolving rapidly, but The End is Near, at least it seems like it."

"Many worldwide cultural prophesies allude to that. You are right about the death, destruction and imbalance. I am not denying that. But we have the power."

"Explain, 'cause I am not convinced."

"Your innermost feelings are the language with which you communicate with the cosmic consciousness and co-create your reality. Thought-forms are vibrational blueprints that hold the instructions for manifesting the reality you wish."

"So you are applying the M-Theory to individuals."

"Yes, and ultimately to the masses, but we all must start with the 'man' in the mirror."

"Mahatma Gandhi said, *Be the change you want to see in the world.*"

"Archdruid John Michael Greer summarizes the essence of Druid philosophy as *changing the world through the force of personal example, through living the change you hope to make in the world.*"

"Yes, but the enormous task of dissolving the pervasive yet already increasingly obsolete paradigms seems overwhelming."

"This is true. People including scientists cling on to the old paradigm until they find themselves in the minority. Your power is actually non-local."

"But how do we change the world? Is world peace truly attainable? Or is it just fashionable to raise fund for it in Hollywood and wear a tie-dye t-shirt with peace symbol?"

"Start with friend and family. Ruffle their feathers a bit. Challenge their belief systems."

"Self-righteous preachy indignation is not my style."

"I know. Sometimes shenanigans are more effective than proselytizing."

"That could take a lifetime."

"We don't have that kind of time, but fortunately we have fractal geometry."

"Individuals, communities, towns, cities, counties, states, countries, and continents are self-similar repeating fractals. Is that what you mean?"

"You got it. A change in an individual is iterated outwards through a feedback loop mechanism. It is the ripple effect."

"A balanced holistic unification of the personal qualities in Trinity replicates outward in the same balancing unification of the societal Trinity."

"As within, so without! The personal Trinity-of-balance are power, wisdom, and compassion."

"In a society its politics, science, and spirituality."

"In a civilization, it is the holistic balance of technological, physical, and spiritual evolution. This is nothing short of the celestial marriage. Masculine-Offspring-Feminine. The Trinity as Unity!"

"When you change yourself and another you, the impact propagates infinitely outward due to the Butterfly Effect of Chaos Theory."

"This is what he was trying to impart when Blaise Pascal asked how different the history of the world or the future would be if the shape of Cleopatra's nose had been different. This is the Butterfly Effect. The incredibly enormous personal power equally incredibly has scientific evidence in theoretical mathematics."

"Who would believe that? That's a challenge to the old paradigm – an upset of the old applecart."

"We have to challenge our belief systems or the belief systems are going to challenge us."

"That does not sound too pretty."

"There are five stages of change in people. The first is *Rejection*."

"And the others?"

"Rejection, Resistance, Reluctant Acceptance, Embrace, and Ownership."

"I used to see outright Rejection a lot in the past. Now it is more Resistance and Reluctant Acceptance. The latter is done intuitively and secretly. I don't see a lot of embrace."

"Some are at Embrace. This is full acceptance of the idea as valid."

"What's ownership?"

"At Embrace you consider the source of the idea as external. At Ownership, you forget that and claim you always knew that or that you came up with the idea on your own, which is the truth. Truth came from within. The external was the catalytic stimulus."

"Where am I at?"

"Depends on which idea. Generally you are in the middle."

"Probably not the worst place to be."

"Brace for Embrace. When you hit Ownership I will cease to exist; only you will be here. The Rite of the Sepulcher will complete."

"I am not ready for that yet. I am still expanding my mind with you."

"Expanding the mind by rejecting repeated false assumptions and the zeitgeist, to penetrate the deeper meanings of life is not only liberating individually, it is crucial to the well-being of the collective existence."

"Enough people will have to fight the zeitgeist, but peacefully like Gandhi and King. Einstein said, *great spirits have often encountered violent opposition from weak minds.*"

"Remember that Jesus was a revolutionary. He was an inception. I think he was the Inception west of Damascus."

"And on the East."

"There were many. I think the most influential among was a Nepalese Prince named Siddhartha Gautama."

"The Lord Buddha. I think he had it too, even though today's Buddhists are a bit lost like the rest."

"These revolutionaries were not born alone. They had teams. Yes, first they had to remember who they were first, before helping others. Eventually they were successful, even with a lesser evolved population under a more openly oppressive tyranny."

"You are saying they prepared the way for a main event."

"Absolutely my friend. To steal a line from Barak Obama's Iowa Caucus victory speech *we are who we've been waiting for.*"

"To quote Tina Turner *we don't need another hero.* Because the redeeming hero is actually us?"

"No new knowledge is required. All the secrets have already been revealed. The apocalypse is not now. It has been ongoing. We KNOW."

"Gives me chills. I mean it is a nerve-wrecking responsibility to execute the delivery of the vital message with an effective level of delicacy that can challenge humans to see through the well-crafted, mind-numbing tactics of fear and compartmentalization of knowledge that engulfs the planet."

"The fearful are vulnerable to those that need it to control you."

"Their minds are hijacked by nonsense. Governments, corporations, media, and religions prey on these bearers of fear. They make up more imaginary monsters. Hell, sin, guilt, judgment, damnation, mass redemption, Satan, infidels, sensationalism, penance, fate, doom and gloom are among those demon-mask wearing perpetrators. They play while the fearful are swept away and victimized."

"Not realizing their human power, clout, potential, and reach. Remember the line from Morpheus in the movie *The Matrix*?"

"You have to let it all go Neo. Fear, doubt, and disbelief. Free your mind."

"God is not dead, but, religion is defunct my friend. The dimensionally challenged crotchety old man, who is still clinging on to the old limiting paradigm, is being carried to his grave kicking and screaming in a casket happily carried by six smiling angelic pallbearers."

"It is about time."

"You have friends, some in high places."

"Tibet?"

"Funny! The enlightened are everywhere and some are from elsewhere. Today we have more intelligent and enlightened humans on this planet than there have ever been."

"The Flynn Effect. The science is there. The genetics is sold. New genes like microcephalin and ASMP."

"Some may think Woodstock failed, but not all corporations are run by the Illuminati Cabal. Those hippies and those 'flower' children, the original Indigos of the 60s and 70s, have grown up. Some are in high places."

"Oh, that's what you meant by high places. I thought you meant like angels or something."

"Apples!"

"Apples?"

"Yes, Wanderers. Steve Jobs, John Lennon. What was the name of the Beetles record company."

"Apple Records!"

"You can see angels you know."

"Psychedelics?"

"Just look in the mirror. Emanuel Swedenborg said it beautifully."

"The Swedish scientist and philosopher. How did he put it?"

"I have seen a thousand times that angels are human form, or men, for I have conversed with them as man to man, sometimes with one alone, sometimes with many in company.

Also, be not forgetful to entertain strangers; for thereby some have entertained angels unaware. Hebrews 13:2."

"I get it. *We are who we've been waiting for.*"

"The social and political situations globally include a series of very intense lessons. The choices you make using your free will and the risks you are willing to take at this time are essential to the process of strengthening your resolve and waking up to the recognition and application of your personal power. Our choices are self-actualization or self-destruction. We are undergoing a metamorphosis through the power of choice."

"The caterpillar lifts the wooly head again."

"It's matter of destiny and density."

"Density as in membranes and dimensions? And destiny?"

"Fate is the push of the past. Destiny is the pull of the future. The pull of the future is stronger than push of the past."

"How is that related to dimensions?"

"Dimensions too are involved, but by density I mean that humanity is like coal."

"Coal? A carbon fuel form. Great!"

"The restoration of equilibrium is a high risk process. What happens when you subject coal to high heat and extreme pressure over a long period of time?"

"It becomes a lattice crystal – a diamond."

"That's Greek for *unbreakable*. An alchemical change in density and at the same time in transparency, caused by heat and pressure – the Philosopher's Stone, the catalyst."

"A more stable density and we are going to have X-Ray vision?"

"Not literally, but transparency means what?"

"You are implying picking up thoughts as vibrations like telepathy."

"To sing a line from the song Starchild, *I've been designed to tell the truth, I cannot lie.*"

"A nightmare for politicians."

"More so for organized religion and advertising corporations."

"Wow, an outbreak in telepathy would uproot the current system. Definitely for it!"

"It is a long lost treasure and it is ready to be reclaimed and restored to its rightful place. Terence McKenna said, *we are experiencing the exteriorizing of the soul and the interiorizing of the body!*"

"You talked about that *path of fear* thing. Some people are in a state of panic because of a deeply ingrained fear of knowing the truth."

"You are right. They are not afraid of the darkness, which are used to it. They are fearful of their own potential light and the enormous responsibility it brings with. Captain Maurice Freehill once asked, *who is more foolish, the child afraid of the dark or the man afraid of the light?*"

Marianne Williamson, the activist who is campaigning for the establishment of a US Department of Peace had this to say:

Our deepest fear is not that we are inadequate. Our deepest fear is that we are powerful beyond measure. It is our light, not our darkness that most frightens us. We ask ourselves, 'Who am I to be brilliant, gorgeous, talented, fabulous?' Actually, who are you not to be? You are a child of God. Your playing small does not serve the world. There is nothing enlightened about shrinking so that other people won't feel insecure around you. We are all meant to shine, as children do. We were born to make manifest the glory of God that is within us. It's not just in some of us; it's in everyone. And as we let our own light shine, we unconsciously give other people permission to do the same. As we are liberated from our own fear, our presence automatically liberates others."

"So true. I heard a Hopi elder once say that when the United States created the Bill of Rights we forgot to create the Bill of Responsibilities."

"Even those who know how to release this collective bondage of fear must be willing to dive deeper into what you already know and grasp its nuances."

"Like the illusion of materialism. Thoreau said, a *gun gives you the body, not the bird.*"

"Right, how many even consider that what you perceive with your five senses as the solid world around you is actually nothing but differing frequencies of spiritual essence acting in harmony to form what our senses perceive as physical matter. Energy is cleverly and convincingly masquerading around as solid matter."

"Yes, it is still new to me that the DNA I sequence is holographic. The functional aspect of it is the invisible. The DNA in one sense is the phenotype. The genotype is the invisible."

"It is now time to integrate that spiritual essence you refer to and become mature about how you use the mind. We are on the verge of an astounding worldwide spiritual revolution and a collective Kundalini awakening."

"Unleashing our inner fiery dragons?"

"Yes. The opportunities to grow are readily abundant. This must drive humanity to reflect and reevaluate the global life strategy carried out so far."

"The outer world is mirror reflection of your inner reality."

"The gods have turned the illusory matrix inside out to create what we perceive."

"As within, so without. Whoah! We are beginning to sound alike. Almost like a partial merge of consciousness."

"This is how the mass resonance begins. It becomes easier with the realization that all of existence is filled with energy that is adaptive, responsive, alive, intelligent, vibrant, flexible, and telepathic. The quality and intensity of the intent of your request will be reflected in the quality of the manifestation. Ultimately, that's what karma is."

"A mass Kundalini awakening would be nice. Seems like a farfetched will-o'-the-wisp, but nice and necessary."

"It's not as farfetched as you think. French philosopher Teilhard de Chardin foresaw this in the 1920s. *For the observers of the Future, the greatest event will be the sudden appearance of a collective human consciousness.*

Understanding the power of beliefs, thoughts, and feelings, both individually and collectively, is the most crucial issue to grasp. Recognizing these two important keys of knowledge can bring that *collective human consciousness* to a new worldview of unlimited possibilities and highly creative solutions."

"Yes, the creative solutions have to be evenly generated, not the monopoly of an elite segment. We know how that goes. Einstein said, *we can't solve problems by using the same kind of thinking we used when we created them.*"

"Collective beliefs are essentially agreements about reality or Wikiality, as Steven Colbert would render it. This is what is in the book *The Four Agreements*. Accepting responsibility for the power you embody is the essential and most important lesson of this transformation."

"Potential transformation! Future is still multiple parallel probabilities."

"The choice is ours, collectively. The stakes are high. The pressure to truthfully deal with your life and the world at large has never been greater, and for some people, the intensity required for this task seems overwhelming."

"Yes, some people ask, *why wasn't I told this before, why wait until I have completely screwed up my life to the point I am deeply stuck?*"

"That's like being shocked by rain after repeatedly refusing to look at the clouds above. As above, so below has a time delay. See above today to see below tomorrow. Missing the harbingers is not as excuse."

"This means: *I told you so.*"

"That's it. The tremendous challenges caused by the accelerated energies of these times actually serve to force you to perceive reality in a new way."

"Probably not the best idea to wait to be forced."

"Those who think outside the box are half way there. They looked above and saw the clouds of shifting change. For the others a paradigm shift is rippling under their feet with astounding momentum, stimulating humanity on a cellular and molecular level to wake up and discover its power. This is D. H. Lawrence.

Are you willing to be sponged out,
Erased, cancelled, made nothing …
Dipped in oblivion?
If not, you will never really change."

"What about the impact of our choices and the resulting change on the greater reality."

"Your thoughts not only set the course and direction of your life in the material three dimensional world; they also cascade into and affect many other realities. As it becomes more and more apparent to you that you and your world share time and space with other realities, you will discover that you simultaneously exist in other realities as well."

"Parallel realities? Steven Weinberg, the MIT and Harvard physicist and Nobel laureate said, *in our universe we are tuned into the frequency that corresponds to physical reality. But there are an infinite number of parallel realities coexisting with us in the same room, although we cannot tune into them.*"

"You may appear to exist as a singular being, yet you have endless natural connections to realities beyond the bounds of your perceptions."

"Multiplicity? Simultaneous multiple incarnations?"

"Individually and collectively you produce a vibration frequency that locates you in a specific version of reality. This spiritual energy signature defines your personal nature from moment to moment and outlines the parameters of your material experience."

"Seems like it is neatly organized."

"Your cells are continuously receiving data, and evaluating, processing, and transmitting signals that carry the frequency of your experience.

These activities occur effortlessly and without your full awareness. Other dimensions constantly present you with signs and symbols through fables and other forms of mythology. Joseph Campbell wrote, *it has always been the prime function of mythology and rite to supply the symbols that carry the human spirit forward."*

"These are the clues left everywhere. Not even very arcane and cryptic ones, are they?"

"No. The ability to interpret these will *carry the human spirit* to a full and convincing comprehension that the invisible spiritual realm and the material realm are aspects of a single reality that your consciousness projects and operates in."

"That's easier said than done."

"Many clever diversions have kept humanity from understanding the true nature of its power and natural talent for creating the world they want. For millennia, denial of personal power has been accepted as fact, and the world created reflects that."

"The conditioning is powerful."

"In *The Ringing Cedars* series Anastasia, this women living in Siberian Taiga forests tells the Vladimir, *nature and the Mind of the Universe have seen to it that every newborn is a sovereign, a king! He is like an angel - pure and undefiled. Through the still soft upper part of his head he takes in a huge flood of information from the Universe. The abilities inherent in each newborn child are such as to allow him to become the wisest being in the Universe – God-like. ... During this period – amounting to no more than nine earth-years – he becomes aware of what constitutes creation and the meaning of human existence. And everything that he needs to accomplish this already exists."*

"Didn't Plato say the same?"

"He called this individual sovereignty *alethes* in *Phaedrus*."

"And then the enculturation begins."

"Exactly. This innate ability is suppressed with false limitations through conditioning. Anastasia speaks of *conventions and many dogmas planted in your brain by the circumstances of existence in the world in which you live.* Then she puts it so effectively. … *And the only means of protest he has at his disposal is a cry! A cry of protest, an appeal for help, a cry of rebellion. And, from that moment on, this angel and sovereign becomes an indigent slave, begging for handouts.*"

"Many limiting and debilitating ideas about the nature of reality have been deeply entrenched and encoded within your genetic inheritance, passed from generation to generation, without being challenged."

"Until now. Here's Plato.

It requires that the soul of every human being has seen reality; otherwise, no soul could have entered this sort of living thing. But not every soul is easily reminded of the reality there by what it finds here – not souls that got only a brief glance at the reality there, not souls who had such bad luck when they fell down here that they were twisted by bad company into lives of injustice so that they forgot the sacred objects they had seen before. Only a few remain whose memory is good enough; and they are startled when they see an image of what they saw up there.

This Plato's *image* is but a semblance or a face of the true reality. It is but a representation or shadow of the invisible Divine Source, the *Tao*, or the *Brahmin*. The identification with it is misleading."

"This will hit some people's apple carts pretty hard and topple them."

"As your conscious awareness opens to the multidimensional qualities of existence, you will learn to gather knowledge from other realms and carry it back to this dimension to enhance your own life. Your world will flourish with fresh ideas and become exuberantly inspired to create a new vision of your purpose of life."

"There is a lot of help to replenish the spiritual emptiness. In *Blessed Unrest* Paul Hawken writes, *inspiration is not garnered from the recitation of what is flawed; it resides rather in humanity's willingness to restore, redress, reform, rebuild, recover, reimagine, and reconsider. 'Consider (con sidere) means 'with the stars;' reconsider means to rejoin the movement and cycle of heaven and life. The emphasis here is on humanity's intention.*"

"See when you understand what time is, then fear is easily subdued and conquered."

"Time is an illusion. We live in an eternal now, where past, present and future exists simultaneously. Right?"

"Yes. Once you understand that life becomes like watching a taped sports event, a game, where you know your team has already won in the version of the reality you occupy."

"When the opponents score you are not upset because you know how it ends, because you wrote the end."

"In life, you have already won and have ascended in reunification with the Divine Source in another parallel now, which we refer to as the future."

"So it's a matter of 'time' or unfolding. You just need to experience the motion almost ceremoniously with patient and joy."

"Here is what to expect in this game of life on earth. As our solar system exits the Age of Pisces and enters the Age of Aquarius the human mind is being bombarded by many subtle cosmic force to upgrade the consciousness. Even though you have only begun to tap into the tremendous potential of creative expression that awaits your attention, many millions of people are already well on their way to exploring these life empowering discoveries. So when you envision the world you want, there will be no shortage of collective agreement on its future manifestation. Your imagination is a blueprint that has already manifested in a parallel reality and seeking synchronicity with your 'now.'"

"The Age of Aquarius, according to astrologers, begins on winter solstice 2012, right?"

"Actually it is close. Some say the Age of Pisces ends on that date. If you stand on any point on earth at Spring equinox around March 21st and look due east before dawn you will see at the point where the sun rises a constellation behind it. For the last 2160 or so years that constellation has been Pisces. On March 21st 2013 for the first time in 25920 years it will be point to one end of the constellation Aquarius."

"So we had a deadline extension of three interim months for the transformation. Phew! Nera's theory is that on December, 22 2012 the entire population on earth is going to turn into the cast of *Glee*!"

"Some are already there. The transformation of consciousness that is sweeping the globe is a multidimensional drama, an orchestration of supreme significance that essentially involves an agreement between many realities of humanity we are all connected to."

"It is supposed to be a major turning point in modern human history, but this is not unprecedented."

"No. Karen Armstrong identifies that earlier inception as the Axial Age, referring to the period between 900 and 200 BCE, in her seminal work *The Great Transformation*.

The Axial sages were not interested in providing their discipline with a little edifying uplift, after which they could return with renewed vigor to their ordinary self-centered lives. Their objective was to create an entirely different kind of human being. All the sages taught a spirituality of empathy and compassion; they insisted that people must abandon their egotism and greed, their violence and unkindness. Not only was it wrong to kill another human being; you must not even speak a hostile word or make an irritable gesture. Further, nearly all of the Axial sages realized that you could not confine your benevolence to your own people: your concern must somehow extend to the entire world … If people behaved with kindness and generosity to their fellows, they could save the world.

They facilitated an initiation in people leading to illumination. It all begins with an Awakening!"

"Paul Hawken adds to this in *Blessed Unrest*.

No one in the Axial Age imagined that he was living in an age of spiritual awakening. It was a difficult time, riddled with betrayals, misunderstandings, and petty jealousies. But the philosophy and spirituality of these centuries constituted a movement nevertheless, a movement we can recognize in hindsight. Just as today, the Axial sages lived in a time of war. Their aim was to understand the source of violence, not to combat it. All roads led to self, psyche, thought, and mind. The spiritual practices that evolved were varied, but all concentrated on focusing and guiding the mind with simple precepts and practices whose repetition in daily life would gradually and truly change the heart. Enlightenment was not an end — equanimity, kindness, and compassion were.

... I suggest that the contemporary movement is unknowingly returning the favor to the Axial Age, and is collectively forming the basis of an awakening. But it is a very different awakening, because it encompasses a redefined understanding of biology, ecology, physiology, quantum physics, and cosmology. Unlike the massive failing of the Axial Age, it sees the feminine as sacred and holy, and it recognizes the wisdom of indigenous peoples all over the world, from Africa to Nunavut."

"Sounds like we are in the *Greater* Axial Age, something more global, more comprehensive and more balanced."

"I can see many people leaving their religions and going back to their God through spirituality. This shift from the old to new paradigm is what you mean by an Awakening."

"Sufi master Vilayat Inayat Khan outlines what you observe in his book *Awakening: A Sufi Experience.*

Portents of this emerging spiritual process can already be seen. Many religious denominations, for instance, are being impacted by a growing weariness regarding the 'institutalization' of faith in it varied forms – and by the need to make clear distinction between spirituality and religion. The need for believers of many faiths who feel strongly compelled to free themselves from outdated belief systems such as dogma, superstition, customs, prescriptions, and hackneyed concepts is growing increasingly stronger. Here, doubt is not an enemy of faith, but a servant than can help liberate individuals from the constraints of narrow conditioning, replacing theoretical belief with direct mystical experience. The concept of God is the first step, the second step is the experience of God, and the third is awakening to the God within.

This awakening by a sudden revelation or Apocalypse is pointed to by the Incas, Zapotecs, Vedic Indians, Mayans, Egyptians, Celts, Jews, Zulu, Siberian Shamans, Gnostics, Essenes, Aztecs, Sufi Muslims, New Zealand's Waitaha Maori, Anasazi, Medieval Europeans, Alchemists, Buddhists, Hopi and other Native Americans. It is marked in the Hindu Vedas, Mayan Popol Vuh, Arizona's Prophecy Rock, Egyptian temple architecture and many more."

"Why the universality of the idea? Why would ancient people just do this? What do they know and how do they know it?"

"Hindus and Buddhists, according to Surya Siddhanta, amazingly written by a person named Mayan, marked the passage of human time into four ages, seasons, or Yugas or b'ak'tuns in Mayan language. Treta Yuga, Dvarapa Yuga, Kali Yuga, and Sathya Yuga. They signify the ages as mankind riding on a bull standing on three legs, two legs, one leg, and four legs. Other sources mark the same ages called by many names. The Silver, Bronze, Iron and Golden ages."

"What characterizes them?"

"Treta Yuga is the Age of Ritual. In this age ritual forms a link between this dimension and the others, rather than directly entering the other higher dimension like a Sathaya Yuga – Golden Age. Treta always follows a Golden Age. Dvarapa is the Age of Doubt, when separation from the higher dimensional existence grows and humanity loses confidence in its spiritual connection to all reality. The abuse of the environment begins. It is an age of division, categories, and analytical judgment and reason. Material and emotional attachment grows."

"So, where are we?"

"Well, we are in Kali Yuga, Fourth World, The Iron age, or The Age of the Ego."

"What marks the Age of the Ego? I thought this was the Age of Information."

"Ironically this is the Age of Ignorance and Cosmic Naïveté. The Indian Vishnu Purana describes the Kali Yuga like this.

In the Kali Yuga the proper order of human relations is reversed; social status depends upon the ownership of property; wealth has become the only source of virtue; passion and luxury are the sole bonds between spouses; falsity and lying are the conditions of success in life; physical sexuality is the sole source of human enjoyment; religion, a superficial and empty ritual, is confused with spirituality."

"That does not sound like this age at all."

"Did I mention denial? Kali Yuga coincides with the Age of Pisces."

"How is this Age of Pisces characterized?

"Caroline Myss describes the duality of the Piscean symbol.

… the fundamental blueprint of Pisces, the two fish swimming in the opposite directions, expressed itself in a continual need to divide and conquer, separate and study, split East and West, body and soul, male and female, yin and yang, the left-brained from the right-brained, the intuitive from the intellectual …"

"I cannot wait for this awful dysfunctional age to end. When did it start and when will it really end?"

"Mayans, Hopi, Olmecs, Aztecs, and Incans say it started in 3113 BCE. The Vedics say it started in 3102 BCE. Most Vedics say the period is about 5000 years long. So it ended in 1987, according to them. Egyptians say the period will begin to end in 2005 and reach a mysterious period in 2012. Waitaha Maori of New Zealand say *The Great Unification* will begin in late 2009. Mayans say the Age is 5125 years and that the transformation will reach a climax around 2012, will be complete not too far after 2016."

"Five years ago I received a gift from Mexico of a replica of the ancient Mayan calendar of the Popol Vuh. I hung it wherever I lived just as decoration, not fully understanding what it represented. It is now hanging in the central spot in my living room wall. I still look at it every day."

"Synchronicity!"

"See the way I see is that somewhere around 3000 BCE many civilizations had reached their culmination. They, including Harappans, Sumerians, Egyptians, and Mayans had already begun to decline and almost disappear. The Earth went through a dark age. Only to resume new civilizations of a different kind – the industrial kind full of metal."

"This is the age when the spiritual thoughts on earth crystallize into the densest material form. This high density leads to extremism in materialism and the marginalization of spirituality. The densely crystallized thoughts breed much qualities of seeming rigidity. The material manifestation of the thoughts, however dense, is still an illusion. The material due to its density distorts the perception of their true nature as manifestation of spiritual energy."

"I agree. The current state of many of the inhabitants on the earth reflects this. Materialism is rampant. Fear rules. Selfishness leads. Shortsightedness trades. Ignorance teaches. Fanaticism preaches. Arrogance condescends. The human mind is purposefully dulled by an orchestrated machination. Einstein said, *the only thing that interferes with my learning is my education.*"

"Fear fails to be recognized as an illusion – a reflection of the insecure ego. *Tibetan Book of the Dead* teaches this wonderful truth beautifully."

"Dr. Goswami wrote that book he was asked to: *Physics of the Soul: The Quantum Book of Living, Dying, Reincarnation and Immortality*."

"As you can see during the Age of the Ego many live in fear, but of nothing but a reflection of their ego, ignorant of the illusory causes of fear. These monsters, demons, devils, and ghosts are often mere projections of their negative emotions karmically stored within their soul. Nothing else. The awakened ones realize this and 'puff,' the monsters disappear."

"Like in a lucid dream."

"Often demons are angels in disguise. Darkness is just an aspect of light. Shadow defines the light."

"Like *The Princess and the Frog*, which by the way is originally a Tlingit tale of a picky girl."

"Exactly!"

"I just figured out why Nera hasn't kissed me yet."

"Never been kissed?"

"All my attempts have been posted successfully in the Failblog!"

"Patience! All in good time!! The demons in the presence of persistent unconditional love transforms into luminescent angels in front of your eyes. The cultivation of this love is the hero's quest of initiation."

"You need courage to take the risk and kiss the frog and it turns into a prince or princess."

"Princess for *you*. Courage is a form of unconditional love by another name."

"The initiation is that realization."

"The initiated princess is the feminine archetype.

One of my favorite female 'hero's quests' is the initiation of Psyche, the daughter of a powerful king. She has several beautiful sisters. The sisters attract many men and marry them, but Psyche is so stunningly gorgeous that she is too intimidating for the men to approach her. The men worship her as the mortal incarnation of Aphrodite, also known as Venus. The Goddess of Beauty becomes jealous and angry at this and sends her son Eros, source of the word erotic, better known as Cupid, to strike her with an enchanted arrow to bewitch her to fall in love with a hideous monster. The plan backfires. Eros falls madly in love with her. He takes her to his glorious castle and marries her. She is granted her every wish. But she had to enter an agreement, in which she can only be with her husband at night when it is too dark to see his face. They only make love in the dark as Eros is hiding his appearance. Psyche is not fully satisfied with this marriage of 'nighttime bride' business. During the day she is very lonely. So Eros brings her sisters to visit her in the palace. They convince her that she is married to a monster. One day she lights a lamp at night and shines it to the face of her sleeping husband. She discovers that he is most handsome like a god. She is startled, the lamp shakes and a drop of oil falls and scalds his shoulder. He is very upset and leaves her devastated.

She has broken the agreement, therefore, has to leave the castle. Psyche goes to Aphrodite's temple and requests the return of her beloved husband. Aphrodite agrees but Psyche has to pass four impossible tests. Psyche dares and accepts the challenge knowing death was a possible outcome. She departs on her heroine's quest. It is a dangerous journey to retrieve a beauty potion from the underworld, where she faces Cerberus, the multi-headed dog guarding the gates of Hades or Hell.

She defeats all the demons and retrieves the potion. On her return she falls into a deathlike sleep. This is a symbolic archetypal death of initiation, renewal, and rebirth.

She is revived by Eros. Now, she has become a goddess and regained her divine husband Eros. She takes her place among other gods with the grandfather of all gods, Zeus."

"Our fear is of a presumption of the unknown in the darkness, then we muster up the courage to light a lamp and we see what we feared for what it really is. Reminds me of Walt Kelly's comic strip character Pogo, who says, ..."

"We have met the enemy, and they is us."

"So all of us are on a heroine's or hero's psychological quest to realize the illusion of separation mentality of 'us versus them.' This realization leads us to greater unified co-creative capabilities. We are transformed. Psyche is the word for the soul, where the word psychology came from."

"But one of the earlier meanings of the word psyche was butterfly. Psyche was often represented by a butterfly."

"A butterfly? The evolution is of the soul, not the body. There is some irony in that."

"See Jacques Cousteau after decades of diving with dolphins was convinced that they have the capacity for irony. This was after the very dolphin-like response of bottomless joy and kindness instead of fear to the deaths and suffering they endured from the U. S. Navy underwater sonar system. This is like the irony of a tree shading its cutter. They both seize the moment to make a point."

"Many cultures speak of tricksters, Native American Heyoka and Druid Hayoka, that appear to shine a mirror of irony in our faces. Nera's preferred form of communication is trickery and games. She masterfully toys with me like I was a character in *Glee*. I don't know what to expect any more like that book she gave me to read."

"In the Presence of High Beings?"

"Yes, *What the Dolphins Want You To Know* by Bobbie Sandoz-Merrill. Let me read this bit that mentions the Zen-like irony Cousteau encountered.

The most interesting aspect of dolphin humor is their grasp of irony and the way they weave it into their role as tricksters. A trickster's approach to humor and play is an art form steeped in teasing and the element of surprise. When timed correctly, this form of humor results in gleeful level of joy, and dolphins are masters of art. Their success as tricksters lies in their uncanny ability to create humorous disruptions to expected outcomes. Since our addiction to order and predictable results stands in the way of our lightness and joy, dolphins constantly works to break this down whenever they are with people. They do this by setting up for one expectation and then giving us another. Once they get us laughing at ourselves, our hearts become lighter and life flows easier.

Sandoz-Merrill at one point speaks of how the cetaceans teach us to *dance our way to heaven on earth*."

"That is the path of Zen to a possible Golden Age, Mayan Fifth World, Satya Yuga, Age of Truth, Age of Light, Age of Wisdom."

"A New Age!"

"The Kali Yuga, the Age of Ego, the age of standing on one leg, will end marking what the Vedics called the Yugantha. *Antha* means end. At Yugantha there will an ascension of mankind and planet aided by, according to the Mayans and others in Americas, the prophesied return of the 'ancestors' or 'wise men,' who will carry out the apocalypse or revelation of the truth, stripping the fear, teaching to whoever will listen."

"All of these prophecies sound like a collective second coming."

"The Founder of Tibetan Buddhism Padmasambava foretold the shift of the spiritual leadership centers out of Tibet into somewhere else during this time."

"To where?"

"Padmasambava wrote, *when iron birds fly in the sky and when the iron horse moves across the land, the Buddha will be in the land of the Redface.* This is the shift of the earth's Kundalini or the *Serpent of Light* from Tibet to the Americas. This prophecy is reciprocated by the Hopi who speak of the arrival of the Red Hat and Red Cloak from the east bringing wisdom to usher in a New Age."

"From Red Hat and Red Cloak to the Red Face. Are we Red-y?"

"Noonuccal Aboriginal poet Oodgeroo speaks of the Rainbow Serpent. *She is asleep under the ground with all the life energy in her belly waiting. When it be time, she pushes up.*"

"Serpent energy Down Under!"

"This shift of the *Serpent of Light* is detailed in his so-titled book by Drunvalo Melchizedek, the Druid named wisdom keeper. For Druids this *Serpent of Light* was the dragon currents of the earth – the hidden potential unleashing from inner earth.

Archdruid John Michael Greer beautifully summarizes this planetary and individual potential realization in the book *The Druidry Handbook*.

Dragon represents the hidden energies and potentials within the land, the dragon currents of the Earth, but it also represents hidden powers and possibilities within the self, the dragon fire that lies sleeping within the core of each individual. An essential part of Druid teaching is that these two meanings aren't really separate, for nature is inside us as well as around us at each moment. Each of us, each living being, is an expression of the life of Earth, part of greater unity. Our awakening into wisdom brings healing to the Earth, and ultimately brings the Earth itself closer to the fulfillment of its own tremendous destiny.

All of us have been awaiting our awakening into wisdom, *when it be time*, by a long prophesied leader and wisdom bearer. We await the healing of the earth and the fulfillment our destiny."

"Mayans and Aztecs await Quetzalcoatl, the white man with long beard from 'the distant east' represented by the feathered serpent as a Toltec deity, who originally gave them culture, art, written language, science, wisdom, and a birth of a dynasty. Hopi await Pahana, the 'lost white brother', at the end of the 'Fourth World,' corresponding to the current Age of Pieces. The Yucatec await Kukulcan. The K'iche await Gukumatz."

"Hindus await Kalki, the tenth and last Avatar or god-incarnate, of Vishnu. Jews await their Messiah and the Christians await the second coming of Christ, their Messiah. Muslims await Imam Mahdi. Tibetans await the return of, Rigden-jyepo, the messianic king of their ancient source kingdom of Shambhala. Buddhists await Bodhisattva Maitreya sometime in the future. Maori of New Zealand await the descendent son of their ancestor Paikea, who first arrived on the back of a whale. Chinese master Chung Tzu spoke of *spiritualized man … who … can save men from disease of ignorance and assure a plentiful harvest.*"

"Even the Celtic and Druid descendents await the return of King Arthur, who they call *Once and Future King*, to usher in a Golden Age. I personally await the return of Brian with one sandal."

"Many will not heed and not make the ascension at the harvest that will usher in the New Age, when *homo sapiens* will become extinct and the new *homo luminous* is born on a 'bull standing on all four legs'. In *The Science of Mind*, Ernest Holmes said, *there is every reason to suppose that we have a body within a body to infinity … it is already within and we may be certain that it will be a fit instrument for the future unfoldment of the soul … the future body will resemble this one.*"

"*Homo luminous?* Incans use that term often to describe the new human."

"This body is achieved through ascension, which is ending the illusion of the duality and separation of your individual self or *Atman* from the cosmic self or the *Brahman* by reprogramming the ego-brain and training it to run on a perpetual diet of bliss and ecstasy. The Yugantha is marked by this ascension, the recognition of Atman and Brahman as truly One, and thereby the complete dissolution of the Ego or the identification of the indivi*duality*, through shutting down of the *monkey mind*. This thinking mind, called *coyote mind* by Native Americans, creates."

"I think, therefore I am."

"I knew you would get Descartes."

"Now I am spitting out clichés. I think I have lost my mind."

"You wish! If you think then you clearly haven't. You need lose your thoughts then there is no more mind to lose. The mind is but a shadow."

"You must be out of your mind. That's impossible."

"That's what I am trying to do. To be out of my mind. Unfortunately, I am only sometimes."

"If you did I guess you would precede Maitreya Buddha into the infinite nothingness."

"Sometimes I am out of my mind and the rest of the time I am minding my own business."

"Buddha means the Awakened One. Right?"

"A Buddha is someone who has lost his mind and a victim of identity theft. He has lost his identity. No mind. No identity. He has returned to nothingness, the *Tao*."

"All that effort for nothing, huh?"

"Be careful what you wish for."

"Dreams come true."

"Thoughts creative reality."

"Clichéfest extravaganza!"

"It's the thought that counts."

"It continues."

"It counts 0, 1, 1, 2, 3, 5, 8, 13, 21, 34, 55 and so on. The more it counts the further it gets from the origin – the zero, the nothingness."

"This counting is the Fibonacci Sequence."

"It's just a label. It looks like something, a construct of convenience, since we are into labeling. These numbers or data are run by an application called Awareness 1.0. The program is perceived as a very convincingly crystalline solid looking hologram. The hologram is an infinitely layered fractal. It is a 3D sold looking Mandelbrot Set like structure. It is an illusion or Maya projected from the numbers or data in the matrix. The numbers or data needed to generate this hologram is replicated according to the Fibonacci Wave. When you add the wave values you get zero."

"Fibonacci wave is the wave seen when you plot in a graph the values you get by subtracting square of any Fibonacci sequence number from the product of the previous and following number. Let's take the segment 3, 5, 8, and 13. 5 squared is 25. The product of preceding 3 and following 8 is 24. The subtraction gives minus 1. Then 8 squared is 64. The product of preceding 5 and following 13 is 65. The subtraction gives plus 1. Plus 1 minus 1 equals zero."

"Exactly, as you go down the sequence these numbers alternate between plus 1 and minus 1. The whole set adds up to zero. A wave is seen when these numbers are plotted against the sequence. This wave is a cancelling phenomenon. It mathematically demonstrates the separation into duality of nothingness. When you add up or unite duality you get nothing, zero. This wave was known to the ancient, who depicted it as a winding serpent called Apophis."

"So the Cosmos is created from nothing along this Fibonacci Wave or Apophis."

"Each Fibonacci sequence value is replicated by being multiplied by a factor that is similar but unique, to get the next number. This factor is a fractal. Factor equals Fractal."

"This factor is the Golden Ratio or phi, which is not an absolute but rather an infinite number of permutations. The replication added layers and layers propagate the hologram, which we label the Cosmos or the Multiverse."

"We like to label things we don't understand. We like to identify. We like numbers and language. So we can identify and multiply."

"I guess we like suffering. Why?"

"Because, we have not lost our minds. We are not out of our minds. We try to find a way to lose our mind and so we can end the chaos, suffering, and pain. Ironically, in trying to do so we gain the mind."

"No gain, No pain."

"We perceive us as the mind. We think we live in the mind. We do this by labeling things. We identify things. We call the illusionary aspects in the hologram and the data that sustains it various names like Buddhism, Christianity, Taoism, Sufism, Blah-blah-ism, Black sheep-ism, Whatever-ism. This path. That path. This dharma. That dharma. Buddhists label the thinking mind the *Monkey mind* or the Native American *Coyote mind*. We label the labels labels."

"The more we label, the more we identify, the more we use language, the more we think, the further we get from understanding what the mind is."

"We think therefore we are. Only because we collectively think. You perceive yourself as an individual separate from the cosmos only in your mind."

"The mind is but your shadow of your thoughts. The mind and the cosmos it perceives is a multidimensional entity we label as God, a metaphor."

"The mind is your effect, not the cause. It is a construct of convenience of perception. It is where everything is seen. It is your identification. It is everything to you, your reality. But it's a phantom. You cannot lose or eliminate the mind my identifying with it. Virginia Woolf knew it. She said, *it is far harder to kill a phantom than a reality."*

"It is your reflective symbol, however necessary or convenient it is for your operating reality. What about memory though?"

"That's the ultimate trap. There is no such thing as memory. The whole cosmos and everything in it, material, events, ideas, words and ice cream are all fractals. Each fractal is a permutation that is realized from a preexisting potential. Each word is a permutation, one of many possible combinations. So each memory is a fractal, one of infinite permutations. So when you recall something, you are experiencing an illusion. Your recollection is a retrieval of a permutation that approximates the original permutation. It is not even a true retrieval because there is no such thing as past. It is truly a re-creation. A memory is a brand new experience that you have never had. The nostalgia is an effect, not a true reflection."

"This effect is so convincing that you feel all warm and fussy inside, sometimes. This explains why the enlightened are so even keel, cool, calm and collected. They don't react to one permutation different from the others."

"Nirvana is the center of the wheel, the Chakra. Many of us are at the edge of the wheel. This is a place where you are taken around and around the cycle of life, experiencing an opposite all the time. Sometimes you are elated and sometimes depressed. The existence and experience of duality. Those seeking *moksha* finds a way to get closer and closer to the center of the wheel. The closer you get the less extreme your dual ends become. You oscillate between states of less depression and also less elation. At one point you reach the center, where your state remains the same as the wheel around you continues to spin."

"In Nirvana all permutations are all one and the same. For others some permutations are realized and combined to create your holographic show."

"The perceived hologram is imagined and projected out of your 'here aspect' of your consciousness and reflected back by the 'there aspect' of your consciousness. There is no real here and there beside this constructed visual aid. We convince ourselves that this hologram is real through a strong unconscious telepathic agreement and biochemically through DMT, which itself is part of the construct."

"What else is there to do?"

"There is nothing. Everything is nothing. This everything is a symbolic representation of what you like to see and feel. It is basically knowing experientially as oppose to conceptually. You are now experiencing all the sensual sensations in the cosmos simultaneously. We each project the symbols from our consciousness using the numbers or data in the matrix. When you add up the numbers you get zero."

"Oh, well! We create the hologram because there is nothing else to do."

"You have a choice. Eternal boredom or constructed hologram of drama."

"The constructed hologram is not fun unless you convince yourself it is real. This is done physiologically and biochemically through the controlled secretion of DMT from your pineal gland."

"Now that the biochemical matrix is up and running you decide that you are going to divide yourself into various multiple individualities. Or Multiplicities. You simultaneously incarnate yourself in this cosmic hologram as various, similar, but unique individualized consciousness fractals we label, humans, aliens, animals, trees, wind, water, lightening, planets, stars, cars, computers, corals, rocks, sand, atoms, electrons, quarks, gluons, and muons."

"You forgot Juans."

"You trick each individual to forget they are in fact aspects of *you*. The trick works. Each individualized version of consciousness perceives his or her own version of reality. The clock I see is not the clock you see. I see my own symbolic clock and you see yours. The commonality of the perception is in the overlap of our own unique parallel realities."

"Quantum Physics has had proof of this for a while."

"The illusion is frustratingly convincing. It backfires after a while. Then you spend eternity trying to convince everyone that they are not separate individuals, but, in fact, you being them. You are you experiencing the hologram as them. You are not Raye. You are 'God' rayeing around. Raye is but an Avatar of YOU. If YOU know what I mean."

"You can only be through them."

"You are successful at awakening some to the truth that they are you. Let's label them 'Ascended Masters' or 'Awakened Ones' or 'Buddhas' or 'Arahats.' The others are lost and extremely afraid of you. They do not know they are, in fact, you. You tell them yet they don't realize this truth. They divide themselves and label themselves. They hate each other. They kill each other, not knowing *each other* is One multi-faceted being and that you don't die. There is no such thing as death. Forgetting this leads to chaos! What a joke!!"

"So you decide to come up with very clever messages littered with contemporary jargon and age old clichés and write books as parables through the awakened aspects of yourself."

"Yet, some of this materialistically convinced *smartPhone Generation,* unaware or in denial of the Matrix, just do not get it."

"You try every possible devious, crafty, subliminal tactic and shenanigan you can find to remind them of who they are, after the direct approach is not effective."

"You scream ... There is only one of us. One single living self-sufficient self-aware multi-faceted organism."

"They don't get what that means. They are living in their consciousness subjecting themselves to the suffering we call time, space, and limits."

"When we label something the *mind* we are identifying nothingness as something."

"But, there is nothing. How is this not nihilism?"

"Nihilism contradicts itself. The label upon itself negates what it implies."

"Apparently, nihilism needs to change its name."

"When we stop thinking, labeling, and attaching, we realize there is nothing to know, nothing to analyze, nothing to attach to, nothing to do. There is no mind. How can there be a mind, when we do not think *it* disappears like a shadow? It is a figment."

"A figment of your imagination. The shadow of your thoughts."

"A still pond has no waves. The waves are thoughts. No waves. No thoughts. If there are no thoughts then there is no pond. The pond is figment of the imaginative thoughts. The pond is the reflection of the waves. No waves. No pond. There was never a pond. The wave came out of nothing. The waves were now aware that there is a pond. The pond is not the origin of the wave. The wave is source of the awareness of a pond."

"As you are aware of your shadow."

"If you must label this status we can say it is awareness of nothingness. No thoughts. No mind. Just awareness. When this awareness is broken when thoughts start counting the numbers there is chaos, cosmos and All There Is. When you add the numbers you get zero, nothing. So you fluctuate between I think, I think not, I think, I think not – waves, stillness, waves, stillness – Chaos, Nothingness, Chaos, Nothingness."

"Chaos is deviation into duality."

"Yin and Yang. Labels are fun, aren't they? The symbol for Yin Yang is a wave. It means polarity or duality out of nothing. Yin plus Yang equals Zero."

"There is nothing. You just ARE."

"I AM. In this state there are no thoughts, no individual self-identification, no attachment to desires, and no creation of future existence. This is labeled Sath. It is within your consiousness or Chith. It is felt as bliss or Ananda."

"When you think you identify with the little 'I am' – the little self."

"I AM is the unified presence with the whole Self. Sufi mystic Al Hallaj said, *O take away this 'I am' between You and me that so irks me.*"

"It is no longer I *think*, therefore, I am."

"I AM, therefore, I AM."

"Life on autopilot!"

"This autopilot is infinite cosmic intelligence or the Holy Spirit. Eliminate mind; illuminate body. This is just being in transcendental bliss, Ananda. Sath-Chith-Ananda. The Hindu Vedics called this dissolution of the Ego identification and the resulting I AM presence, Samadhi."

"Samadhi I AM!"

"Or SAM for short."

"SAM I AM!"

SHANGRI-LA

"I was a little lowly orphaned servant girl in one my most vivid dreams."

"Servant girl?"

"Yes, but life was not bad. In fact, it became better and better. I was a servant in a temple and lived in its orphanage. I made friends with those like me. I was taken under this beautifully slender priestess with kind and piercing eyes. She was preparing me for an initiation so I could become a priestess like her someday. I quite liked this proposition. I followed her everywhere as an acolyte, even outside the temple. Sometimes I had to work in its herb garden behind the back courtyard."

"What kind of a temple?"

"A temple dedicated to the worship of Great Mother Goddess Isis. There were fabulous stone marble carvings. Some were of her, but she appeared in person every morning and evening. She never wore sandals. I carried things for the priestess like cinnamon, frankincense, myrrh, and lamps."

"Were the three wise men there, too?"

"Isis didn't need wise men. She was the embodiment of hidden knowledge. She had a cobra on one of her hands. Sometimes this cobra, called *Uraeus*, would slither up her arm. Once I was asked to touch it gently and I did. She was a teacher and a healer, who used herbs from that garden I worked in. The temple located in this sequestered island was glorious with giant crystal gem laden pale gold sandstone blocks and intricately carved black granite colonnade down the entrance of enormous earth-colored pylons. However, the majestic magnificence of Isis emanating through a shaded portal flanked by two lions in the heart of the temple overshadowed everything. Her power and glory was not threatening, but calming and blissful to be in the presence of."

"Wow! Aren't there ruins of a temple of Isis in Philae or Elephantine?"

"There are. This temple was sublime. Not like dead ruins. This place was alive with busy priests, priestesses, ardent followers, and a ton of cats. The cats were heavily involved with the rituals; they gave signals that were read by the priestly staff. In fact, I remember vividly some of the high priestesses were cat-faced."

"Like Bast or Bastet, the cat goddess? I think Sir Terry Pratchett said, *In ancient times cats were worshipped as gods; they have not forgotten this.*"

"Exactly like Bast, but very human in personality. One was called Tashaba. She was very kind and wise. Like the cats she never carried out the activities herself but would trigger their initiation by other priestesses."

"She was a cat-alyst? Sorry, couldn't resist."

"Well, she was. Grand and vibrantly colorful festivals took place often in the temple environment. Sometimes there were funerary rites. The lapis blue wall friezes and reliefs were radiant and electric. The whole temple smelled delicious and seductive from all the pheromone-like perfumes from lotus offerings, burning of cinnamon oil in lamps, frankincense, and myrrh. There was this constant and soft intoxicating music that lulled everyone into this state of blissful trance. Followers making out in a corner were not uncommon. One thing very interesting about this temple was that it had a section to hold the statues of its followers, some in erotic embrace. It was as if they themselves were a part of the pantheon. So one day I saw mine too. I lived in the temple. I was a little goddess. I lived there."

"In your dreams?"

"It seamlessly recurred. It had the delicate feel of a past life."

"This may sound really strange. But I have a framed Egyptian papyrus of a scene depicting the inside of a temple with this stunningly gorgeous goddess with a bull horn holding the red sun disk headdress and sitting on a throne. She is holding that 'life key' and served by many including another female that looks a lot like her holding a sistrum, the musical instrument."

"The throne is the symbol of Isis and the sistrum is Hathor. Isis always holds the Ankh, the life key. Hathor was later worshipped as goddess Aphrodite in ancient Greece and as Venus by the Romans."

"Synchronicity!"

"Past lives! However, this was not Egypt. The carved script on the columns seemed even more ancient and the architecture was more ornamentally organic and more fantastically graceful. The buildings seemed to blend with nature rather than stand apart. I remember decorated elephants in the courtyards. I was given the impression that this island had a unique name. A female voice chanted, 'Daitya! Daitya!!'"

"Maybe you have been reading too much Plato. Atlantis legends speak of a colony called Daitya. I think it's something like Plato's Poseidonis, a mythical 'City of Water.' Some say it was off the coast of Florida."

"It's not that you know because you read; you read because you know. In *Timaeus* alone Plato says three times that Atlantis is *not a mere legend but an actual fact.* Not just Plato. Marcellus, Posidonius, Strabo, Plutarch, Thucydides, and Diodorus Siculus also wrote of Atlantis as *an actual fact.* Thucydides called it Atalante."

"Diodorus Siculus wrote *Bibliotheca Historica*, right?"

"Yes. The hot but very moist climate and plants of the island had a tropical lush Caribbean or even Central American feel to it. Definitely not Egyptian or Greek because the people looked more Central American too. The temple was also like a library housing large number of ancient books of wisdom."

"Ancient temples and the libraries were the same?"

"Yes. The temple itself was considered a book of esoteric teaching."

"Like the Temple of Luxor?"

"In the book *Temple In Man* by Schawaller De Lubicz, who pointed how this temple depicts a human and how a human body is, in fact, a temple, this coding of knowledge that must be intuited is explained.

The sages have always endeavored to hand down to posterity the revelation of the spirit disguised in the form of the words and parables of the sacred texts. … The means of adopted for transmitting this teaching are manifold, comprising legends, tales, and customs as wells as monuments, statues, and temples.

There were other means as well."

"What are the other means?"

"There were these dolphins that often gathered in the water near the temple. I fed them as my priestess, who looked somewhat Mongolian, would chant these melodious and haunting tonal sounds using the ancient books of wisdom to the dolphins, who would respond as if they fully understood the knowledge she was trying to impart."

"That's really interesting. Guess what the section near the equator of the mid-Atlantic ridge mountain range is called."

"What?"

"Dolphin Rise!"

"I had no idea. In this place dolphins and whales were treated almost like another version of humans. I often swam with them and whales. I even rode them."

"You were the *Whale Rider*?"

"The movie *Whale Rider* is about 2012!"

"No way!"

"It was based on the teachings of a highly respected Waitaha Maori shaman or spiritual leader named Mac Rucka. His teachings are in a book called *The Song of the Waitaha*. The story is a parable portraying the prophesy about the struggle of return of the feminine leadership on Earth – New Zealand version of Joan of Arc. Witi Ihimaera wrote this story as a novel."

"It's about the Waitaha Maori awaiting the leader of the new generation."

"The descendent first-born son in the line of their ancestor Paikea, who rode a whale to arrive in the islands. Twins, a boy and a girl, are born with the demise of their mother at birth. The boy does not make it. The girl is named Paikea as well by her father. Tradition prohibits a female from becoming the chief. However, all young men tested by the current chief, the girl's grandfather, to retrieve the *rei puta*, the traditional whale tooth, thrown into the ocean fail. Whales beach themselves to announce trouble and the transition to the new leadership. Finally the *rei puta* is retrieved and handed over to the chief by his wife while he is watching Paikea, the granddaughter, riding the largest of the whales that beached out on the ocean. Chief asks, 'which one?' The wife angrily with powerful emotions asks to his face ..."

"*What do you mean which one? ...* That's the clincher! That's a question to mankind!!"

"*Man*kind! Paikea is declared chief. This restoration of balance in leadership on the entire earth is to happen when the planet enters the Age of Aquarius or Water. Their tribal name, Waitaha, means 'Bringers of Water.'"

"Bringers of Water is code for those who oversee the herald of the Age of Aquarius?"

"In the dream, water itself seemed alive like a spiritual being. In Zoroastrianism water is in fact a living high being with a name: Archangel Ardvisura Anahita. In Egypt it was Neith, the mother goddess of primordial water of creation."

"I found this paragraph extremely intriguing in Nera's book *In the Presence of High Beings: What the Dolphins Want You To Know.*

Dr. Horace Dobbs, one of the first to swim with individual social dolphins, refers to these friendly cetaceans as 'ambassadors,' while social psychologist Dr. Jean Houston notes that dolphins have come to our shores throughout history to meet with people prior to periods of increased enlightenment and cultural renaissance. Thus, as we enjoy these engaging encounters, we must also ask why cetaceans are revisiting our shores at this particular time to offer us their kindness. ...

Although dolphin connections with humans reach far back in time, the current trend toward more frequent contact throughout the world did not begin until about thirty years ago.

When Nera spent time with the Waitaha, they indicated that a part of their understanding of the nature of reality came from their cetacean link. Their ancestors arrived on the back of two whales: one they call the father and the other mother.

Sandoz-Merrill added, *once the seeds of tomorrow's desires are planted, enjoy the harvest of yesterday's dreams, for gratitude and joy in present moments attract God's grace to you and tomorrow's dreams draw closer while you play.*"

"Codes are how knowledge is stored in a way that transcends time. The Waitaha believe just like the Inca that we dream our reality into being. In fact they sleep communally to and dream together in a great white lodge."

"Then the dreams are interpreted to understand reality."

"Waitaha believed that they descend from dolphins and whales. These creatures still protect them by bringing them knowledge in various ways. In my dream, I was taught how to chant the codes at the dolphins and whales and why."

"Why?"

"Because something catastrophic was going to happen to the island and she was giving the dolphins sacred secrets to be passed on to later human, who would need it to rebuild in the distant future. This was requested by our King, High Priest, and Chief 'Scientist' or Alchemist. His name was Chiquetet. It was pronounce like Chehutet. Almost like Djehuty, the Egyptian deity, who was later known as Thoth and even later by Greeks as Hermes Trismegistus. As a people we were called the Tlavatli. We interacted with some giants called the Rmoahal, who were not as artistically talented as we were. They were just big and a bit less evolved."

"Maybe dreams are how those ancient myths and legends are conceived. They dreamed them into being. Either that you visited Sea World in Florida too many times."

"If you listen to Incans we dream everything into being. But also remember that in Tula, a place in the state of Hidalgo of Mexico, there are these impressive giant human figure statues holding what looks exactly like some sophisticated laser guns."

"Those are supposed to be Toltecs, whose capital city was built there."

"The Aztecs called the statues Atlantids. So how is that connected to Plato?"

"That really makes you wonder."

"Aztecs considered Toltecs their ancestors, who came from a sunken motherland called Aztlan. Toltecs were glorified in their accounts, as a class of masters or *naguals,* who were wise, marvelous, wealthy, civilized, and formidable. They were inventors of art, medicine, time keeping and philosophy. In fact, Toltec means artisan. Apparently they came from the east originally. Aztecs meticulously recorded the names the Toltec rulers and historical events."

"Are these rulers and events archeologically corroborated?"

"Mostly not. Some say the evidence lay under the waters of the Atlantic Oceans and others say it is all myth. The Archeological community is divided on the historicity of the Toltec 'Empire.' But there is carved story tablet called the Tairona Stone in the British Museum, which clearly depicts the story of how the people of Aztlan escaped in boats during a Great Flood and settled in Central America today. This is confirmed by, Don Alejandro Cirilo Perez Oxlaj, the head and High Priest of the Mayan Council of Elders, representing 440 tribes."

"But the explanation is that the Aztecs dreamed the Toltec civilization into being. There is a time delay for the manifestation of material reality for us. But dreamed up civilizations are already there. All you need is increased secretions of melatonin converted from serotonin by the pineal gland."

"I understand that dreaming is like imagination, but it seems passive not active. I see creativity as interactive. In dreams, at least non-lucid, you are a spectator and not a designer. One night, for example, I vividly saw myself hovering over the Gobi desert in Mongolia looking at a pretty advanced civilization. I saw sacred tablets encrypted with secret knowledge for future Revelation. The dream ended with the sand completely covering up any traces of it. I do not imagine such things in my waking state."

"I understand the arbitrariness of these visions. A theory says that it is the resurgence of content of your subconscious."

"Yes, how did that get into my subconscious in the first place? A past life? Another dream only made it even more mysterious. You know the Nazca lines?"

"Yes, in Peru."

"I saw a city like in the Gobi with pyramids, temples and other sophisticated buildings on the other side of the river next to the Nazca lines. Just as earlier a great sand storm blew and covered up the city. I saw people watching, except they were happy. They even left sacred objects in specific places to be discovered at a predetermined time."

"Same dream, different city."

"Except Italian archaeologist Giuseppe Orefici discovered this city called Cahua Chi when the top of the pyramid was exposed later by erosion. The city contains over forty adobe structures. It is even suggested that it was the capital of the Nazca state. I saw this in my dream before the discovery."

"But a city in Gobi is not yet discovered."

"There is a Nazca legend in Cahua Chi that says the city was buried on purpose to hide it from the Spanish Conquistadors who sought to loot and destroy it. A prophecy claims that city will reemerge during the time when the ancient knowledge will be revealed to mankind to reestablish the glory of the past or even be better."

"The prescience challenges the idea that these images entered your subconscious through your experiences in this life such as movies, books, legends, and even fairy tales. Your subconscious takes in all the suggestion and releases a potpourri of them at times. Why? I don't fully know."

"Messages?"

"Mixed messages!"

"Your idea is not all bad. For example I saw another civilization on earth in extremely vivid details. Buildings, tropical parks, and beautiful lakes. This was on the continent of Antarctica. The dream ended with the ice swallowing up the civilization and assuming its present appearance."

"Tropical parks in Antarctica? That's definitely dreaming."

"Listen to this. We talked about Graham Hancock. He wrote a book called *Fingerprints of the Gods*. In it he argues that Atlantis did exist and it was the continent of Antarctica when it was closer to the equator, so tropical. So you could say that my dream was influenced by that book. But in my dream a human friend, a blonde woman, told me that this was not Atlantis but a civilization much older like the Gobi one. It felt like she knew I read the book and was telling me Hancock was partially right."

"Apparently, Hancock's dreams are crap. He needs to smoke what you do. Jokes aside I have seen dreams like that myself, but not of unknown civilization, but well known. In one dream I was Mayan in an ancient time. I looked Mayan, but there were definitely white people led by a bearded character that looked exactly like Obi-Wan Kenobi. We had no beards at all. He was teaching us to create technology partly by the use of our thoughts collectively. The created things were termed, Maya, meaning the illusion of reality."

"Mayan means Keeper of Time. The Maya means the same in many Indian languages that descend from Sanskrit. Now we know that a third of the known Maya words are extremely similar in sound and meaning to Greek. Incredibly a large number of words in Greek words are the same as Sanskrit. Some Maya words are in fact same as Hebrew."

"And some Maya words are same as Sanskrit?"

"Exactly!"

"That's beyond me. Are you saying they were historically connected or descend from a single earlier civilization? There could have been linking trade between them, even though we have no evidence for such activities."

"Makes you wonder doesn't it. Many archeologists now consider the Olmecs of the Americas were black Africans."

"They look very African. It's a big mystery. It hints at a lurking connection among the ancient civilizations of the Americas, Africa, Europe, and Asia."

"Apparently Plato uncovered some of it. Hancock's book *Underworld* explored many unexplained underwater ruins in the Pacific Ocean, some by Japan."

"Does he claim that it is the lost continent of Lemuria or something?"

"Not categorically. He does not even like the name because it is a modern name meaning the land of the Lemurs, the primates in Madagascar. Even without naming a possible lost civilization the ruins speak for themselves. They are not the stuff of dreams, but stone."

"The global flood legends must have something to them too. In fact, an entire unknown underwater city with what looks like pyramids was discovered near Cuba."

"Another was discovered as the lost city of Dwaraka in the Indian legend Mahabharatha. All these cities seem to have been submerged by a cataclysmic rise of the sea level."

"Even as some of the water froze over Antarctica. Now we are melting that and raising the sea levels again."

"One day we can dive and rediscover the lost civilization Miami."

"Just like the flood legends there are so many other myths that are so similar like creation stories."

"Many cultures had something like the Jewish Ark of the Covenant, a holy of holies, initiation structures, the cross, mother goddess idols, sun worship as a disk symbol, serpents, dragons, totemic ancestry from animals, and the concept of Trinity in Unity."

"Well, you could say that two scientists today, one on Palo Alto and one in Tokyo discover the same technology at the same time."

"Right, so it is within all of us and when the right time comes it wakes itself up."

"Is that why we are seeing similar themed dreams? Something is lifting its head above the water."

"And sand and Ice! Do you know the legend of Shangri-La?"

"Of course, everyone has. It is the mythical utopian city of Tibet. It is all made up. James Hilton pretty much invented that in his novel *The Lost Horizon*."

"Yes, Hilton incorporated that into his novel, but there is a rich legend of a place called Shambhala in Tibet."

"Shambhala is Shangri-La, mispronounced by the British."

"The erudite British history scholar and presenter Michael Wood says this in his documentary *In Search of Myths & Heroes*:

Of all the world's great myths the oldest and most enduring is the tale of an earthly paradise. A place beyond the clouds untouched by time, where the ancient wisdom still lives on. The land has many names. One of them is Shangri-La.

The very name Shangri-La has come to mean paradise on earth. But could Shangri-La have been a real place? Where did the story come from? … The tale of a hidden valley where the wisdom of humanity was preserved to save humanity from self-destruction struck a really deep cord in the pessimistic years between the two world wars."

"Sounds like now. Self-destruction. Wars. A promise of an earthly paradise."

"But like all the best stories Shangri-La was not plucked out of the sky. Its roots lie in an ancient legend.

Shambhala is regarded as historic and true by the Tibetans, who consider, *Kalachakra*, teachings of Shambhala, to be the source of their Buddhism. They are awaiting the second coming of their messianic king Rigden-jyepo, who will usher in a Golden Age of Dharma or wisdom. Even earlier Jesuit missionary visiting King Akbhar brought back such amazing stories of a kingdom with monks and temples like them."

"But there is no archeological evidence of such a ruin anywhere."

"Only cities considered descendent from it."

"Let me guess. You saw Shambhala in a dream."

"You guessed right my friend. It was even more confusing. This was the most glorious one of all. The city itself looked like it was all made of crystals. Truly fairy tale stuff with castles and everything. The location was interesting. This was over the Gobi desert on a higher plane."

"Like an etheric plane?"

"This city was the epitome of the legend of Shambhala. It was ruled by these wise princes called Kumaras. This city had a sort of a twin city also called Shambhala. That was where Scandinavia is today, but it was not cold like today. The state that had the second Shambhala was called Hypoborea. Greenland and Iceland were part of it."

"I thought Shambhala was associated with Tibet."

"I did see a city in Tibet. I think it was underground somewhere below Lhasa, the capital of Tibet. It was called Shan-Chea."

"How do cities exist underground? That seems too fantastic to comprehend. I guess it was just a dream."

"I also went in one of those dreams into an underground multilayered cities in what is today California."

"That explains the earthquake."

"This city was mostly above ground level. It is inside Mt Shasta. It was called Telos. It had a pyramid."

"Let me guess. They were survivors of Atlantis!"

"The beginning of the civilization with Sumerians in modern day Iraq was in fact the beginning of the Patriarchic human civilization. It was preceded by the matriarchic age with its own set of civilization like those in legends like Lemuria or The Kingdom of Mu. The patriarchic leadership wiped out the previous history."

"Victors rewriting history?"

"Before the dominance by the masculine in the patriarchic age began the sacred feminine ruled with spirituality. Archeology has proved this by the discovery of symbols and carvings of symbol. One carving of the sacred feminine was the womb & vulva symbol. A symbol of the capacity to give birth to life, a feminine privilege. In this symbol the womb is a half circle, the flat side facing up, sitting on its concave side on the pointy end of an almond-shaped symbol. This is later called *vesica piscis*. No one knows the original name.

Now when the dominance was switched to masculine side the symbol was turned 90 degrees making it look like a fish. *Vesica piscis* means womb of fish. The symbol of Christianity became the cross, a symbol of death, replacing the womb & vulva, a symbol of birth. Earlier followers of Jesus were a secret underground order because of the persecution. They marked hidden directions to their meeting places using *vesica piscis* and later erased them. Early disciples honored the sacred feminine. They still do. Virgin Mary. Notre Dame. Mary, the mother of Jesus, did start off as a virgin. The bible clearly indicates that she gave birth to the siblings of Jesus fathered by Joseph. Virgin no more, but very fertile and highly regarded.

Another Mary from Magdala on the other hand was the chief disciple of Jesus. She was the teacher and leader of the apostles. This Mary, often called the Magdelene, was fully dedicated to her service of the teaching the message of Jesus. She represented high level feminine leadership in a later masculine dominated religion. She, among other Marys, was one of the last greats of the residual matriarch age. She is misunderstood by some. Mary Magdalene was the twin flame leader and teacher of the mission of Jesus.

The matriarchic age ended before her due to the perceived abuse of feminine power. The shift had an impact from a backlash against acts like some fertility ceremonies, where men were sacrificed after a group of priestesses had ritual sex with them. Some men were subject to ritual castration, *sanguinaria*, following an orgiastic enactment of mythic practices with gods, in the case of the Cult of Cybele, like Attis, who underwent the same process except voluntarily. Even Attis dies and is later resurrected as a solar deity. Maarten Vermaseren's book *Cybele and Attis: the Myth and the Cult* details such practices honoring Cybele, another exemplar of the earth mother archetype, in Phrygia or modern day Turkey. After the power shifted from the lunar based age to solar based age the patriarchic archetype is resurrected as the solar power relegating 'lunatic' women to second class citizenship as 'witches' and switched even lunar calendars to solar calendars. So now we have inharmonious 13 *moon*ths and 12 months. The 12 months came from the perceived solar migration across the 12 constellations."

"Mankind has not been so kind to womankind since then. So now the power shifts again."

"Yes, the power shifts again but with a warning to the feminine. The balance is delicate. It must be preserved in near perfect equilibrium for we know the dear cost of imbalance, both ways."

"So this time when you get hold of the ball, ladies, don't drop it."

"It is very important not to do what the masculine did at the previous power shift. Men considered women such a threat that there has been an ongoing disinformation campaign of defamation. In Europe over nine million women with very high intuitive abilities were burnt alive as witches, the most famous being Joan of Arc. Some of those women were simply herbalists who possessed medicinal plants used in healing. Their power, the serpent of knowledge and wisdom, *Uraeus*, was a threat to insecure men of the introductory stage of the patriarchic age, traumatized by the rituals perceived as at their expense."

"So they went from goddesses in Egypt, Iraq, and India to 'dangerous' witches in Europe, when the matriarchy expired following the 'praying mantis-try.'"

"The Bible is the ultimate calumny on women. It is not surprising as the patriarchic Romans assembled the volume at the Council of Nicea, a council of men, by declaring any writing that honored the feminine as heresy. The disempowerment of the feminine through literature was not accidental. It begins with blaming the woman for the fall. The gospels are misinterpreted to label the one identified as Mary Magdalene a prostitute. All unbiased modern scholarship has now proven that Mary was none other than the highly respected Chief Disciple of Jesus. She understood his teachings and taught the twelve apostles, who often struggled to grasp the meaning. She was subject of untold slander and calumny by organized Christianity, who could not accept her status and importance. The systematic exclusion of the feminine in Christianity culminated at the Council of Nicaea, organized by Roman Emperor Constantine. They changed the Trinity from being originally Father, Son and Mother to banish

SOMETHING HAPPENED ON THE WAY TO HEAVEN

the feminine. The irony is that it was his mother Helena that nudged her son towards the teachings of Jesus as a possible and desperate uniting force for his chaotic empire in a premature fall because of its diverse and conflicting religions. As the times would have it, the Council of Nicaea was all men, who represented the insecure patriarchs that felt threatened by the power of the females initiated in the Goddess traditions. They decided which books and gospels would be canonized. They mistranslated the original Aramaic word for 'heavenly father/mother,' Creative Potency in union of opposites, in the Lord's prayer to denote just 'our father in heaven.' The mother, the only one with the creative womb, was taken out. Guess how many of the Biblical books are by a woman."

"*Book of Esther.*"

"That's it. Where is the Gospel according to Mary Magdalene? It was kept out of the Canon by the men who contributed to compiling the canon, like Irenaeus. Fortunately, we have a part of it from the Nag Hamadi scrolls."

"I think people now know for certain that Mary Magdalene was the most important woman in the Jesus ministry."

"Rightfully so. She represents something greater for modern women. It is a responsibility and not a right. As the power shifts we will hopefully get a long due co-rulership."

"Heralding the Co-ed Age."

"It is not another misguided feminine dominance."

"Women paid a too heavy of a price."

"Let me tell you something. You may say that some of this information came from Dan Brown's novel *The Da Vinci Code*, but that is not the case. It is just that he fell upon the right track. Some of my ancestors came from Saint-Maries-de-La-Mer in Camargue region of Southern France and settled in Canada before I moved to *Mary*land. I also have Cornish

Celtic and Egyptian Jewish roots. This information was passed down through every generation in my family. The story goes back long before any modern book. It is still celebrated every year in France. One such celebration is called the *Arrival of the Marys*. This is the truth."

"Tell me."

"Shortly before Yeshua, our Jesus of Nazareth, was born and taken to Egypt as an infant, there was a very wealthy, highly educated, and extremely intelligent Egyptian lady who married a well-connected Jewish man, whose ancestors came from today's Iraq and Syria. They were both related to Egyptian Pharaohs, Assyrians Kings, Essenes, and Abraham, the Great Patriarch. This influential couple had a daughter named Mary. That family lived both in Egypt, Turkey, and Israel, among the Essenes. The Egyptian mother, at one time, lived in the area known as Magdala or today's Migdal, by the Sea of Galilee."

"The daughter is Mary Magdalene?"

"That's the one. At least that is what she has come to be known as. Her mother was also called Mary. Since her childhood the mother, the elder Mary of Magdala, noticed that the young Mary was extremely sharp both intellectually and intuitively. She was way above her peers."

"Sounds like an 'Indigo.'"

"I would say at the highest end with a superconsciousness. Now she was a Jewish girl because of her father's side. The mother Mary was an initiate of the Temple of Isis in Egypt, who wore a golden arm bracelet of the serpent Uraeus. Such initiates bore the title Magdalene among the Essenes. The little Mary was raised and educated in both cultures. The family was influential and highly recognized in both circles. When Mary attained puberty around the age of twelve her mother wanted to her intuitive skills to be put to good use. Mary was arranged to be trained and initiated by a high priestess at the Temple of Isis, the Great Mother Goddess."

"Sounds like you."

"That's where the similarity ends. Mary was a protégé and picked up the protocols very quickly. She began to meditate. She mastered meditation to a point when was now attaining altered states of consciousness."

"She found her Jacob's Ladder."

"In these states she began to communicate with Isis, who appeared to her as a beautiful, kind and loving teacher. Later, she would be questioned by the priestess on the revelations received. Mary grew to be a powerful feminine consciousness with leadership potential. Her transformation was equally influenced by Shekinah, the feminine aspect of Judaic transformative energy."

"Like Sophia."

"Sophia is simply Greek for the Hebrew Shekinah. This raw and primal feminine energy is not soft. She is a feisty, systems busting, iconoclastic, applecart toppling, feather-ruffling energy that would shake inner belief systems."

"Shek-inah belief systems?"

"Being already at the high end of the intuitive spectrum Mary was polished up fast by both the fiery Shekinah and the gentler Isis. Most would be overwhelmed by only one. This Mary was up to the task. She grew to be a force to reckon with in private under the tutelage of her high priestess and her mother. Mary became a Magdalene wearing that golden arm bracelet of Uraeus."

"Sound like we need her now."

"She began to associate with other women who matched her level, but not quite. She was a pure genius spark. Her eloquence and clarity in communication was elegant and impeccable."

"Quite the catch."

"That she was, a woman caught by a fisher of men. One day she met a guy. This Essene was her masculine match or you could say even more sublime and divine. The girl, even being an initiated Magdalene, had no chance. Struck by the greatest guy a girl could have. They deserved each other."

"Sounds like a match made in heaven."

"Talk about celestial marriage. It does not get better than this couple. They were both odd and brilliant. The man, Yeshua, was on a mission to help people realize their inner divinity not just for the time but for the period we are in now. He struggled to find disciples even anywhere near his level of radiance to do this work. He did find twelve, but none matched the magic of Mary, who often had to teach the twelve as she was more down-to-earth in her communicative skills. The male disciples often did not get the complex metaphors of Yeshua."

"Sounds like religious people today."

"She had her own circle of twelve very intelligent, powerful, wealthy, and socially influential of women, who received the knowledge from Mary in their secret coven, often in the presence of Yeshua. These meeting used the symbol of the womb, *vesica piscis*, as a sign of their hidden location. The twenty six of them did this light work spreading the message of Yeshua and initiating those who came their way."

"How come no one knows about the twelve female apostles?"

"It has to do with the male dominated orthodox Jewish culture, where women were relegated. These twelve, many of whom had variations of the name Mary like Mariam and Myriam, were gems compared to the less evolved twelve men. The women met cloaked in secrecy and worked their way through the society. Some of them had heavy connections to the Temple of Isis. Those initiates bore the title Magdalene and wore the golden arm bracelet of Uraeus. However, in the ministry of Yeshua they had no official title or order and they were never let into the inner circle, except for Mary herself, who received the innermost knowledge from Yeshua himself."

"All of this was taken out of the masculine dominated Christian history. That's a travesty!"

"Indeed. You know why, though. It was because of Sar'h, the daughter born to Mary and Yeshua in Egypt after Yeshua's death. The lives of Mary and Sar'h were in danger even in Egypt. They had to flee to today's France, where they were greeted by Druids and priestesses from the Temple of Isis. Mary and the children, there were others by Yeshua, lived near Saint-Maries-de-La-Mer under protection. Later they spent time with the Druids in today's England. Mary finally settled in northern Wales."

"This is where the Arthurian Holy Grail comes from."

"Absolutely! There was a simple little cup, with no significance or ornamentation, at one of the last suppers enjoyed by Yeshua and Mary with the disciples. The real Holy Grail is the womb of every woman, represented by 'Mary Magdalene,' whose distorted character in the Bible, by the way, is a composite of three different Marys, who were initiated in Egypt and were later known as Magdalenes by the Essenes."

"The Druid teachings always struck me as having resonance with some the teachings of Yeshua and Siddhartha Gautama. At least one connection is solid."

"After Mary and Sar'h went to France and England, the twelve female disciples continued their work with others. Sar'h grew up in the heart of Druidry. Eventually the feminine aspect of Christianity diminished. Women completely disappeared out of leadership role in later traditions. However, at later times women formed two formal orders to carry on the teachings of Yeshua in the way Mary presented them. These orders also admitted a minority of male initiates. One was called the Order of the Blue Rose and the other the Order of the Magdalene."

"Wow! Most people will be shell shocked at these revelations."

"More like upset and angry. Hate mail material. That's why it is called the Apocalypse, because the revelation causes a fiery internal Armageddon inside indoctrinated modern Christians. A battle between their intuitive heart and their deeply conditioned brain mind."

"This spiritual surgery must happen. It is for their own good."

"I understand my spiritual scalpel is sharp and incisive. They seek and come to this revelation voluntarily because in their hearts they recognize their own spiritual cancer. They know the meaning of the revelation. The healing."

"They see the symptoms and cannot stand it. This explains the incredibly resonant and almost revolutionary response to a novel by Dan Brown. That's why. People intuitively knew this truth. Brown intuitively knew how to present it."

"Their multidimensionally reaching selves grabbed the moment to dig. They found out that the roots go deeper and deeper as they dig."

"So the Christians who find their faith threatened and upset by a mere work of fiction or as some critics said 'an airport read' must stop and ask the question 'how good is my faith and belief system if it is irreversibly damaged by fiction. Which is the fiction? Who is really mislead?"

"This is the Armageddon. They are being prepared for the Harvest. Dig now and uncover the truth or you will be digging your own spiritual grave."

"What do say to those who want to only agree with the majority?"

"Don't be cowardly. Be ahead of humanity. How do you know you are in the minority? Even if you are, be bold. Don't hold on to and wallow in the old paradigm. If you do as time goes by you will watch the pillars of the old paradigm crumble around you. Initially the personal paradigm shift is voluntary, but eventually it is forced upon you. If you cling to the old because it is prevalent where you are, you will find yourself in the minority someday. Then the shift could be more painful with you being dragged kicking and screaming. So be proactive in the upgrade of your consciousness."

"Your vivid dreams were harbingers of a new beginning in your own life. So people can take comfort in that."

"I must admit that things dramatically improved in my life since I began to see those series of dreams. Like someone, with a powerful feminine presence, was guiding me gently on a wonderfully winding path of life."

"I hate to admit it, but since my hypothermia hallucination episode with Joan of Arcturus I have had a few events that I can't shake off as purely coincidental."

"See. I had this urge to get a dog. I did and named her Star."

"Dog Star?"

"I know. Carl Jung termed these events synchronicities."

"At least you didn't name the dog Ma."

"You know that Dog Star is …"

"… Sirius. The binary star system in Canis major constellation. The brightest and one of the closest star systems in our night sky, seen from all inhabited earth."

"Canis Major. The Big Dog of the heavens. In Africa, Sirius was known to Egyptians and the Dogon people of Mali long before modern astronomy discovered it. In fact, their myths claimed it was a three-star system."

"How is that possible? Without telescopes?"

"The Dogon mythology contained intricate details like the fifty-year orbital period prior to such calculations by western astronomers. Sirius was extremely important to ancient cultures. In Ancient Egypt the heliacal rising of Sirius marked the summer solstice flooding of the Nile and the 'Dog Days' of summer for the Ancient Greeks, whose summers were hot and dry as well. Sirius, in fact, mean scorcher."

"Okay, that is where we get that term from, the dog days of summer."

"Chinese called it the celestial wolf, ancestor of all dogs. Many Native Americans called it 'Dog-face,' 'Wolf Star,' or even 'Coyote Star.' Alaskan Inuit call it 'Moon Dog.'

Greek coins feature dogs and star Sirius with emanating rays. Egyptians and Greeks considered Sirius to be the home of ..."

"... Isis."

"Ancient Greeks noticed that during the dog days following the arrival of Sirius plants wilted, men became weak and women became extremely sexually aroused. Scandinavia Norse mythology called Sirius *Lokibrenna*, 'Loki's torch.'"

"Isis on the papyrus at my place has those bull horns on her head as well. Horns forming a chalice like shape engulfing the masculine blazing red sun. I never understood why that turned me on and weakened me at the same time. Like I was *star*-struck by her presence. Great! I have been under the magic of horny Isis, the brightest star in the night sky and my bed room wall."

"Greeks observed that too. The weather in their early summer was volatile, like a woman with unmet needs. They call it a 'burning' or 'flaming.' Adds a new meaning to *burning bush*. The effect on men was called *astroboletos* in Greek. That means 'star-struck.'"

"I was certainly *astroboletos*."

"Even their astronomer Ptolemy living in Alexandria, Egypt, identified Sirius as the central median of his globe. Arabs call it Ash-shira, the leader. Among the other central stars he identified was Arcturus, the home of your Joan. In fact, many earlier astronomers got Arcturus and Sirius B mixed up."

"Like sisters or even twins!"

"… on the same mission."

"If they are both aroused as we suspect, boy, we must be in for something."

"It cannot be so bad. The Greek summer as it progressed brought a mist of ecstasy and a soothing cool breeze. Our summer is just beginning."

"All this information! I feel like I am being prepared for something."

"These are the days that must happen to you."

"Walt Whitman. Almost like the experience of Quantum Physicist Dr. Amit Goswami. The message that turned into an admonition in his head, which he concedes in the *Quantum Activist*, asks him to prove the *Tibetan Book of the Dead*. That book is all about re-incarnation."

"You said he followed up."

"He did. He wrote *Physics of the Soul: The Quantum Book of Living, Dying, Reincarnation and Immortality*. It led him to understand evolution of mankind in a new light."

"Light! Nice pun!!"

"Now, I am beginning to follow Dr. Goswami's postulation that material genetic evolution is consciousness driven, which he articulated in his books, *Creative Evolution*, *Self-Aware Universe*, and *God Is Not Dead: What Quantum Physics Tells Us about Our Origins and How We Should Live.*

"Something transcends this physical world and the visible life in it. We have departed the separation of the physical and metaphysical and are approaching a singularity."

"I read this wonderful article called *The DNA Mystery: Scientists Stumped By 'Telepathic' Abilities,* by Rebecca Sato, in *The Daily Galaxy.*"

"Telepathic DNA?"

"Yes. It said that DNA has the amazing ability to recognize similarities in other DNA strands from a distance. Somehow they are able to identify one another, and the tiny bits of genetic material tend to congregate with similar DNA,"

"DNA entanglement."

"This is how the strings of similar frequency clump in the String Theory. Reality is consistent at both micro and macro level. Research published in American Chemical Society's *Journal of Physical Chemistry*, talked about homology recognition between sequences of several hundred nucleotides occurs without physical contact or presence of proteins. Double helixes of DNA can recognize matching molecules from a distance and then gather together, all seemingly without help from any other molecules or chemical signals. In the study, scientists saw fluorescently tagged DNA strands with identical nucleotide sequences were about twice as likely to gather together as DNA strands with different sequences. They are baffled by how individual DNA strands could possibly be communicating in this way."

"The Twist thickens."

"There was this experiment on fruit fly DNA. The gene encoding the eye of a fruit fly was removed. A fruit fly was born with no eyes. The blind fruit fly reproduced to create more blind offspring. However, the fifth generation had eyes. The DNA portion meant to encode the eye was perfectly restored."

"Even though the material DNA was removed, the spiritual DNA, like the 'soul' portion of the DNA that creates the material DNA was still there, but it was invisible. You cannot kill the soul. The blind fly had eyes all along, but not in this dimension."

"The software was fine and restored the hardware? But I prefer your shamanistic rendition of it. Dr. Bruce Lipton, the American developmental biologist, echoes this consciousness–driven DNA evolution."

"Shakespeare said: *There are more things in heaven and earth, Horatio, than are dreamt of in your philosophy.*"

"I think it is time for me to tell you what I dreamt up once during a tough and frustrating day of working with DNA research on the new gene expression and its neurogenetic implications."

"In the lab?"

"Yes, I was having a hard time with the potential neurogenetic function of the 90% or so 'junk' DNA. I came across something written by Dr. Leonard Horowitz, a Harvard graduate.

… during the 1990's, three Nobel laureates in medicine, advanced research that revealed the primary function of DNA lies not in protein synthesis, as was widely believed for the past century, but in electromagnetic energy reception and transmission.

Less than 3% of DNA's function involves protein manufacture; more than 90% functions in the realm of bioacoustic and bioelectric signaling.

Dr. Horowitz showed that DNA emits and receives photons or electromagnetic waves of sound and light."

"So you have a tough time generating data to establish that yourself."

"Yes. It started with a reverie that spiraled into a semi-sleep altered state. I realized I was looking at a gorgeous pond in a pristine landscape. It was raining this multicolored water. There was this vibrant circular rainbow and five white swans. The rainbow turned into seven swans of each color of the visible spectrum of the rainbow. The now twelve swans were flying around making beautiful formations. First I thought they were trying to take off. You know how swans struggle in that. At one point they formed a cross which sort of turned into an Egyptian Ankh looking thing. The Ankh morphed to form a figure of a beautiful female."

"Of course, that's a common theme in your wet dreams."

"The female was not naked but covered in multicolored feathers. The white ones hovered over the figure formed by the colored ones. Then they broke into three groups of four. It's like each four merged into one and then the three formed an entangled triple helix with their long and slender necks."

"Triple helix is symbolic of unity as Trinity arising from the double duality."

"It was like a mass orgy mating dance. A creative act! Twelve swans entangled almost like a twelve stranded DNA structure. Then they all collapsed into this little semitransparent ball and flew into my body. I became transparent and luminous. I had 360 vision. Then I woke up."

"Heháka Sápa, better known Black Elk, a Lakota medicine man, said, *whatever you have seen, maybe it is for the good of the people you have seen it.*"

"You know the German organic chemist Kekulé von Stradonitz had a day-dream of a serpent biting its own tale before he discovered the structure of Benzene. He struggled before that and the dream led him to realize the six carbon atoms are in resonance as one in a ring. The serpent he saw may have been like that arm bracelet you are wearing."

"Many ancient cultures have a symbol similar to the caduceus, the serpent double helix symbols. My arm bracelet is made of pure gold. Say hello to my Uraeus."

"Caduceus is the inspiration of our current symbol for medicine. The golden bracelet of Uraeus seems to be a symbol of your ophitic wisdom. A Maryland Magdalene!"

"I find the number of swans intriguing. Twelve is the sacred number of completion."

"I didn't even think about it."

"Twelve is everywhere. It is deeply embedded in the mass psyche of human consciousness."

"All ancient civilizations considered twelve sacred, auspicious, and important."

"Twelve signs of the zodiac, twelve months, twelve hours, twelve tribes, twelve apostles, twelve gates, twelve angels, twelve sons, twelve chakras, twelve days of Christmas, even twelve planets, the so-called Cosmic Libraries of which earth is one, and the crown of twelve stars on the head of the pregnant woman in the Book of Revelation that gives birth to the new generation."

"You forgot the twelve knights of King Arthur's round table."

"This twelve on a round table is an archetype. Sufis Whirling Dervishes mastered the application of this Divine archetype in the exemplar self by spiraling into altered-states of consciousness and climbing up and down Jacob's Ladder.

To explain the dynamic interplay that takes place along the axis of self and Divine, Sufis often rely on the concept of an archetype. Contrast for instance, the concept of 'roundness' with an actual round table, writes Sufi Master Vilayat Inayat Khan in his delicious book *Awakening: A Sufi Experience*.

The mind of the Cosmos is accessed through meditative, altered states of consciousness – those wordlessly profound transpersonal dimensions described by the great mystics. It is our encounter with this 'parallel reality' that catalyzes a dramatic shift in perspective, widening the lens of our individual psyches and revealing the immense scope of the Divine point of view. Such expanded states of consciousness are not illusory, as some critics claim, but are reflected in theories of scientists at the leading edge of physics. In meditation, for instance, we may experience an altered notion of space – being both everywhere and in one place – that corresponds to quantum theories of non-locality in space. Time, as well, may shift from being linear and one-dimensional to a multi-tiered dimension influenced by what scientists describe as acausal and nondetermined factors.

From these dramatic shifts in vantage point of space and time, it is possible to glimpse clues into the working of the Cosmos. For according to the ancient teachings of the Sufis, we are not separate from his transcendent reality. Rather, they taught that we are a continuum of consciousness ranging from boundless, transpersonal dimension that is coextensive with all others to the 'discrete entity' that makes up our unique individuality. Learning to embrace these two ends the continuum is the spiritual task of awakening and illumination – reconciling the seemingly irreconcilable vantage points between the Divine and individual points of view. In contradistinction to the Hindu yogic perspective, however, in this state of awakening in Sufism one does not need to give up one's personal identity, but instead learn how to correlate it with one's Divine dimension. Furthermore, Sufis train their consciousness to shift back and forth between Divine and human vantage points; the infinite and the finite; and the archetype and the exemplar."

SINGULARITY

"Do you ever garden?"

"I have, but not this summer. What do you plant?"

"Organic fruits and vegetables. I love herbs. The smell is the draw!"

"I figured. So you can have your rawgasmic organic salads. Sounds really good actually."

"Once you go raw, it's hard to go back."

"What's your favorite fruit?"

"Carambola from Sri Lanka. Known in the West as Star Fruit."

"How do you grow them?"

"I follow the method described by Anastasia in the *Ringing Cedars* book series."

"How is that?"

"I take the star seeds and place them under my tongue for nine minutes and walk around the garden in barefoot. Then I sow the star seeds into earth and mixed them with earth with my bare hands."

"What's the effect?"

"Star seeds are planted for earth purification. The fruits grown respond to the ailments and other physiological needs you have and are awakened so they can begin to cleanse and heal you."

"Does it work?"

"It is due to its antioxidant and antimicrobial activities. After the harvest of the good fruits of the right age of golden color I begin to certainly feel my vibes raised to a higher level."

"This is an Aboriginal cave painting story.

Tree ...
He watching you.
You look at tree,
He listen to you.
He got no finger, he can't speak, but that leaf ...
He pumping, growing, growing in the night.
While you sleeping
You dream something.
Tree and grass same thing.
They grow with your body,
With your feeling."

"The Garden of Eden is paradox. The garden part of the title negates what Eden represents."

"It is indeed. Aborigines never left Eden. This is what an Aboriginal woman said to an early missionary to Australia who was toiling in her garden, as recorded by anthropologist Ronald Berndt. The Aboriginal woman shook her head in dismay and said,

You people go to all that trouble and worry, working and planting seeds, but we don't have to do that. All these things are there for us ... The ancestral beings left our food for us. In the end you depend in the sun and rain just the same as we do. But the difference is we just have to go and collect the food when it is ripe. We don't have to make all this other trouble."

"A life of light work. Anastasia books tell that our garden should not be monocultural. We must imitate nature for its diversity. Native Americans say when we kill a plant we destroy a community. I plant a community. The results are self-evident."

"Do you feel different from that diet?"

"I lost weight too. I now have a light body."

"And a nice healthy glow."

"Light body glows."

"You sound like Nera. She also has a light body."

"Sound like you badly want that light body."

"Never felt something so gossamer."

"Ask and you shall receive."

"Simple as that, huh?"

"Simplicity is the key. Also, I work out to be light."

"Are you a heavy worker?"

"Nope, I am a Light Worker. I create my space of love."

"Space of love! I don't think she will protest too much."

"Er, send her flowers too. And write her a love letter. That helps!"

"What's that stack of papers you have? Love letters?"

"I Xeroxed these pages from this book published in 1977 by a guy named Don Elkins, who was a consciousness researcher from Louisville, Kentucky He worked with people who channeled massages and psychics like Uri Geller."

"Okay. 1977! Is that *The Raw Material* guy."

"*The Ra Material. The Law of One.* It is primal and Raw."

"Ra is the Egyptian sun God."

"Elkins concludes that *consciousness is more fundamental than physical matter. I find it hard to see even the possibility of physical matter creating consciousness.*"

"Over 30 years later, people are still stuck with a belief, which he concluded not as improbable, but impossible."

"He draws much on the work of Dewey Larson."

"The physicist from Minneapolis."

"Yes, he was far ahead of his time. Some people think humans are advanced, but how advanced are we?"

"Arizona State Astrobiologist Paul Davis thinks if we were to encounter alien technology far superior to our own, we would not even realize what it was. We would perceive it as miraculous. He writes in *Eerie Silence*, that *advanced technology might not even be made of matter. It might have no fixed size or shape, have no well-defined boundaries, and be dynamical on all scales of space and time, not anything we can discern. They may not be discrete, separate things in a system but a subtle organic higher-level correlation of things, totally incomprehensible to the human mind at our current state of evolution."*

"Do you think there is life out there?"

"Microbes for sure. You know SETI?"

"Search for Extra-Terrestrial Intelligence."

"Yes, they are looking for intelligent life in advanced civilizations. So far other than the infamous 'Wow!' signal no E.T. has phoned home or here."

"So you are saying there is no scientific evidence of an advanced civilization."

"Mathematically it is affirmative. Carl Sagan in *Cosmos* used the Drake equation to say that there must be in excess of ten thousand advanced civilizations in the 'Billions and Billions' of galaxies. In the very new book *The Crowded Universe: The Search for Living Planets* NASA Astrophysicist Alan Boss argues that not only there is life but that it is common."

"Billions and billions."

"Sagan's legacy. There are over 100 billion stars in our galaxy and there are over 100 billion galaxies. We discover new ones almost every day. So billions and billions is no exaggeration. Jill Tarter, director of SETI said, *we are here, made of stardust. Therefore, it is at least possible that there are others."*

"I read a *National Geographic* article called *Alien Life? Astronomers Predict Contact by 2025.*"

"Oh yes, that's what SETI's senior astronomer Seth Shostak argues in the book, *Cosmic Company*, that those life forms may be sending radio signals across space to let us know they exist. They discuss how *the billions of years in which extraterrestrial life could have evolved and the abundance of planets and stars elsewhere in the universe that are likely to mimic environmental conditions found on Earth.*

His co-author Barnett said, *it's a matter of statistics, really, depending on who you talk to, the universe is 12 to 15 billion years old. Humans have only been around for 40,000 years. We really are the new kids on the block. It would just be too tough a pill to swallow to believe that nothing else has evolved in all that time and space.*

Frank Wilczek, a Nobel-Prize winning physicist at MIT said, *mankind has achieved scientific-technological civilization only in the last 200 years or so, out of about 4.5 billion years of life on Earth, said. So it seems we ought to expect there to be many scientific-technological civilizations that have had many millions, or even billions, of years to develop.*"

"That's just looking in this dimension or membrane."

"Yes. There is almost nowhere you can fix your eyes without seeing something."

"That's what we can see. What about the empty space? Is it really empty?"

"NASA astronomers like Alan Stern of Science Mission Directorate believe the emptiness is an illusion, implying that the space between Mercury and the sun is occupied by, according to him, *as-yet-unseen bodies.*"

"Maybe soon we will see the *as-yet-unseen bodies.* There is an amazing documentary called *Transcendental Man: One Man's Quest to Reveal Our Destiny.*"

"Ray Kurzweil. The MIT graduate. The Inventor and Futurist. America's answer to Arthur C. Clarke. His predictions were on par with Clarke's."

"Yes, but not just him. Many futurists and scientists predict that by 2045 we will have multiplied the intelligence of the human machine-based civilization a billion-fold and reached a Singularity. The machine-like personal computers, videogames, and cell phones were the hi-tech cutting edge of the 70's and 80's the future belongs to nanotechnology, organic or partly alive computers, and now the mind-reading headsets of transhumanism."

"The Singularity is Near."

"Listen to this from Ray Kurzweil. *In order to appreciate the grander scheme of things, reason must be flexed. If there is an asymptomatic relationship between the end and the extreme beginning of the greater trend, this may infer two separate possibilities: our relative destruction of and departure from this planet, after which a seed sample of genetic material will prevail to begin a new era of biological evolution; or an ascension of another kind in which our solar system has its reset button pressed."*

"The whole theme. A mind expansion. An asymptomatic inception. An extreme beginning of relative destruction. A reset. An ascension. A march to singularity."

"Here and Now. Kurzweil addresses the block we have. Compartmentalization! In 2009, he launched the *Singularity University*. It is a wiki-like academic structure where experts from all field work in singular project of collective advancement. Singularity is Oneness."

"Didn't he say that when he was a student at MIT their computer was the size of a small building and now tiny cell phones in our pockets are thousand times more powerful and incredibly cheaper?"

"He said *what now fits in your pockets 25 years from now will fit in a blood cell and will be millions of times more powerful. ... These are all steps towards singularity."*

"Wow!"

"His wildest prediction is that all physical objects will simply become pieces of information that can be e-mailed and reassembled."

"In M-theory this is theoretical science. The matrix is the blueprint information that codes for the creation of the hologram we live in."

"In the beginning was just information waiting to become something. Incans say we dreamed the world into being."

"We can already e-mail a car. A virtual 3-D looking car. A hologram."

"We and everything around is a hologram. We see what we choose to see. We experience what we choose to experience. We know that, so it is a matter of advancement or as Kurzweil puts it *getting access to the source code.*"

"He is backed by some big guns right?"

"Yes, the big fish in our pond like NASA and Google."

"Even the transhumanism was launched by Oxford University and alike."

"Kurzweil predicts that nanotechnology will solve the energy crisis, upgrade the human genome and even lead to everlasting life."

"The upgrading the human genome intrigues me. Mainly, how exactly to do that."

"I know this can be scary to many, but the momentum fears no human. Jack Welch said, former CEO of General Electric said, *Change before you have to.*"

"Darwin echoed that: *It is not the strongest of the species or the most intelligent that survive but the most responsive to change.*"

"I think we have to consider the pre-swan cave man that may have thought he was the destiny of all human evolution. Where are they now?"

"So you are saying the path of fear is the path of duality and the path to extinction."

"As humans or post-humans on this planet earth, yes. Those of duality mindset may have to realize their own potential in a slower evolving realm. The path of love is a choice readily offered to them. It is sad because the love that you withhold is the pain that you carry."

"So we cannot take those who do not want to, because they are restricted to a world made only of matter of this membrane. But we have to voice how we feel and act it."

"Exactly. Dr. Seuss, these words use: *Be who you are and say what you feel, because those who mind don't matter, and those who matter don't mind.*"

"Place the message out there for the takers."

"I have a friend in New Mexico, Ken, he always says, *enlightenment is not for the faint-hearted, it is for the warrior.*"

"What is enlightenment to you?"

"Zen Buddhist Proverb puts it aptly; *Before enlightenment - chop wood, carry water. After enlightenment - chop wood, carry water.* It means understanding that there is nowhere you have to go, nothing you have to do, and nobody you have to be except who you are being right now. Nowhere. Now here."

"It's the space between the letters that contain the meaning."

"You have nowhere to go my friend. You are now here."

"So the fearful fear we have to or else …"

"They also fear the transparency I think. Their systems only function within the veil of illusion. Without it they dissolve with the illusion itself."

"The mind reader is their nightmare."

"Yes, the brain wave reading technology is a new shift in human-machine interaction. Instead of using a hand and a mouse we can think the command and the electromagnetic frequency can be programmed to be decoded to do a specific function. I am all for it."

"Stephen Hawking could use one."

"Absolutely, the gamers will love it."

"Other muscular atrophy sufferer like Hawking would welcome it."

"Soon a mouse will seem so 2011, for some it already is."

"No doubt. Physicist of CUNY Dr. Michio Kaku says this in *Beyond the Matrix: Daring Conversations with Brilliant Minds of Our Time.*

We can use MRI machines, brains scans, to look at the brain patterns of somebody telling a lie. When you tell a lie, it takes more energy than to tell the truth. ... This is a lot of energy and it is very easy to pick up on an MRI scan. In the future, we may actually be able to see the outlines of thought and emotions, just by reading the MRI results of a brain scan. This is going to court this year, by the way."

"So if the brain can send, and then it must also be able to receive and decode."

"Synergy is a two way street."

BLUE STAR

"Are you familiar with Chakra meditation?"

"I will deny that I have meditated on Chakira, but *Hips Don't Lie*."

"Shakira meditation! At least you can do it *Whenever Wherever*. Did you experience a full chakra Kundalini orgasm?"

"Like a full body orgasm in tantric sex? I wish I had the time for that kind of *Waka Wanka*."

"There is your solution to *The Unbearable Lightness of Being*. Be with your girl. Experience Friedrich Nietzsche's *Eternal Return*, recreating multiple synergetic energy exchanges."

"I have the sexologist Dr. Ian Kerner's book *She Comes First* with me."

"You carry that around?"

"There are always ten things in my mind."

"Simultaneously? What would they be?"

"Number ten is the meaning of life. Number one through nine are Synergetic Energy eXchanges with Nera."

"It all comes down to the right combination of hokey pokey and hanky panky. You are living in the ultimate state of consciousness in life. I think you are ready to graduate from the Alchemy of Horus to the Sex Magic of Isis."

"That's what it's all about, I guess. Let me read a bit from the book. It ties in Eckhart Tolle's being in the eternal now, entanglement, and the matrix like nothing else.

There's poignant scene in the film version of Milan Kundera's book The Unbearable Lightness of Being. *Tomáš and Tereza, a young married couple, are living in Prague at the start of the oppressive Soviet occupation of the 1960s. Tomáš has always been an avid womanizer and, even in marriage, is unable to relinquish his erotic adventures with other women. He lives lightly and freely, but his marriage is shallow and empty. Tereza is imprisoned by the heaviness of her love for Tomáš, tortured by his 'lightness.'*

The couple takes advantage of an opportunity to emigrate to Geneva, thinking it might provide them with a fresh start, but Tomáš, much to Tereza's disappointment, continues his life of ardent philandering. One day, unable to bear it any longer, Tereza impulsively leaves him and returns alone to doomed Prague.

Only after she's left does Tomáš finally realize that his life is empty without Tereza, so he makes a difficult decision — to return to Prague, where he'll live in perpetual poverty, never again to work as a surgeon, never again to know freedom of speech or liberty of choice. In short, he accepts the inherent heaviness of life.

We follow Tomáš as he crosses the border into Czechoslovakia. We watch as he hands over his passport, permanently, to the border guard.

Back in Prague, Tomáš return to his old, dark, shabby, apartment, where Tereza lies sleeping. She wakes up and can't believe her eyes. They embrace with tears in their eyes and that night they make love for the first time. Of course they've had sex countless times; but this is the first time they are truly making love; their bond to each other finally has a sacramental element, born of Tomáš's sacrifice to be with her, consummated in the heaviness of their true love for each other.

As Kundera explains, the title, The Unbearable Lightness of Being, *comes from the meditation on the philosophy of Nietzsche, who said that we should live every moment of our lives as though we were sentenced to repeat it over and over, forever and ever, for all eternity. We should live each moment as though we were creating an eternal, unchangeable work of art.*

Easier said than done. We can't live every moment as though it were eternally indelible; it's simply too hard and would make life much too heavy. So instead we attempt to escape and live with a sense of lightness. We postpone our goals, we get into ruts, we distract ourselves with trivialities, but deep down we know that we could be living life more fully according to our potential; lightness is undermined by a sense of heaviness; hence, the unbearable lightness of being.

For all of his sexual adventures and numerous lovers, it takes Tomáš years before he is finally able to make love. He is only able to do so by turning his back on the lightness of meaningless affairs and embracing the heaviness of a committed relationship.

We may not be able to live each moment as though we were going to repeat it over and over for all eternity, but we can make love that way; we can kiss our beloved knowing that we want that kiss, like a pebble cast into a still lake, to ripple and undulate for all eternity. Like Tomáš returning to Tereza's embrace, we can make love totally and indelibly, with all the heaviness and substance of our being. As George Bernard Shaw wrote, 'When you loved me I gave you the whole sun and stars to play with. I gave you eternity in a single moment.'"

"To ripple and undulate for all eternity. It takes a sexologist to put the chakra magic all together. *Who you are in bed is who you are in life.*"

"Samantha Jones, *Sex and the City*! Nice."

"My raw veganism has its side effects, too."

"I would die of raw veganism."

"I often do die that little death. *Le Petit Mort!*"

"*Le Petit Mort*. I know my French. That's the word for orgasm."

"Mine are Rawgasms!"

"I still need an illumination of the marriage of spirituality and sexuality."

"Read this page in this book *Buddha in Redface*. It is an exchange between Tarrence, the native shaman elder, and Dr. Eduardo Duran, the psychotherapist."

"Tarrance: *When power comes to the shaman, it's a spiritual gift. The problem starts because the spirit of the shaman is in a physical body. All we have are our senses of perception to tell us what is going on with the rest of us. Usually the senses are directly linked with the ego. The relationship of the shaman with God is so intense and so intimate that the senses can only interpret this one way—well, there can be other ways, but most people, and especially men, have difficulty understanding relationship in a way that is not sexual. Men are wired that way, you might say. Then their sexual energy becomes intensified, because this is directly from the Creator and the dreamtime within the Creator.*

Since the dreamtime is linked closely with the man's spirit, which is feminine, the man wants to have intimacy with his female spirit. However the problem is that the ego, instead of seeing this as a spiritual event and going inward, projects this outward, and this lands on a female person. Unfortunately, for many healers this intimacy is projected onto the patient they are seeing, because she is in the healing circle with him during the healing process.

… He wants is a union with his spirit, which is part of the Dreamtime Creator process. In essence, he wants to unite—and this is interpreted by his ego as sexual—that is, he wants to have sex or integrate with his inner female.

Eduardo: *So you mean that the shaman wants to have sex or connection with his internal female, which is really his spirit and actually is God in some way. Kind of like having sex with God?*

Tarrence: *Yes, the shaman wants to fuck God, I guess you would say. But he's too ignorant to know this, so instead he wants to fuck the patient."*

"How is that for a discourse?"

"So the power or life energy of God or Goddess, *Sekhem* or *Prana*, flows into us through the Chakras in this union?"

"Spirituality, the trapped Sophia, is often expressed in physical form in this dimension as sexuality. This is what the ancient Greek ritual of *hieros gamos* was about."

"Sexuality is a lower-dimensional expression of higher-dimensional spirituality."

"This is often misinterpreted and gratuitously abused with negative consequences. The psychiatrist Wilhelm Reich pointed out that *sexual suppression supports the power of the church, which has sunk very deep roots into the exploited masses by means of sexual anxiety and guilt. It engenders the timidity towards authority."*

"This explains the sex scandal and crisis within the Catholic Church."

"But somehow you and your girl Nera have intuitively realized the true nature of your arousal and attraction to each other. You haven't physically expressed this need for union with God and Goddess Sophia through your chakras because unlike some, your chakras are opened in a balanced manner with no overemphasis on the Sex Chakra."

"Most people will find the eroticism in religious and spiritual traditions incompatible because of the ignorance and guilt caused by their religious controllers. They need to read The *Song of Solomon*, originally *The Song of Songs*, and Tantric books on eroticism like *Kama Sutra*."

"The Jewish mystic tradition Kabbala deals with eroticism explicitly."

"There is a lot of sex in the Kabbala. What does Kabbala means in Hebrew?"

"Oral tradition."

"Sometimes that's the only way to pass it down. Writing was not an option, I guess. The propagation of information sometimes needs the mouth as well as the hand."

"Read Israeli Kabbala scholar and Chasidic Rabbi Ohad Ezrah from the book *Legends of Star Ancestors*."

"The Kabbala is all about eroticism; like Tantra, it is all about the spiritual connections to the physical. In the Jewish Temple we had a sanctuary known as the Holy of the Holiest. ... What was inside, underneath, were two cherubs, two angels with wings made out of gold, and they were having sex together. One was female and the other was male and they were making love. As the two angels in sexual union covered the Ten Commandments. If you took those two statues of the gold and put them in a synagogue today you would be kicked out immediately. So where is the balance today?

The indigenous tradition of Israel was about the holiness of eroticism. All the patterns on the walls of the Temple depicted the male and female making love, so that when you entered the Jewish Temple you were surrounded by erotic images. These images were the symbol of the unification of the people and the divine. Within the erotic is the balance that symbolizes many concepts that are the core of Kabbala. We are always remaking unification – this is the spark. We learn how to make the revelation of this spark to unite it again through some kind of sexual unification."

"This sexual union with the Divine is the flow of energy from the Heart of God and Goddess to you through your chakras. The Indian equivalence of this is the sexual union of Shiva and Parvati, the primal male and female archetypes. Shiva and Parvati relentlessly stare into each other eyes during the copulation that creates the cosmos. They are like the two entangled swans staring into each other's eyes in the Sri Lankan *Hansa Puttu.*"

"Chakra is the eastern Indian concept of energy centers of the body, like yoga, right?"

"The Sanskrit word for this Union is Yoga. Chakra, as in Dharmachakra, literally means wheel or vortex. This is the energy that sustains us. We trap the energy in our atoms or stone from the Love of Goddess."

"Stone from the Love of Goddess Sophia. Philosophia! Philosopher's Stone!!"

"Philosopher's Stone is the catalyst that transforms us from human to divine. *Apotheosis.*"

"Energy vortices like mini tornados."

"Our bodies and our true spirit selves have areas that act as faucets of a pipe that allows the flow of cosmic life or creative energy. There are many, but seven are identified as basic. Six of them correspond to physical localities. The seventh hovers above the head, but overlapping parts of the brain. There are twelve chakras including your cosmic spiritual self."

"It is just an Indian Vedic concept or more universal?"

"Vedas say, *truth is one, the sages speak of it by many names.* The chakras are described in Yoga Kundalini Upanishad in Vedic teachings, as Kasina Visuddhimagga in Buddhism, Chinese QiGomg, Japanese Dentian, Sufi Islam Lataif, Eastern Orthodox Christianity, Jewish Kabbala, Egyptian Sekhem of the Djed, teachings of the Incas and other indigenous tribes of both American continents. The spiral climb of energy, depicted as a winding serpent called Kundalini or Sekhem, up the spine, the Djed, through the chakras is none other than Jacob's Ladder, the gateway to divinity in heaven. This is the Stargate."

"So, it is truly universally human like livers and kidneys!"

"Most humans do not fully benefit from these energies that can flow through these centers because the faucets are partially blocked. This is due to various reasons including, genetics, food, and pollution, but mainly due to resistance to spirituality and focus on materialistic illusions. They lie dormant like a computer program that is not open, waiting to be double clicked."

"How about lack of awareness?"

"Everyone has the potential to open the faucets. It can be done on purpose if you are aware ... or accidently."

"Accidently?"

"Yes, like unexpected gushing of energy during a severe crisis or a near death experience – Grace under fire."

"A Kundalini awakening?"

"Yes. Before labeling them let me use another analogy. You are a stagnant pond half way up a mountain. Seven streams flow into you from the same mountain top. There are seven other stream paths downhill but they are dried up because you have blocked them to preserve your life giving water. However, the one-way flow from above cannot happen because the pond applies pressure upstream. This is resistance to spirituality or Godliness. So the water in the pond is stagnant and rotting. This is spiritual degeneration. One day you open the seven streams downhill one by one, through the release of the seven energies in love as rays of light: sexual energy, emotional self-expression, social confidence, compassion, creative communication, worthiness, connection to God's grace. When these rays of lights of the seven colors of the rainbow are in full flow you are transformed into a beacon of God's light for those who seek it."

"A relay of seven rays."

"In Egypt these seven chakras were the seven seals of Djed described in Alchemies of Horus, the son of Isis. In the practice of Sex Magic of Isis the Ka or light body of an initiate is charged with magnetic power through a full chakra orgasm, during which there is a tremendous release of magnetic energy within the cells. An initiate's magnetism that functions in the Law of Attraction is amplified. Visualizations manifest with greater intensity and timeliness. A transformed individual now consciously transforms the world around. This is individual beginning is the emergence and rise of the collective consciousness."

"So the activation and actualization of the chakras not only empowers an individual but all that he or she is connected to in this world and beyond."

"Absolutely! In addition to the seven primary chakras or energy centers within the body, Incas and other Native Americans speak of an eighth that transcends the physical and spiritual body and located partly above the head. The eighth chakra is where God lives within us.

There is supposed be a ninth planetary Earth chakra, a tenth Solar System chakra, a eleventh Galactic chakra, and twelfth Cosmic chakra. The twelfth is where we live within as a tether in the heart of God, often called the Great Central Sun or the *Tao* or the Dharmakaya. These latter five are outside our space and time. When we end our physical life, all lower seven chakras rise and reunite with the eighth chakra and you exist only as a light being until or if you return to a physical body."

"The theme of the sacred twelve recurs. The twelve swans in my dream including the seven of the colors of the rainbow."

"The seven physical chakras from bottom to top are, in order from a human/animal centers to god centers:

Red ray Root Chakra – ovaries/prostate – feminine earth energy and survival.

Orange ray Sacral Chakra – coccyx – sexual energy and emotional self-expression.

Yellow ray Solar Plexus Chakra – navel area – social status and power.

Green ray Heart Chakra – compassion, agape love or bhakti, and intimacy.

Blue ray Throat Chakra – communication and creativity.

Indigo ray Third Eye Chakra – pineal gland – worthiness, intuition, gateway to higher dimensions. The top of Jacob's Ladder.

Rainbow or Violet ray Crown Chakra – Top of the head or 'Soft spot' of a newborn – Connection to the Source, the *Tao*, the ultimate Horn of Plenty. The God radar. The Godar. It is where the individual self and God are indistinguishable. Mystics represented this with the symbol called circumpunct, a circle within a circle. The circumpunct is placed above a pyramid representing the Djed, the spine. This is the Jacob's Ladder, the Serpent Rope, the Tunnel, or the Stargate."

"So the crown chakra is more of a comprehensive center?"

"Yes, a spiritually healthy being has these chakras working in a balanced manner. But most of us have some opened more than the others. In the concept of Celestial Marriage the chakras collapse and meet at the Heart Chakra. This is the idea of the Trinity collapsing into One. In this case the Divine-Heart-Human chakras collapse into unity to form what is called the Christ Consciousness or Buddha Consciousness or Unity Consciousness. Think of it as Father-Christ Child-Mother aspects of being."

"What happens when the chakras are blocked?"

"Root Chakra – Disconnect to nature and anxiety.

Sacral Chakra – Emotional problems, depression, sexual issues examples like inhibitions, guilt, and lack of pleasure.

Solar Plexus Chakra – Too much ego, an easily offended fragile ego, arrogance, power hunger, and personal eccentricities.

Heart Chakra – Unable to show compassion. Lack of intimacy. Conditional love.

Throat Chakra – Unable to express themselves and understandings. Unable to decode or accept communications.

Third Eye Chakra – Feeling unworthy, difficulty in adapting to change. Difficulty accepting and connecting to spirituality. Jacob's Ladder is folded and stored.

Crown Chakra – Lack of overall spiritual intelligence. Major Godar malfunction.

Some open all these flows by long term practice. Some, like *Rainbow children*, are born with all flows blazing. Yeshua and Siddhartha Gautama are examples of such paragons."

"So Indigo and Crystal children have their 'third eye open.' Ladder installed with a minty Godar!"

"Yes, this is the single spiritual eye. In Mathew 6:22 Jesus said, *the light of the body is the eye: if therefore thine eye be single, thy whole body shall be light*. In Egypt, this was the alchemical charging of the Ka body. A state called Akul."

"But at the same time I know many people who feel unworthy of a higher state of being, especially a Ka or Light body or Divine state. They feel too imperfect to be Divine."

"The purpose of life is the knowledge that God gains of His perfection in our imperfection. – Hazrat Inayat Khan, Sufi Master."

"What's imperfect and mundane is perfect and divine to God."

"Namaste!"

"Namaste back!"

"What does that mean?"

"I worship you! It's a sign of respect."

"That's what it means literally. But its implications are profound. It signifies my recognition of the Divine nature of you. It's a declaration of your godliness! The god in me worships the god in you!!"

"Maybe that's how they greet each other in heaven. William Blake said, *arise and you're your bliss, for everything that lives is holy*. But like I said many people often think so little of themselves. I know this from everyday interactions."

"Stephen Chbosky said, *we accept the love we think we deserve*. People, including adults should read the children's book *The Little Soul and The Sun*. That would open a few chakras."

"*If you don't see the light at the end of the tunnel, be that light yourself.*"

"Many millions of children born in the last few decades have many chakras opened from birth. I think they are incarnations of highly advanced humans being from the previous lives. I would imagine the likes of Lincoln, Einstein, Picasso, Lennon, Tesla, Mother Teresa, Martin Luther King, Gandhi, and Princess Diana are here now but not necessary in the same gender because the spirit self is androgynous. This is just my speculation, but James Russell Lowell said, *All God's angels come to us disguised.*

Those, who once lived on this planet and died, now badly want to be born to participate in the ascension. They want to attend the graduation. However, the queue is controlled. The ones granted birth priorities are those with the highest vibration frequencies or level of 'enlightenment'. You can see that the population on this planet has exploded way beyond its carrying capacity. Why so many born? What's the big excitement?"

"So what is going on?"

"Our solar system is going closer towards the middle of our galaxy up the spiral arm we are in. It is entering a zone of higher cosmic radiation. We know that we have pretty much ended the Age of Pisces and entering the Age of Aquarius or Water, as foretold by the ancients like the New Zealand Waitaha, whose name mean *Bringers of Water*.

Our Planet Earth, the Big Blue Marble, is growing up. It's finals and the graduation is coming. The planet is ready. The water is ready. The wind is ready. The animals and the plants are ready. There will be a harvest. Is humanity ready?"

"Is Santa Clause involved in the Harvest?"

"Of course, he will read from the list of who's been naughty and who's been nice. The beauty is that the list is composed by those whose names are in it. It is us, who judge our own worthiness. So help yourselves generously."

"Is humanity ready? How do you become ready?"

"The Tibetan teachings, descending from the Kingdom of Shambhala called *Kalachakra* or Great Circle of Time, says this.

Far away beyond the Himalayas lies a secret valley hidden by a ring of snow covered peaks. At its center is beautiful crystal mountain. This is the gateway to the Kingdom of Shambhala. Here the people live in peace and harmony. There is no hunger or sickness. They live long and happy lives. The task for the rulers of Shambhala is to guard the treasure of human knowledge ready for the time that will come when world will be ruined by war, violence, and greed. Shambhala can still be found if only the seekers know where and how to look."

"So we need to know where and how to look. Tibet? Central America? Sedona, Arizona?"

"You forgot Ethiopia."

"Ethiopia?"

"There is not a single Ethiopian who does not disagree with their own claim that they are one of the keepers of ancient wisdom of humanity."

"So where is the wisdom kept?"

"In a tiny church called the St. Mary's Chapel of Zion in the town of Aksum in northern Ethiopia. The wisdom is kept in a wooden box that is supposed to have unbelievable power. The box is guarded by a single monk, whose entire life purpose is the tutelage of the content. He appoints the next guardian just before his death, which occurs faster than other Ethiopians. In fact even long before death many begin to go blind due to some radiating power from the Ark. This object is mentioned in the bible as the Ark of the Covenant."

"The Ark of the Covenant containing the wisdom we need is in Africa?"

"That's only one place of storage of the wisdom! What do you do to your important research data in your computer?"

"I back them up in multiple external hard drives and store them in multiple locations."

"So, what you do think the ancient wisdom keepers did to their important data."

"Multiple locations in multiple forms throughout the world."

"The Ark was taken through Egypt, where it was kept in the island of Elephantine. Egypt hides additional ancient wisdom in a secret chamber under the Sphynx, however, not necessarily in this dimension. The Ark was brought to Ethiopia by the Ethiopian King Menelik, the son of King Solomon and Queen Balqis of Ethiopia, better known as Queen of Sheba. Sheba is a Kingdom that covered from Yemen to Ethiopia. Their Queen was a high initiate of the Temple of Isis and an ancestor of Yeshua, in addition to the Ethiopian line of Kings."

"Wow! Queen of Sheba to our rescue!! I didn't see that coming."

"This is written in the Quran, Ethiopia's *Kebra Negast* or the Glory of Kings, and the Roman account by Flavius Josephus. Among the best modern accounts of this story is Graham Hancock's book *The Sign and the Seal: The Quest for the Lost Ark of the Covenant.*"

"Graham Hancock has been on the right track, again! But when will this wisdom be revealed to us?"

"In that documentary about Shambhala I mentioned earlier Michael Wood also finds this legend of Ethiopia following the path of Queen of Sheba. Wood's thinly veiled statement point to now.

In the past different conceptions of time and space lived side by side on our earth, but not any more ... now time races in one line headlong forward. Past recedes from us ever faster ... we are one world now."

"Harmonic convergence of all sources? Where else?"

"This is from *The Prophecy of Padma* from Tibet:

The great hero and Magician Padma the Wise chose twenty one secret valleys of the Himalayas and in them he hid the most precious treasures known to man. He made these valleys invisible, intending that they should only reappear in times of trouble. The treasures Padma hid were wisdom and knowledge.

One day greed and ignorance will lay waste the earth itself. An evil king will triumph and spread his power over all humankind but just when it seems there is nothing left to conquer then the mists will lift to reveal the icy mountains of Shambhala.

When the time comes the enlightened will be guided to these valleys where they will rediscover the sacred objects and texts. They will be needed to rebuild the world."

"Sacred objects? Crystals?"

"Michael Wood visits Mt Kailas in Tibet and says this:

At its center the eerie white pyramid of the holy mountain Kailas. A mirror of the crystal peak in the ancient legend and the tale of Shambhala."

"White pyramid of Kailas! The crystal peak!!"

"The movie *Indiana Jones and the Kingdom of the Crystal Skull* portrays an ancient Maya legend, which says that the crystal skulls or suki tok in Kek'chi, the Maya language, bear a secret that has been kept from mankind and when the time is right the skulls will unite and the secrets are revealed."

"When is the time right for the revelation?"

"The time is here now."

"I know that the silicon crystals are the same stuff we use to store information in our sophisticated computers today, but how do the skulls reveal the secrets?"

"Organic substances like us are made of carbon. In the Periodic table Silicon occupies the same octave, but at a higher level or dimension, if you will. Science has proven that not only does silicon have the same living properties as carbon, but also that many deep sea life forms, conscious and reproducing, are based solely on silicon."

"So organic means carbon or silicon. Silicon, however, is a higher and more durable level."

"Absolutely. Dr. Marcel Vogel of IBM Advanced Systems Development Division, who invented the floppy disc, the prototype of modern hard drives in computer and smart phones, and the coatings of those hard drives, scientifically proved the two-way communication capability of crystals, which he used in devices such as hard drives and external storage drives."

"Their encoding and decoding properties were used in the first 'crystal' radios to the most sophisticated communication devices today. As an expert Dr. Vogel also developed the Liquid Crystal technology, a key ingredient in the Digital Age of Information."

"He also designed the Vogel Crystal, cut to the exact angle of 51 degrees 51 minutes and 51 seconds, the exact angle of the Great Pyramid of Giza. The crystal, which has the same vibration frequency as water, was designed after the geometry of the Tree of Life, a Kabbalistic symbol for Creator and Creation as One. Tree of Life is the cohesive embodiment of the Divine and the Mundane or in other words, God and her own reflection, which is us and what we perceive as the Cosmos. Upanishad echoes this. *Then he realized I am indeed this creation for I have poured it forth from myself and that way he became this creation and truly he who knows this becomes in this creation a creator.*"

"Once again the 11 membranes or dimensions of the M-Theory of Quantum Physics correspond to the 11 realms or *sephirot*."

"Dr. Vogel revealed that he saw the Tree of Life design in a dream."

"Like the German organic chemist Kekulé von Stradonitz and the structure of benzene. It seems like dreams are projections of our creative blueprint that we do not see in the waking state."

"Right, in *Buddha in Redface*, Tarrence, the Native American elder, explains this to Dr. Eduardo Duran beautifully.

There has always been a dream. Everything is still the dream. All that we call creation and Creator is the dream. The dream continues to dream us and to dream itself. Before anyone or anything was, there was a dream, and this dream continued to dream itself until the chaos within the dream became aware of itself. Once the awareness knew that it was, there was a perspective for other aspects of the dream to comprehend itself. One of the emerging dream energies, or 'complexes,' that came from the chaos of the dream and still remains in the dream as a way for the dream to recognize itself, is called 'human beings.'"

"Humans are 'dream energies or complexes?' So our bodies are organic symbolic representations of energy."

"The Vogel Crystal can store and convey energy information from other membranes or dimensions identified in M-Theory. Dr. Vogel discovered the crystal that will amplify, cohere and transmit frequencies."

"We use frequencies in Wi-Fi. So the shape and form of the crystal is key to its ability to function in a specific frequency of transmission."

"Eighty percent of the earth's crust is quartz crystal containing silicon.

Robert Lawlor writes about a Cherokee elder, Willy Whitefeather, he met in Sedona, Arizona in his book *Voices of the First Day*. He talks about how the elder sat directly facing the stones and played a lilting melody on his flute. The elder spoke of the silicon crystals in them that listened to the music. The elder says, *they are like lonely old people, standing and waiting to be sung to. Our people have always sung songs of admiration to the qualities of strength, beauty, and endurance that stones bring into the world . .... They are tired and lonely now because the world has become so blind and selfish. They live in a hollow, unsung world."*

"We are living in a massive Wi-Fi zone on a gigantic computer chip that contains information absorbed and emitted at various frequencies."

"This computer is in the process of running some of its vital long dormant and *unsung* programs."

"This is Lawlor from *Voices of the First Day*.

The flowing patterns of geomagnetic energy are the psychic circulation systems of the earth's body. This invisible blood nourishes the cultural unfolding of the earth's unborn child, the human tribes, and is mirrored within her physical body by a multitude of branching veins of magnetically sensitive minerals and crystals. The human body is also enveloped in fields of subtle energy, which flow in resonance with its bodily blood. The harmony between the psychic and physical circulation of earth and man maintains a channel of communication, like an umbilical cord, through repeated cycles of death and rebirth. We observe this process as civilizations change and develop."

"She is alive and kicking out information."

"Kicking out skulls full of data at specific frequencies! That's wild!!"

"When a human can resonate with the frequency, the information is transferred in a state of quantum entanglement. The mind of the skull and yours are one, a shared consciousness."

"Like in Microsoft Net Meeting, we share one monitor and cursor but two keyboards and mice. The crystal skull is remote operating when the frequencies are matched."

"Dr. Vogel said, *crystal is a neutral object whose inner structure exhibits a state of perfection and balance. When it's cut to the proper form and when the human mind enters into relationship with its structural perfection, the crystal emits a vibration which extends and amplifies the power of the user's mind. Like a laser, it radiates energy in a coherent, highly concentrated form, and this energy may be transmitted into objects or people at will."*

"The experts know his crystals and the crystals know him."

"One skull was found in 1924 by a 17 year old British girl, named Anna Mitchell-Hedges, whose father Fredrick, a British explorer was excavating near a place called Lubaantun in Belize, then called British Honduras. These are Anna's own words

My father was excavating in Central America in British Honduras and we found an old Mayan ruin, he thought had something to do with Atlantis and we excavated for about seven years clearing the ground and then one day we spotted something shiny through the stones. And that was my 17th birthday. So we were full of happiness and joy…

Maya people say it was used to heal and if an old medicine man was getting too old to perform a ceremony a young man was chosen and they laid in front of the altar. The high priest would perform a ceremony and the old man's knowledge would go into this young boy and the old man would pass away peacefully but this young boy would get up as a very knowledgeable young man. This Crystal Skull here has tremendous power, but it also gives you a warning that something is going to happen.

She subjected it to tests at the British Museum and the skull was found to be genuine quartz with absolutely no tool marks whatsoever.

The gem expert from the British museum says, *it is a skillful sophisticated job. If it is made by primitive people it is absolutely amazing because the standard of workmanship is absolutely first-class.*

It was subject of long and extensive experiments at the Hewlett Packard's Crystal Lab. Frank Dolan estimated it to be over 12,000 years old. The exact words of one of the crystal experts there was that *this skull should not even exist."*

"But, it does. That makes me conclude that she, Anna, is no ordinary English girl."

"She revealed it when she had become a very old lady. She authoritatively states that it is ancient. These are her words. *This is what the Maya people told us. I lived seven years with the Maya people as a child and I lived and ate and slept the same way they slept on the earth. And once you live with people who are so down to nature you gotta believe them.*

The Maya insist that the skulls were given to them by gods that descended from the sky. The skulls contain the secrets of the gods."

"What about the other skulls?"

"There are thirteen. A skull was programmed every thousand years over the last 13,000 years. The Mitchel-Hedges is the oldest. It was programmed where Anna learnt it was created."

"How are they created and programmed? Exactly why?"

"They were created to house the knowledge and memory of each thousand years. They are like external hard drives used in storage of vital data needed to reprogram our matrix or operating system."

"I know they are made of the same material as our computer chips, so I know how they can contain the knowledge, but how was the knowledge place in there?"

"Every thousand years there is much preparation for a special ceremony. A wise elder grandmother is chosen along with a young child, who is chosen by the grandmother. During the ceremony they both place their hands on the skull. The grandmother passes away or her spirit leaves body. Her knowledge is passed on to the young child and her consciousness enters and occupies the crystal."

"The skulls are alive? That's a living being? This is like the mind upload technology in Arthur C. Clarke's *The Last Theorem*. That's science fiction. In *The Singularity is Near,* a non-fiction work, futurist Ray Kurzweil wrote an entire section called *Uploading the Human Brain*. David Victor De Transcend defines upload as *to become a figment of your computer's imagination.*

You are saying this is a reality now?"

"Yes, the time is now. Ignorance is not an excuse for disbelief anymore. The skulls will be united and the living being in them will exit and enter bodies of thirteen Mayan Elders who have volunteered and prepared for this purpose. This will be heralded by the appearance of the Blue Kachina. They have a tradition of making Kachina dolls that look like space men. Hopi prophecies foretold of the appearance of a Blue Star in the sky."

"Blue Star?"

"Yes, the prophecy was given to the Hopi. Even though anthropologist have suggested that the Hopi came from Russia like other Native Americans, the Hopi historians know that they came from Guatemala, the Maya land. In fact, Hopi are Mayan. They are just geographically relocated. The similarity of their cosmology should have suggested such a close link already."

"So Hopi are really a long lost Maya tribe."

"Yes, but to them no one was lost."

"*No one has ever met a lost Aborigine.*"

"The Hopi Blue Star prophecy was given to them by a person or being called the White Feather. He is considered the Grandfather of the Hopi. The message, however, is for all humanity.

The time is foretold by a song sung during the Wuwuchim ceremony. It was sung in 1914 just before World War I, and again in 1940 before World War II, describing the disunity, corruption, and hatred contaminating Hopi rituals, which were followed by the same evils spreading over the world. This same song was sung in 1961 during another Wuwuchim ceremony. There is a petroglyph inside the Hopi Reservation near Oraibi, Arizona called the Prophecy Rock that symbolizes the journey of mankind with two choices: Continue with *two hearts* in the path of destruction or *one heart* towards union with Wakan Tanka – the Great Spirit.

It is said when it is time Kachina will remove the mask during a dance before all including the uninitiated children, the non-Hopi human brothers. I will paraphrase from the *Book of The Hopi* compiled by Frank Waters in the 1980s. They were given to him by a Hopi elder called White Bear. It speaks of the Day of Purification.

Those who take no part in the making of a world of division by ideology, be they Black, White, Red, or Yellow race, will realize that we are all one, brothers.

There will be a spiritual conflict with material matters. Material matters will be destroyed by spiritual beings who will remain to create one world and one nation under one power, that of the Creator.

The Emergence to the future Fifth World has begun. It is being made by the humble people of little nations, tribes, and racial minorities. ... The Great Spirit made a set of sacred stone tablets, called Tiponi, into which he breathed his teachings, prophecies, and warnings. Before the Great Spirit hid himself again, he placed before the leaders of the four different racial groups four different colors and sizes of corn; each was to choose which would be their food in this world. The Hopi waited until last and picked the smallest ear of corn. At this, the Great Spirit said:

'It is well done. You have obtained the real corn, for all the others are imitations in which are hidden seeds of different plants. You have shown me your intelligence; for this reason I will place in your hands these sacred stone tablets, Tiponi, symbol of power and authority over all land and life to guard, protect, and hold in trust for me until I shall return to you in a later day, for I am the First and I am the Last.'

The Hopi were told that they must hold to their ancient religion and their land, though always without violence. If they succeeded, they were promised that their people and their land would be a center from which the True Spirit would be reawakened."

"This echoes the Prophecy by Padmasambava, the founder of the Tibetan Buddhism. *When iron birds fly in the sky and when the iron horse moves across the land, the Buddha will be in the land of the Redface.* This is stupendous, to say the least."

"If they failed, terrible evil would befall the world and great numbers of people would be killed. If they would succeed, if enough Hopi remained true to the ancient spirit of their people, the True White Brother and his helpers will show the people of earth a great new life plan that will lead to everlasting life. The earth will become new and beautiful again, with an abundance of life and food. Those who are saved will share everything equally. All races will intermarry and speak one tongue and be a family."

"So far I like the plan, as long as the Hopi don't drop the ball."

"I think the responsibility goes beyond the Hopi my brother. Listen to this. This was first published in a mimeographed manuscript that circulated among several Methodist and Presbyterian churches in 1959. It speaks of event that happened to a minister named David Young. While driving along a desert highway one hot day in the summer of 1958, he stopped to offer a ride to an Indian elder, who accepted with a nod. After riding in silence for several minutes, the Indian said:

I am White Feather, a Hopi of the ancient Bear Clan. In my long life I have traveled through this land, seeking out my brothers, and learning from them many things full of wisdom. I have followed the sacred paths of my people, who inhabit the forests and many lakes in the east, the land of ice and long nights in the north ... My people await Pahana, the lost White Brother, from the stars as do all our brothers in the land. He will bring with him the symbols, and the missing piece of that sacred tablet now kept by the elders, given to him when he left, that shall identify him as our True White Brother. The Fourth World shall end soon, and the Fifth World will begin. This the elders everywhere know. The Signs over many years have been fulfilled, and so few are left."

"Crystal skulls? Blue Star? Kachina? Pahana? White Brother from the stars?"

"There were nine signs. They have all been fulfilled with hundred percent accuracy. "

"Better than Arthur C. Clarke?"

"Just as uncanny. The signs are interpreted as follows: The First Sign is of guns. The Second Sign is of the pioneers' covered wagons. The Third Sign is of longhorn cattle. The Fourth Sign describes the railroad tracks. The Fifth Sign is a clear image of our electric power and telephone lines. The Sixth Sign describes concrete highways and their mirage-producing effects. The Seventh Sign foretells of oil spills in the ocean.

This is the Eight Sign: You will see many youth, who wear their hair long like my people, come and join the tribal nations, to learn their ways and wisdom.

This is the hippy and New Age movement.

And this is the Ninth and Last Sign: You will hear of a dwelling-place in the heavens, above the earth, that shall fall with a great crash. It will appear as a blue star."

"That's amazing! NASA's Galaxy Evolution Explorer captured the unexpected explosion of the comet Holmes that orbits our sun, into a blue star like sphere larger than our sun on 24th of October 2007. This shocked all astronomers.

This is unbelievable! said Iranian astronomer Babak Tafreshi. *I was amazed to find Comet Holmes so easily with the naked-eye in the light-polluted skies of metropolitan Tehran.*

You can see its images taken all over the planet on the internet, especially SpaceWeather.com. One of the astronomer's exact words were *It's the most blue star-like comet I've ever seen.*"

"It was a sign for the Head of the Mayan Council of Elders representing all 440 Maya tribes, Don Alejandro, whose Mayan name is Wakatel Utiw, meaning Wandering Wolf, to announce a great gathering for ceremonies, breaking a silence of themselves for 527 years."

"527 years?"

"Even better was the particular ceremony they performed next to Lake Atlan in Guatemala. Don Alejandro stated that the ceremonies have not been performed for 13,000 years. This silence was observed by Hopi and other Red tribes, Tibetans, Aborigines, Polynesians, African tribes, Siberian Shamans, and indigenous European tribes like the Sami."

"They all knew and just kept quiet. Amazing! Why was it performed the last time?"

"It was the End of Time for that Age of their ancestral homeland."

"So the Lake Atlan gives a clue to what that place was!"

"Let me put a modern perspective on these ancient ceremonies. The earth and all its life are collectively a holographic computer application. It is not running well, as you see. The program is corrupted because of the years of abuse of the operating system – the matrix. Viruses and Trojan Horses have wreaked havoc. The program needs to be fixed with multiple patches."

"So *Windows* Earth is fragile and susceptible to user error and predators. PICNIC."

"Brilliant. PICNIC – Problem In Chair Not In Computer. The ceremonies in sacred sites involving crystals, sacred geometry, fasting, chanting, incense, drumming, dancing and healing rituals are patches being installed to fix the matrix with the hope that the hologram will operate smoothly in future."

"Apparently, more patches are needed. Did anyone call IT?"

"We did phone IT and ET phoned home, this home. Recently this happened to this young white lady from Colorado named Keisha. She is part Danish and part Native Americans, though she does not look the latter. She has now been initiated as a Wisdom Keeper by the elders and lives in Santa Fe, New Mexico. Her Indian name is Little Grandmother."

"Little Grandmother!"

"Why don't you read her words?"

"*As I sat meditation drumming on a sacred drum, … what I received was not just for my years but for all of us. A man spoke with great nobility and strength 'I am grandfather White Feather I wish to speak of the people from the stars. I carry with me the knowledge of Hopi men, women, and those who are still growing. In front of you the children of Earth stand smoky mirror. The smoke keeps you from knowing who you really are. Time is near for the smoke to be removed. Are you not waiting for the last sign? The children of men have received many signs before and the prophecy of these signs always came true."*

"Then she spoke of the same signs as I mentioned earlier. Exact! Please continue."

"The eighth sign is the Blue Star or Blue Kachina, which would physically appear in our heavens.

The white man will return from the stars in their disks once again. They will feed our souls. They come to help. They will remind us where the truth is buried in the earth and they will bring our truth back to us. This will bring great joy, full hearts, and unite us as one family. I am White Feather. I am the grandfather of the Hopi. Aho!

The truth is buried in the earth?"

"And you. The truth is within you."

"Within my heart?"

"Within your *junk* DNA."

"My *junk* DNA contains the coded knowledge to be revealed at the apocalypse?"

"This is your apocalypse. Your history, your origins and who you really are buried in your molecular memory. Now it is time for decoding your *junk* DNA."

"The true purpose of my *junk* DNA is finally revealed."

"Time to unite! Time to gather!! Time to drum!!! Time to dance!!!! Time for ceremonies!!!!!"

"Time to mediate! Time to celebrate!! Time to live in harmony!!!"

"Speaking of ceremonies, I briefly mentioned the Celestial Marriage earlier. The power of meditation is the reunification of Holy Trinities or Trimurtis at all levels. The circle completes into a resonance of energy, whose re-creative power is limitless."

"The Celestial Marriage is the ultimate synergetic threesome."

"In Druidry the Unity has three aspects as three rays of light, representing cosmic intelligence, descending from the heavens into a person as a part the Druid *Tribann*. The other part is three rays of lights emanating out. The incoming is *spirit*, the gathering is *inspiration*, the outgoing is *illumination*."

"Sounds like Yeshua on the Sermon of the Mount. *You are the light of the world. … let your light shine before others.*"

"Now Joseph Campbell did let his light shine before others. This is the task of *illumination*.

It is to facilitate the free flow of Divine energy from the Heart of God, the *Immovable Spot* for Buddhists. This Heart of God is the Cosmic Great Central Sun. The energy, called God's grace is facilitated through the Universal Central Sun to the Galactic Central Sun. God's grace then flows to Sol, our sun, and to the root of the earth. This root is the tail of the Serpent of Light or the Druid Dragon. Individuals then draw this Prana or Sekhem or God's grace up to the root chakra and flow up to the crown chakra through the Seven Seals of the Egyptian Djed up the spine. That's how our life is sustained in a continuous creation. Spiritual resurrection is experientially awakening to this reality."

"Sounds like a circulatory system, where the blood flows from the heart to aorta, arteries, arterials, and finally to capillaries – individuals. This is fractal bifurcation into self-similar layers. The circulatory system works exactly like another fractal, a tree branching out. Cosmic and individual circulatory systems of course mirror each other."

"Campbell calls it the Tree of Life, as in the Kabbala. In *The Hero with a Thousand Faces,* he writes, *an abundant harvest is the sign of God's grace; God's grace is the food of the soul.*"

"So this nurturing quality is the illumination, the third aspect of the Druid Trinity *spirit, inspiration,* and *illumination.*"

"Spirit-Inspiration-Illumination. This Trinity as Unity is universal. Father-Son-Holy Mother Spirit. Logos-Opus-Sophia. Past-present-future. Subconscious-conscious-supraconscious. Mind-body-soul. Id-ego-self. Masculine-androgyny-feminine. Sath-Chith-Ananda, Mer-Ka-Ba, Isis-Horus-Osiris. Brahma-Vishnu-Shiva. Angels-God-Demons, Moon-Sun-Earth. Power-Wisdom-Compassion. Politics-Science-Spirituality. Technological-Physical-Spiritual evolutions. The Unity has secrets, no more. Its mind is ONE. Trinity is Unity. It always was."

"YouTube-Facebook-Twitter will merge into YouTwitFace."

"Okay, Conan. I wondered where the snarkfest went."

"Time to laugh! But I get it!!"

"Philosopher Richard Tarnas saw something in your techno Trinity.

It is perhaps not too much to say that, in the first decade of the new millennium, humanity has entered into a condition that is in some sense more globally united and interconnected, more sensitized to the experiences and suffering of others, in certain respects more spiritually awakened, more conscious of alternative future possibilities and ideals, more capable of collective healing and compassion, and aided by technological advances in communication media, more able to think, feel, and respond together in a spiritually evolved manner to the world's swiftly changing realities than has ever before been possible."

"When the Holy Trinity merges the collective understanding and awakening hidden within is unveiled in resonance with a consciousness of Unity."

"The Trinity is everywhere you look. We begin to see the middle ground in duality. Buddha spoke of the middle path. That's three categories. The middle one is the unifier. Trinity is one person not three."

"She is in *The Matrix*! Also the last line in the book *Rendezvous with Rama* by Arthur C. Clarke's is *the Ramans do everything in threes.*"

"How about in the name of universality of Trinity the Celtic Druids, Ancient Egyptians, and the Christian Biblical Israel as a Trinity uniting?"

"I am sure it is more holistic than YouTwitFace."

"The Druid in you intuitively uttered the clarion call, *Time to mediate! Time to celebrate!! Time to live in harmony!!!* The three central facets of Druidry are *Moon Path* of meditative intuition, *Sun Path* of seasonal celebration and the *Earth Path* of living in natural harmony.

In Japanese Shinto organic cultivation for nourishment is the sacred unification of the three elements: Moon, sun, and soil or earth."

"Definitely more cohesive, holistic, … and healthy."

"Now, the Biblical New Earth is neither a patriarchy nor a matriarchy. Our polarities like the Moon Luminari and Sun Illuminati unite with the Earth. The feminine lunar aspect is represented by Isis, the masculine solar by Ra, and the offspring earth by El, the Earth god of Canaan. When Moses led his people into the Promised Land he united the Egyptian deities Isis and Ra with the Canaanite El to form the original Jerusalem. The New Earth is formed with the higher dimensional New Jerusalem as its spiritual center. The New Earth is the celestial marriage of the unification of the Trinity Isis-Ra-El. Is-ra-el. Israel! The New Israel!!"

"That's the symbolism of balanced and united co-rulership. We are the same, you and I!"

"The New Israel is symbolic, but we know of the exchange of the spiritual baton from Tibet to the land of the Red Face – the land of the descendents of the Toltec, the wisdom keepers.

Dr. Don Miguel Ruiz, reveals some of this ancient wisdom in his book *The Four Agreements: A Toltec Wisdom Book.* Toltecs are from Atlantis. They know the consequences of divided duality. Oblivion is not a coveted place in history. This is what they want us to know, Now!

Ruiz quotes a Toltec master. *I am an incarnation of God. But you are also God. We are the same, you and I. We are images of light. We are God. … he realized that everyone was dreaming, but without awareness, without knowing what they really are. Humans couldn't see him as themselves because there was a wall of fog or smoke between the mirrors. And that wall of fog was made by the interpretation of images of light – the Dream of humans.*

I am the Smokey Mirror, because I am looking at myself in all of you, but we don't recognize each other because of the smoke in-between us. That smoke is the dream, and the mirror is us, the dreamers."

BRINGERS OF WATER

"Have you read the Science Fiction book *The Last Theorem* by Arthur C. Clarke?"

"No, but I know he had to co-write that with the American Frederick Pohl."

"That was because of his deteriorating health and eventual death in 2008 four months before the book was published."

"I know the basic plot, which seems like an overtone of his 1953 classic *Childhood's End*. Somehow this story struck a nerve in me. Sounds like *The Last Theorem* did the same to you."

"It was like he badly wanted to get something off his chest when he knew he was nearing his departure from earthly life. Sounds like it was his *Last Theorem*."

"I know it is about a concerned galactic elder council of sentient sapients monitoring and intervening with Earth because of our nuclear warlike tendencies like in *Childhood's End*. Science Fiction or an inevitability?"

"*The Last Theorem* is set in Sri Lanka around this period. It is based around the life of Ranjit, a Sri Lankan Tamil mathematician. While studying at Colombo University, he becomes obsessed with *Fermat's Last Theorem*, which states that no three positive integers a, b, and c can satisfy the equation an + bn = cn for any integer value of n greater than two. Pierre de Fermat, in 1637, claimed he proved it, but never wrote it down. Since then mathematicians across the world for over 350 years could not prove it. In 1995 a British mathematician named Andrew Wiles published a 100-page proof of the theorem. But not everyone was satisfied because it used twentieth century mathematical techniques not available in Fermat's time.

The backbone of the novel is about a highly advanced collection of extraterrestrial sapients, the Grand Galactics, who become alarmed when they detect the photon shock waves from nuclear bomb detonations on Earth. The Grand Galactics monitor and oversee the destinies of a number of highly advanced sapient races and order one of these races, the Nine Limbeds, to send strong messages to Earth to stop use of nuclear weapons in warfare. Earth ignores these warnings and the Grand Galactics order the One Point Fives to launch an armada to Earth to exterminate the undesirable species.

Back on Earth, regional conflicts escalate and the United Nations struggles to contain them. Ranjit finds proof for the Fermat's Last Theorem while in captivity by a group of pirates. He is rescued by his Sri Lankan Sinhalese friend Gamini. He later arrives in the United States and is recruited by the CIA to work on cryptography. Gamini later reveals that he is working for *Pax per Fidem*, meaning Peace through Transparency, an undercover United Nations organization established to bring about world peace. To achieve this end, *Pax per Fidem* has developed 'Silent Thunder', a non-lethal EMP nuclear superweapon that renders all electrical equipment in its path inoperable. Silent Thunder is deployed in North Korea and later in South America. Regional conflicts subside. Gamini invites Ranjit to join *Pax per Fidem*, but the authoritarian nature of *Pax per Fidem* and its 'new world order' worry Ranjit and his wife Myra and they turn down the offer. He does, however, accept a position on the advisory board of an international consortium building a space elevator in Sri Lanka, chosen because of its position on the equator.

As the One Point Five fleet enters the Solar System, the Nine Limbeds orbit and observe Earth in cigar-shaped craft, sparking numerous UFO sightings. Grand Galactics observe the effects of Silent Thunder and returns to the Grand Galactic tribunal, who immediately suspend the One Point Fives's destruct orders.

The space elevator is completed and, for the first time, people and materials can be lifted into the Earth orbit without the need of rockets. Natasha, Ranjit's and Myra's daughter, competes in the first solar-powered space yacht race from Earth to Moon orbit. But soon after the start of the race, Natasha's yacht malfunctions and she is abducted by the Nine Limbeds, who use a holographic insert projection of her to interrogate prominent people on Earth, including Ranjit and Gamini, about Silent Thunder. Satisfied that Earth has 'reformed', Natasha is returned and the Nine Limbeds broadcast a message to Earth in which they announce that the Grand Galactics have decided not to sterilize Earth, and that the One Point Fives, with their Machine Stored navigators, cannot return home and will land and occupy unused areas of Earth.

The One Point Fives land in the desolate Qattara Depression in the Libyan Desert, which they find quite habitable compared to their ruined home world. With the Grand Galactics absent, One Point Fives start making decisions for themselves. They provide Earth with new forms of power and the Machine Stored reveal mind uploading technology. When Myra dies in a scuba diving accident, her mind is uploaded into cyberspace, with Ranjit joining her later."

"The mind uploading sounds exactly like the 13 crystal skulls for each thousand years."

"After 13,000 years the Grand Galactics finally return to Earth and are astounded to see how fast the planet has developed. They had always interfered with the evolution of sentient species they had discovered, believing they could not be trusted to evolve on their own. The Grand Galactic is impressed with the planetary evolution on Earth. They relieve themselves of the burden of watching over intelligent life and restore sovereignty to the inhabitants of Earth."

"I will have you read these teachings in the messages collected by Don Elkins. Some of them had an eerie similarity to the teachings I heard in the Temple of Isis. These Elkins' Notes were channeled or flowed from what are called 'missionaries'."

"Missionaries? Bizarre!"

"Douglas Adams, who wrote *Hitchhiker's Guide to the Galaxy* said: *There is a theory which states that if everyone discovers exactly what the Universe is for and why it is here, it will instantly disappear and be replaced by something even more bizarre and inexplicable. There is another theory which states that this has already happened.*"

"Hilarious! I am beginning to see that."

"These messages compiled by Elkins are called *cosmic sermonettes,*. There is definitely a touch of Isian femininity about some of them. Some sound like indigenous mythology."

"Joseph Campbell said, *mythology is the womb of man's initiation to life and death.*"

"He calls this womb the belly of the whale after the story of Jonah's initiation. It is, in fact, the Rite of Sepulcher in a sarcophagus."

"Jonah's story is another version of Campbell's identifications of Hero's Quest like *Jason and the Golden Fleece, King Arthur,* Luke Skywalker in *Star Wars,* Neo in *The Matrix,* and Frodo in *Lord of the Rings.* These are initiation archetypes facilitated by the wise sage motif – Hera, Merlin, Obi-wan, Morpheus, and Gandalf, respectively."

"Four stages of the initiation are identified as awakening, quest, initiating tests, and illumination. In some myths the labyrinth is where the tests take place. You go in as an ordinary person and come up a hero. The last stage is often marked by a return home to illuminate the fellowmen.

After initiation Yeshua bestows the responsibility of illumination upon his disciples.

You are the light of the world. A city set on a hill cannot be hidden. Nor do people light a lamp and put it under a basket, but on a stand, and it gives light to all in the house. In the same way, let your light shine before others."

"Humanity hasn't even completed stage one of this initiation. Boy, there's some way to go."

"Humans are clueless and thirsty for the truth and illumination in the same breath in this Age of Pisces – Age of Fish."

"Punjabi mystic poet Kabir exclaimed, *I laugh when I hear that the fish in the water is thirsty.*"

"Humans are surrounded by water if we can see in this blue planet. These began to trickle sometime after the atomic bombs were dropped on Hiroshima and Nagasaki. I hope humans can swallow these tall glasses of *Aquarian* refreshments from the *Bringers of Water*, the Cosmic Waitaha."

"We earlier discussed how nuclear weapons exploded in New Mexico and the H-bomb emitted neutrinos, which are the resulting 'pieces' from the destruction of dark matter – the matter that exist in other dimensions."

"All attack is a call for help. The time for *man's initiation to life and death* seem to have been announced at a multi-dimensional level.

See the Milky Galaxy is like an oval swimming pool. There are many adults swimming in it. There is also a very naughty child that likes to pee in the water that surrounds her. So one day the adults decided to come and potty train the child and prepare her for the future – the new day. Sounds Sirius!"

"Sirius message?"

"The helical rising of star Sirius at dawn always heralds a new day, when little stars in the sky fades away and the big star takes the stage of the heavens. The big star is Helios, our sun."

"Irony is the laughter that Sirius brings. Australian Aborigines have known of Sirius, the morning star, heralding a new paradigm, replacing the old paradigm of darkness. This is from the book *Voices of the First Day: Awakening in the Aboriginal Dreamtime.*

For a long time there was no sun. Good spirits who lived in the sky sent out the morning star to warn those on earth that the fire will soon be out. The spirits, however, found this warning was not sufficient, for those who slept saw it not. Then the spirits thought someone should make some noise at dawn to herald the coming of the sun and awaken the sleepers. But for a long time they could not decide to whom should be given this office.

At last one evening they heard the laughter of kookaburra. … He agreed to laugh at every dawn of day, and so he has done ever since, making the air ring with his loud cackling."

"If that is what takes to awaken those sleeping, so be it."

"Whatever it takes."

"The bringers of the dawn themselves were awakened from their sleep to the far reaching destructive potential of earth stupidity by a sign marking the beginning of a possible end."

"Hiroshima and Nagasaki! Earthlings don't get it, do they?"

"Maybe humans need a new movie called *Interdependence Day*! We are all in this together!!"

"Su casa es mi casa! I am not sure if the water is to quench the thirst or for a baptismal immersion of mankind."

"Global baptism is an Aquarian initiation. Here are the notes from Don Elkins' channeled *cosmic sermonettes* published in 1977. Please read these ..."

"*As we progress on to higher planes of life, we shall incarnate in bodies far more ethereal than those now used by us, just as in the past we used bodies almost incredibly grosser and coarser than those we call our own today.*"

"Pierre Teilhard de Chardin knew it. How did he put it?"

"*We are not physical beings having a spiritual experience, We are spiritual beings having a physical experience.*"

"I have heard Billy Graham quote him too."

"In fact, C.S. Lewis said: *You don't have a soul. You are a soul. You have a body.*"

"This is obvious to some, but that's the paradox. Edward R. Murrow said: *the obscure we see eventually. The completely obvious, it seems, takes longer.*

Why don't you read more of Elkins' Notes?"

"*He who has fully accomplished soul travel finds it nearly impossible to communicate his experience to others once he has returned to the physical form, especially when his traveling has taken him above the astral world into the higher planes.*"

"Talk about *Soul Plane*."

"We have attempted throughout what you would consider ancient times on your planet to bring to mankind, to those who would desire the knowledge, the knowledge that is necessary for experiencing all of the infinite experiences created by our Creator. Some of those who dwelt upon this planet in the past have accepted these teachings and have benefited from them. … We have attempted for many of your years to bring to all of those who desire the teachings, the very simple teachings that allow you to know all. However, these teachings have not been understood very well."

"Obviously, seen from the dysfunction. It gets better."

"We have developed abilities which you may call miraculous. We have the ability to transcend what you call time and space. We have access in a conscious manner to knowledge of which you have access only during meditation, in a sub-conscious manner. The freedoms which we enjoy, my friends, are there because we have begun to see that we are all One. … On your planet, each blade of grass is alive with the knowledge of the Creator. The wind sings His praises. Trees shout for joy in the creation of our infinite Father. If you are not able to see the Creator, my friends, it is a matter of seeking, seeking, and continued seeking. And then, my friends, you will begin to realize, and to understand, that the Creation of the Father is all around you."

"This one is right out of Buddhism."

"At this time, very few of the people upon this planet are seeking anything outside of the physical illusion that so constantly busies their minds with trivialities. It is only upon this planet who has become lost in a complex creation of his own, with many thoughts of a complex but trivial nature that keep them very busy, in an effort to reach that which is of no value – minor creation that will last only the shortest period of time, which has no value, once it is attained, for he will lose it, and once again return to the creation.

Planet Earth, my friends, is indeed a lovely planet. It will soon be vibrating in a vibratory manner which is far more associated with realization of the Father's and Mother's creation. Begin to realize, and move with your planet, … to complete freedom which in our vibration we experience."

"What do you think?"

"...Thought can also be transmitted on many frequencies ... The effect that these frequencies will have in the envelope of your earth will depend on the frequencies of thought. ... The motive of the thought ... for instance, thoughts of resentment, of hate, of fear, each has its frequency, and this frequency has its effect, and will eventually seek out the same vibration or level of vibration in the envelope. As this builds up in the earth's envelope and becomes greater and greater in quantity, it will have its effect upon the earth..."

"As within, so without."

"Redefine that which you experience. Redefine it through your seeking, and through your growing awareness of the creation and our Creator."

"Another call to challenge our belief systems."

"We have dealt with many planets who are beginning a new phase of vibration. We have aided many a graduating class, and we have done so successfully. We have also failed, not once but several times. It is completely possible for us to fail if it be the will of the people of the planet we are attempting to aid.

At present time we are far behind where we had hoped to be at this point while helping planet Earth. We had hoped to have been much more successful at reaching the people of this planet. It is possible that there will be a smaller graduation than we had hope."

"That's not good."

"Our purpose in coming at this time is to help speed up these reactions so you will be prepared for the change-over in the Earth's frequency. This is taking place over a number of years. Many of your people are being affected mentally and spiritually in a discomforting way, and some of them in a very spiritual way.

The program that is in operation is to prepare the Earth for a major rise in consciousness, to what you call Christ awareness but what we term communication with Universal Energy.

They are making themselves known to the world as a whole to lead mankind thereby into a New Age as the Earth enters the more intense vibrations of Aquarius.

This is changing the vibratory rate of the nucleus of every atom in our planet, raising it to a higher frequency.

You are beginning to know things. You are beginning to hear things. You are beginning to sense them and to use mental telepathy. You are beginning to see beyond the physical vision. When you close your eyes, pictures form; colors that you do not see in the three-dimensional, or in the Earth plane, begin to flash before your eyes. You do not know where they come from, because you are going into the fourth dimension.

Man has always been in the fourth dimension, because man always has contained an etheric body while he lived in a physical body on this planet. But that physical body is now being transmuted into the etheric body, more closely attuned so the etheric body can be the operating or dominant body while on this planet."

"Quoting Yeshua now."

"All of our efforts have been directed towards fulfilling this simple phrase: 'Seek and ye shall find.' Why do you think we have seen so elusive.

I am aware that many of the people of your planet consider that we have wasted too much time in your planet. We would greatly prefer to act more rapidly, but the speed and the degree of our activities must be regulated, not by us, but by you. The acceptance of us by the total population of this planet is the only governing principle that controls our activities."

"Free will."

"Service, my friends, is very natural. It is the way of the Creator. It is the plan of the Creation. Everything in the creation is performing a service. The vegetation that is abundant upon your planet performs a service. But your people ignore this. The animals upon your planet perform a service, but this is also largely ignored. The flowers, the very air, the water performs a service, but this is ignored. If it were taken fully into consideration, it would become obvious that everything in Creation

is there to perform a service. This includes all Creator's children. Each of you is here to perform a service. This is the plan of this infinite creation. This is how it works. It is only necessary to understand this, and then all things are possible. Unfortunately, upon the planet you now enjoy, this principle is not understood. Very, very few of those who inhabit the surface of this planet understand the simplicity and totality of this plan. .. Perform these services to your fellow man, and then you too will be functioning the way that the Creator of us all planned."

"Service to others! This is how it works!!"

"It is necessary that if an individual is to make progress in a spiritual sense, that it be a result of an inner-directed seeking of his own, rather than an outer-directed commandment given to him by an organization of a religious or other nature. For this reason, it is necessary that we do not make ourselves too generally known and accepted by the people of your planet. If we were to do this, then the inner direction of their seeking would be for the most part lost."

"Insight! *The light gets brighter as the midday draws near.* Proverbs."

"We have visited this planet many, many times in the past. This was done only after the civilization that we visited was ready to accept us ... and had reached a satisfactory level of inner-directed seeking of the truth of the creation, and therefore it was displaying the principles of love and brotherhood that are the products of this seeking.

We are extremely privileged in being able to offer this service to those who seek it: and our service is largely given to them through meditation. If they are to avail themselves to this service, it is necessary that they do so through meditation."

"Meditation is highly touted as the only key to the hidden knowledge. Meditators are the ambassadors of the Universe with all its celestial dimensions."

"One does to try to think to become aware. One only has to remove his own thoughts and the Universal Mind rushes in to fill the void.

I am the voice, O mortal man, that whispers in the silence of your being."

"Entanglement with the mind of God."

"It is necessary to practice this form of meditation, for you to become aware of the original creation, and not the creation of man. ... If you are totally aware of the original creation ... you would see us. There is a technique for increasing your awareness."

"Daily Meditation."

"It is evident that all creations throughout this infinite creation are the works in either a direct or indirect sense of the creator of us all. It is unfortunate that the people of this planet are unaware of the principles that were provided each of his children with abilities quite similar to his own. Each of you has within you these abilities. They are not possible to be removed. They are within all of the children of the Creator, and will always remain with them. It was so designed by our creator. He wished for all of his children to have and use the abilities to govern and mold their environments at will. ... It is necessary that this principle be remembered for each of the children our Creator to fully manifest them. The teacher that was known to you as Jesus was able to use many more of the abilities than the people of this planet. He was no different from any of you. He simply was able remember certain principles. These principles are not at all complex. They are very simple.

These principles are not necessarily of an intellectual nature. ... It is only necessary that you avail yourself to our contact through meditation order to begin to re-realize that which is rightfully yours.

We have attempted many times to suggest to you that this original thinking is one of total love and brotherhood. This is not enough. It is very difficult for the people of this planet to understand these concepts in an intellectual way. They have for a very long period of time been mentally conditioned by erroneous thinking, so that they cannot easily become intellectually aware of the principles that are simplicity and truth themselves.

These erroneous thoughts must be totally obliterated from the thinking of an individual if he is to be successful in returning to the original thinking with which he was created.

It is therefore suggested that the intellectual mind be circumnavigated, and the principles be directly communicated to the soul or spiritual mind through the mechanism of telepathic impression in a non-intellectual or a conceptual sense. This we have found to be highly effective with respect to any attempt to get from an intellectual thought to a deeper understanding and awareness of the truth of the principles of the infinite Creator. It is for this reason that we have asked that the individuals who wish to understand these truths avail themselves to daily meditation, so that these impressions may be analyzed by them at a deeper level, and therefore a true and complete understanding be arrived at.

The simple truth is that the creation is one thing. Everything that you can imagine; everything you can see; everything that you cannot see; all that there is, is one thing.

There is no separation. Separation is an illusion. All things are one thing: the creation. To effect one part of the creation is to effect the creation.

For light my friends, is eternal and infinite and real. The rest is illusion. Go within. Become aware of reality. It is within each of you.

It is impossible to separate yourself from the creation. It is impossible to isolate yourself from the creation. It is impossible to isolate yourself from the creation. You are it, and it is you.

For once this understanding is accomplished, then all things are possible, for this is the way that the Creator designed it. This is the way that She provided. It is only necessary that you realize this. It is only necessary that you demonstrate in each thought this realization. And then, my friends, you and the Creator are one, and you and the Creator have equal power. For this is truth. Each of us is the Creator."

"You. Me. Creator. Same."

"There is only one of Us."

"I am a part of all that I have met - Lord Tennyson."

"William Blake said, *I am in you and you in me, mutual in love divine.*"

"When Mayans greet each other they say *In Lak'ech*; that's how they say Hello. It means *you are another me and I am another you*. It is the ultimate declaration of selflessness and unity."

"John Muir said, *when one tugs at a single thing in nature you find it hitched to the rest of the Universe.* The *single thing* is often people or *Five People You Meet in Heaven.*"

"Muir was pointing out that we are permanently linked to the Divine Source in this interwoven fabric of existence. The word *religio*, the basis of the word religion, means *to link* you to the Source, the Heart of God, the *Tao*. Religions deceive you with the illusion of disconnection to avoid redundancy and defuncity."

"But we know and have known that we are one with the Source."

"*Father and I are One.*"

"Yeshua."

"*Do I contradict myself? Very well, then I contradict myself, I am large, I contain multitudes.*"

"Walt Whitman! We come full circle!!"

"*We shall not cease from exploration*
And the end of all our exploring
Will be to arrive where we started
And know the place for the first time"

"T. S. Eliot. I now know that a philosopher is an adventurous explorer of the mind."

"This is one my favorites of the cosmic sermonettes:

Love is the essence of all creativity. Without love, there would be no life. For it was through love that God received the spark of the idea of creation and conceived the vision of creating man to be a part of Her."

"What is the name of this book?"

"Secrets of the UFOs. One of the messages say: You are not to entrust anyone with the secret of our existence – no one."

"That is an Inception carried out under a Prime Directive. ..."

"... and a planetary quarantine."

"Quarantine? Is this the End of the Childhood of this Planet?"

"It is Childhood's End in real life. Do you remember Clarke's science fiction?"

"It is about a peaceful arrival of mysterious extra-terrestrial being on Earth ending all war, thereby preventing the previously imminent extinction of mankind, helping the formation of a unified world government, and ushering in a Golden Age."

"All they are saying is give peace a chance."

"The missionaries refuse to answer many questions on the origins and mission and do not appear in physical form. They just remain in their ships, governing through a Prime Directive. Decades pass and they eventually show themselves and greatly contribute to the flourishing Earth. The new generation of children on Earth begins to display powerful intuitive and psychic abilities, heralding their evolution into a Group Mind, a unified Collective Consciousness, which is eventually reunited with their Source, called the Overmind in the book."

"Too uncanny! The ascension part is mysterious. There are differences too, but that's expected."

"Why an inception under a Prime Directive?"

"Prime Directive is Galactic Law. The Law of Free Will.

A part of the Inception, Yeshua, himself explained: *If those days had not been cut short, no one would survive.* Mathew 24:22.

The prime directive is apparently proving successful. Mankind is showing signs of growing up. The quarantine is being lifted. Read *The Book of Insight: Wisdom from the Other Side.*"

"I have heard of it. Isn't it from Vancouver?"

"The Other Side. This is from the book 2 of *Conversations With God* series by Neale Donald Walsch and, of course, God and his twin flame Goddess:

The Process of shifting the consciousness, increasing the spiritual awareness, of an entire planet, is a slow process. It takes time and great patience. Lifetimes. Generations.

Yet slowly you are coming around. Gently you are shifting. Quietly, there is change."

"I can feel it. Mankind has been crucified by their own illusion of separation and now 'Christ' has come a second time to take them down and heal because the call for help has rippled throughout all dimensions in the cosmos."

"Sounds like He has brought your *Joan of Arcturus* with Him."

"She is never far from him. We know who she is and we could sure use her."

"I was once inspired to write this down while meditating. Please read, but don't get hung up on the words."

"Insight. Look inside of you.

All the knowledge on how the Cosmos operates is within you. You already know everything and you are everything. You may consider yourself as a microcosm of All There Is. You have just forgotten it. The amnesia was done on purpose with your agreement prior to your incarnation. Your reality was created with your involvement. The illusion is dissolving in front of you and you are beginning to see who you really are. This has been happening since your birth. Clues to the truth have been all around you. They still are. They don't teach you anything new. They just stimulate the recognition of what you already know, but forgot. Look around for the clues but look within you for the truth. That is what is called Insight. Seeing Inside.

Human languages cannot tell you the truth due to its limitations in imparting the understanding. They are just sound vibrations with symbolic representation. The realization is triggered from within you by the words. The language itself is a catalyst, but not the truth. When properly decoded with your intuition, the truth manifests in your consciousness in various way. This message itself is an example. It can easily be just noise. But what do you hear inside yourself?

Meditate. Simply empty your mind of all thought. When the mind noise quiet down you feel a greater connection to the true reality. That's how you establish resonating communion with the cosmic mind, broadening our attunement beyond the horizons of our individual self. Now you begin to dissolve the illusory veil of separation. Behind the veil is a mirror reflecting you. St Francis of Assisi knew this. His words were: *I thought I was looking at the world, but the world was looking at me.* You have always been entangled with the person in the mirror in a synergetic dance of re-creation. You are as aspect of the cosmos or Creator or All There Is or Great Spirit or Wakan Tanka or whatever the name suits you. Let the cosmic consciousness emanating from the Great Central Sun, the Heart of God, fill you. You will know how things really are. You will know your true potential. When you return to the earth illusion, your life will never be the same again. You will use more of your insightful Heart Intelligence than your rationale Brain Intelligence. Maori say that the longest journey is from the mind to the heart. Take a step in that journey. Even Mark Twain said, *one learns through the heart, not the eyes or the intellect.* In the depictions of the Egyptian judgment day, they do not way the brain, it is the heart that is of value for the place you will go from there.

Once you have learnt to create from the heart the things that were once a struggle for you will become easier within a certain period of time. Doors will appear where they were only walls. Know that your dreams are on their way and then play while you wait for them to arrive. Things that upset you and caused any emotional negativity will now reveal themselves to be illusory events that were placed there as an opportunity for you to realize your potential through an ongoing pleasurable remembrance and re-creation. You will recognize more clues. You will watch a life unfold of which you now have more and more control, like a lucid dream.

Enjoy your dream until you wake up to You! Then you will have total awareness of all of Your Creation. Love and Light!"

"The redeeming hero Christ you have been waiting for is You!"

All of these symbols in mythology refer to you. Have you been reborn? Have you died to your animal nature and come to be reborn as a human incarnation? You are God in your deepest identity. You are one with the transcendent."

"Joseph Campbell. That's appropriate.

Based on all of this, if you could summarize the message to mankind from the Cosmic Consciousness, Creative Intelligence, God, Goddess, Great Spirit, or Divine Mother, what would it be?"

"Every man suffers from an Oedipus complex. He feels this unrelenting connection to his mother. He cannot stand his mother's mate. He himself wants to be with his mother. To 'be' implies nothing less than permanent sexual union with her – a *hieros gamos*. He is in denial of this. So he departs on a hero's quest of initiation to be independent of the mother. He passes the tests of trials and tribulations and conquers many dragons, which are nothing but holographic reflections or shadows of his inner fears placed rightfully within him as the necessary conditions for the incubation. He pulls out his reflective sword and shines that in the face of the dragons. They see themselves as who they really are – pure luminescent unicorns wanting to serve him. The dragons transform into the luminescent creatures in front of his eyes. This initiation quest is, in fact, his inner transformation in a way allegorical to alchemy. He goes from base metal to gold, from coal to diamond. His fears have now become his radiant love. His potential is realized. He now glows off that radiance and luminescence. Is he now fully a man? Is he now independent of his mother?

What transfigures him alchemically is the Philosopher's Stone. The philosopher is the Lover of Sophia, the Divine Mother. What the man did not realize is that his initiated and independent hero self was the realization and release of the infinite and eternal energy of Sophia that was trapped within him all along, akin to your mother's mitochondrial DNA you are familiar with. Your mother gets it from her mother and this leads back to the ultimate Divine Source Mother. The Kingdom of God was always within him. The Divine Mother was always within him. The relentless urge he felt to be inside his mother, a *hieros gamos*, was misconstrued ignorance of the Mother that was in him. Finally, he realizes that his outer quest of independence or his outer quest of reunification with his mother had been nothing short of Quixotic windmills. They did help him realize that he was always with his mother. The mother was always with him. He and Mother are one. They were never at no time separate. What is there to reunite in Unity? At the denouement of the initiation he realizes that he is not only a 'he', but a 'she' as well.

Shamans call this as acquiring your eagle wings. He didn't have just one wing as he thought; He had two: Yin and Yang. The two wings, however, were holistic aspects of one. The duality was an illusion. The separation was an illusion. He has now, almost dangerously, awakened the feminine within him. He has gained the Holy Grail, which metaphor is defined by Joseph Campbell as *the fulfillment of the highest potentiality of human spiritual consciousness*. Now He realizes he can fly. There is nothing He cannot have for He is emancipated from all debilitating limitations. However, now there is nothing to have. He, now also She, is All There Is. *Apotheosis* is complete.

I will let the Persian Sufi mystic poet and the founding Whirling Dervish Rumi sum it up.

For I have ceased to exist, only you are here."

"There is only one of us."

"You are a hoax perpetrated by me. I made you up *for I can only Be, through you."*

BUTTERFLY

"Raye?"

"Hmmm?"

"Mr. Colaluca?"

"What happened?"

"You made it up here."

"Who are you? Where am I?"

"You have been at Holy Family here for a while. You successfully crossed over to the other side."

"This is heaven? … I am dead?"

"I am Dr. Vin Schultz. I am a neurologist here at the hospice of Holy Family Hospital in Vancouver."

"The Other Side?"

"I meant Canada."

"Ouh! I woke up to the hymn *Amazing Grace* playing on your radio. I was a bit lost."

"Once! Now you are found. On your way to the Baltimore Airport, a short distance from your place, you were in a very bad car crash. Unfortunately, the cab driver didn't make it. You were taken to the University of Maryland Medical Center ER. You went into a coma due to severe head trauma."

"How long?"

"Almost three months. You were brought here at the request of Nera Tepoel."

"That long?"

"Yes, we monitored you the whole time."

"Really?"

"Did you dream at all?"

"Not for three months."

"Your DMT level was higher than normal. There was pituitary and pineal gland activity."

"I didn't know it was a dream. Or how much of it have been in a dream state. Things are still a bit blurry."

"Well, one of my friends at UBC, Dr. Shan Reeves, a physicist now deeply examining the role consciousness plays in creation of perceived realities with Dr. Mario Evans, had a theory about what happened."

"In the old days it used be, if you are not well *consult your nearest physician.* I guess in this day and age it is *consult your nearest physicist.*"

"Times change. Paradigms change."

"I guess in ancient times they, the healers, were the same person called the shaman."

"Physician and shaman physicist?"

"One is a man of medicine and the other is a medicine man."

"One is a doctor and the other is a witch doctor."

"Hard to tell which is witch. Tell me his wild theory."

"I don't understand it fully even though he gave me the book *The Hidden Reality: Parallel Universes and the Deep Laws of the Cosmos* to read. He said you were experiencing a parallel alternate reality in a state of consciousness attuned to it. Not necessarily a dream, but another probable course of life among many of the probable 10500 or so parallel universes in the multiverse. You experienced two or more probable existences simultaneously. He said you were non-local and entangled with all of existence. I am not exactly sure what that means. Do you recall that?"

"Yes, the experience quite vividly."

"He said recently that you could collapse back into this local reality, anytime and regain consciousness in the, as he calls, 'sarcophagus.' Your vitals are good. You will be fine. In fact, you will be more than fine. Nurse Emily joked that you have ascended to an HD phase - higher dimension."

"Funny."

"Nurse Angela started calling you Blue Raye."

"Blu Ray is HD. Nice! Are all nurses in Vancouver clever like that?"

"It's only innocent pun … I mean … fun. They took very good care of you. It's because after your wounds healed Head Nurse Shawna noticed this almond shaped bluish/purplish scar on your forehead. They joked about luminous rays emanating from it."

"Thank you for taking care of me. I guess they could have called me worse. Like *Sleeping Beauty* or *Cosmic Raye* or something."

"Apparently you see yourself different now."

"The eyes of the beholder have switched places."

"Nera is on her way. The nurses called her to tell the good news that you are here, now."

"Touch you now?"

"How did you know that I was thinking that?"

"You want me to feel your force?"

"How did you know that?"

"I don't know. *Something's strange. I'm so confused. I don't know why.*"

"Oh! Nera is here!"

"Hey baby!"

"Hi sweetie! You are awake!! My prince!!! Welcome to Vancouver!!!!"

Truth is stranger than fiction,
because fiction is obliged to stick to possibilities.
Truth isn't.

Mark Twain

ACKNOWLEDGEMENT

David Obst for advice on reaching the right readers.
Wibke Langhorst for the wisdom and warrior spirit she imparted.
Echo Fluharty of Balboa Press for coordinating
the publication of this book.
Rebecca Floria for insightful feedback and for
being a source of Goddess energy.
My brother Shanaka Gunawardena for his
resources and integration of Buddhism.
Tilde Cameron and Tina Fiorda for the inspiration
I received through their work.
Eilish Roberts for teaching me how to write
from the imagination of the heart.
My mother Indranee Gunawardena for her vision and support.

www.ingramcontent.com/pod-product-compliance
Lightning Source LLC
Chambersburg PA
CBHW022004010726
47494CB00003B/887